Fantasy Stories for Girls

Unicorns of Balinor:
The Road to Balinor
by Mary Stanton

The Princess School:
If the Shoe Fits
by Jane B. Mason and Sarah Hines Stephens

The Rhianna Chronicles:
The Girl, the Dragon, and the Wild Magic
by Dave Luckett

SCHOLASTIC INC.
New York Toronto London Auckland Sydney
Mexico City New Delhi Hong Kong Buenos Aires

ISBN 0-439-85857-7

Unicorns of Balinor: *The Road to Balinor*, ISBN 0-439-06280-2,
copyright © 1999 by Mary Stanton.

The Princess School: *If the Shoe Fits*, ISBN 0-439-54532-3,
copyright © 2004 by Jane B. Mason and Sarah Hine Stephens.

The Girl, the Dragon, and the Wild Magic, ISBN 0-439-41187-4,
copyright © 2000 by Dave Luckett.

12 11 10 9 8 7 6 5 4 3 2 1   6 7 8 9 10 11/0

Printed in the U.S.A.   40

First printing, April 2006

Contents

DEAR SAMANTHA.

WE HOPE YOU
REALLY ENJOY
THIS BOOK.

LOVE YOU LOTS

OPA + OMA.

JUNE 11TH 2006

UNICORNS OF BALINOR

THE ROAD TO BALINOR

MARY STANTON

For Les Stanton,
A Hero All the Way.

Cover illustration by D. Craig

No part of this publication may be reproduced in whole or in part, or stored in a retrieval system, or transmitted in any form or by any means, electronic, mechanical, photocopying, recording, or otherwise, without written permission of the publisher. For information regarding permission, write to Scholastic Inc., Attention: Permissions Department, 555 Broadway, New York, NY 10012.

ISBN 0-439-06280-2

1

It was dawn in the Celestial Valley. The sky over the Eastern Ridge slowly turned pink. Silver light spilled across the wooded hills, touching the waters of the river winding through meadows and flowering trees, then spreading over the herd of sleeping unicorns.

A few unicorns stirred in their sleep. All slept peacefully. The Celestial Valley was their home, and had been since time began. Above the valley, between the clouds that drifted across the sky, was the home of the gods and goddesses who had created them. Below the valley, by way of a rocky, treacherous path known only to a few, lay the world of humans. In this world, there was Balinor, the country guarded by the celestial unicorns, and then there was the land beyond the Gap. The Gap was haunted by mists and legends. A few chosen unicorns had been down to Balinor, fewer still had crossed over the Gap to Earth. But for thousands of years, after each sunrise in the Celestial Valley, all the unicorns had gathered shoulder to shoulder to form the rainbow. Then they would sing in the new day.

They wouldn't fully awaken until the sun itself peeked over the ridge. And for now, the sun was still out of sight behind the mountains. So they slept, curled horn-to-tail. Some lay back-to-back, others dozed peacefully alone under the sapphire willows that lined the banks of the Imperial River.

All of them slept but one.

Atalanta, the Dreamspeaker, was up early. She hadn't rested at all that night. Just before the sun came up, she gave up trying to rest. She trotted up the Eastern Ridge to the Watching Pool to wait for the visions she knew would come.

Atalanta was the color of the sky before moonrise, a soft blend of lavender, violet, and shadowy grays. Her mane, tail, and horn were of purest silver. She was the mate of Numinor, the Golden One, leader of the Celestial Valley herd. As the Dreamspeaker, Atalanta was the link between unicorns and the world of humans, just as twilight was the link between night and day. Atalanta, alone of all the celestial unicorns, could appear in the dreams of both humans and animals alike. And she was able to call up visions from the Watching Pool, where magic allowed Atalanta to watch events in the world of humans below.

The headwaters of the Imperial River formed

the Watching Pool. The Imperial River began as a small stream trickling from a curiously shaped stone spout in the side of the ridge. This stream flowed into a pond lined with amethyst rock, and from there into a waterfall that fed the Imperial River.

The jeweled rocks — found nowhere else in the Celestial Valley — formed a glittering violet circle, perfectly round and enormously deep. This was the Watching Pool. Atalanta stood there now, hock-deep in the velvety grass that lined the banks. Images formed there, one after the other. The visions remained for a few moments, then sank to the depths of the pool. They disappeared like snowflakes. Atalanta knew she didn't have much time to watch the visions.

She bent over the Watching Pool and touched her horn upon the water, saying, "I, Atalanta, Dreamspeaker, call forth the Princess of Balinor."

The silvery-blue water stirred clockwise, faster and faster. Small waves slapped against the amethyst rock. The waters dimpled, as if an invisible hand scattered raindrops on the surface. Then the whirlpool stilled, and an image formed in the water.

Atalanta saw a slender, bronze-haired girl twisted in pain on a hospital bed. Her legs were bandaged from knee to ankle. "Arianna!" Atalanta called. But the girl made no answer. She slept; a deep, unnatural sleep that Atalanta's dreams couldn't reach. So Atalanta had been right. Arianna had been gravely hurt.

Atalanta's purple eyes filled with grief.

The Dreamspeaker touched her horn twice more on the water. The girl in the hospital bed faded into the depths of the Watching Pool. A new vision formed.

A unicorn stallion knelt in a dark horse stall, head bowed so that his muzzle touched the ground. His coat was bronze, the same hair color as that of the girl on the hospital bed. Atalanta knew him: He was the Sunchaser, Lord of Animals in the world of humans, Bonded to Arianna, and kin to Atalanta herself. Not so long ago, Atalanta watched the Sunchaser, tall and proud down in Balinor. Now he lay wounded on the other side of the Gap. There was a bloody stump in the center of his forehead where his bronze horn once had been.

He groaned once, enduring a pain-filled sleep.

"Sunchaser!" Atalanta called.

The great unicorn raised his head. Atalanta quivered. His bronze horn was gone! A cruel white scar was the only reminder of his former glory. His dark brown eyes were dull. He dropped his head onto the stall floor and lay still. He had heard her Dreamspeaking, Atalanta was sure of it. But he no longer understood the Unicorn's language — he could no longer speak!

Two tears slid down Atalanta's cheeks and dropped into the water of the Watching Pool.

The image of the bronze unicorn sank. Atalanta held her breath, reluctant to see what she had to see next. She shook herself all over, scattering a flowery scent through the cool air. The Sunchaser, greatest of those unicorns who roamed the world of humans, lay broken beyond the reach of the Celestial Valley herd; Arianna, the lost Princess of Balinor, endured the pain of mangled legs, not knowing who she really was. Atalanta couldn't bear the horror of what would next appear in the Watching Pool.

But she had to know: Did Entia, the evil Shifter, know where the Princess and her wounded unicorn were hidden? And if he did, what terrible vengeance would the Shifter seek?

2

Arianna Langley opened her eyes to the dull green of the hospital ceiling. As dim as it was, the light made her head hurt. Her stomach was empty and her throat was raw, as if she'd thrown up after being sick.

"Feelin' better, honey?"

Ari turned her head. This was a mistake. The room swayed, and her stomach lurched.

"The anesthetic made you sicker 'n a *dog*."

A fat woman sat in a chair next to her bed. Large. Large and familiar. Ari narrowed her eyes, trying to focus.

"It's Ann," the large lady said helpfully. "The doc said you might have a little trouble rememberin'." Ann was dressed in blue jeans, a red sweatshirt, and a tentlike denim jacket. A little embroidered horse galloped across the jacket's breast pocket. Ari's head swam. It wasn't a horse — it was a unicorn.

Ann chuckled nervously. "You recall any-thing at all, honey?"

"My name. I remember my name." She rested her head against the pillows. Her stomach was feeling better now. "Arianna Langley."

Ann didn't say anything for a moment. Then, "Right you are, sweetie."

"What happened to me?" She raised herself off the pillow, which was harder than it should have been. It was as if she was pushing a dead weight. She looked down at her legs. Both of them were wrapped in casts. "What happened to me!" she gasped.

Ann patted Ari's hand. "You just rest a little bit now. I'm goin' to find the doctor and she'll explain the whole thing. It's just lucky you weren't hurt worse, that's all."

Ari fell back onto her pillow. A confusion of memories hit her. A tunnel. The smell of dead and dying things. The sound of black flies buzzing. A great bronze four-legged creature plunging in front of her. "Chase!" she shouted suddenly. "Where's Chase?"

"Shush-shush-shush!" Ann's face was pale. She looked nervously over her shoulder. "Chase is fine," Ann said. "It's a miracle, really. I thought that poor . . . uh . . . horse was a goner. But he came out of the accident with a big ol' bump on his head, and that was about it."

"Chase is a horse?" Ari frowned. "That's

not . . ." She trailed off. Her head hurt. And she couldn't remember a thing about who she was or where she'd been. Just her name . . . and the tunnel. She turned her head so that Ann wouldn't see the tears. Her hair lay spread across the pillow, the bronze gleaming dully in the indirect light. There was something familiar about the color of her hair. That color was hers, but it also belonged to someone, something else. Chase! The Chaser! "Chase?" she asked. "Chase is my horse?"

"Horse," Ann said firmly. "He's right at home, in his stall at Glacier River Farm." Ann heaved herself to her feet. Her eyes were small and brown. She gave Ari a thoughtful look. "He's gonna be just fine except for that wound on his forehead. We had the vet take care of that."

"Good," Ari said doubtfully. "A vet is taking care of him."

"Best vet we've got!" Ann said cheerfully.

"What happened to him?" Ari asked.

"Oh, jeez." Ann ran a chubby palm through her scant brown hair. "Don't you fret. I'll go get the doc. Now that you're awake, we can talk about gettin' you back home, too."

But the doctor didn't hold out much hope for going home, at least not right away. She was a tall, neat woman with blond hair pulled into a tight bun at the back of her neck. Her hands were cool and sympathetic on Ari's aching head. She smiled at

Ari, took her pulse, and gazed intently into her eyes with a penlight. "Can you sleep a little now, Ari?" Her voice was kind.

"Yes," Ari said.

"Are you in a lot of pain?"

"No," Ari lied.

"Hmm." She bent over and examined the casts on both legs, one after the other. "I'm going to give you a mild painkiller, okay? Then sleep if you can. Sleep's the best thing for you right now." The doctor took a small syringe from a collection of instruments on the bedside table and slipped the shot into Ari's arm. The needle was so thin Ari hardly felt the sting at all. In a few moments, the terrible ache in her head and legs receded, and Ari sank gratefully back onto the pillows. She could sleep now. And suddenly, that's all she wanted to do. Sleep.

The doctor drew the curtains around the hospital bed and left Ari alone. Sleep began to drift around her. "Retrograde amnesia," Ari heard the doctor say to Ann. "I'm surprised she even remembers her name. She seems to recall a few things about her life before the accident. But it's bits and pieces, nothing more. It's going to take a while. And I have to tell you, Mrs. Langley, her entire memory may never come back."

"She's all right in other ways, though?" Ari heard Ann ask.

9

"Except for the two compound fractures of the lower legs." The doctor's voice was dry. "She's going to take a while to heal."

"Will she be able to walk?"

"I don't know." The doctor hesitated. "There'll be scars, of course. And perhaps a permanent limp. But your foster daughter's very fortunate, ma'am. She's not going to lose either leg. Not if I can help it."

Lose my legs! Ari thought. *No! NO!*

Sleep came like a wave of dark water. She sank beneath it gratefully. She didn't want to think. Not of the past, which she couldn't recall anyway, or of the future, which she feared.

Arianna woke up. The slant of the sun through the window told her it was late afternoon. The pain in her legs was dull, constant but bearable. She made herself calm and tried to think.

She was Ari Langley. She was thirteen. She'd been in the hospital for several days, maybe more. There'd been an operation on her legs.

She had a horse named Chase. She had a foster mother named Ann. And she must have a home, this place called Glacier River Farm that Ann had mentioned.

None of this seemed right. But Ann had said it was right. And Ann was her foster mother. That was what the doctor had said.

But who was Ari Langley? What had happened to her?

She didn't know. She couldn't recall. There had been some sort of tunnel, hadn't there? And an accident. But even those memories, fragmented as they were, didn't tell her who she was or why she was here. Or where she was going. Panic hit her. She was so alone! She didn't remember anyone!

"Calm down," she murmured to herself. "Keep calm." She clenched her hands and relaxed, deliberately. She would take things one at a time.

Okay. She was in a hospital bed. The sheets were clean and smelled of starch. A nightstand was on her left, a plastic chair on her right. The room was — how large was the room? And there was a window. So she could see out. Perhaps discover what this strange place was.

3

Atalanta saw Arianna lie back in the hospital bed and drop into a deep sleep from the drug she had been given by the doctor. Then the image disappeared as fast as a candle blows out. Atalanta reared in distress. The princess didn't know who she was! She barely remembered the Sunchaser! And now the visions in the Watching Pool were failing. Was this the Shifter's work? His evil magic had never before worked in the haven of the Celestial Valley. Only in Balinor. And the celestial unicorns had helped send Arianna and her unicorn to safety on the other side of the Gap — where they should have been safe from the demon Shifter's work.

Driven by fear, Atalanta struck the water in the Watching Pool three times with her silver horn. She had to find out! She chanted the words to the water over and over again until finally she saw Ari, sitting upright in a wheelchair.

Atalanta wasn't sure how much time had passed on the other side of the Gap. It could have been minutes — it could have been days. Arianna was talking to Anale, one of the two servants Atalanta had commanded to attend Arianna on the other side of the Gap. She heard Arianna call her Ann.

Atalanta calmed down. Perhaps things were going to be all right after all.

Suddenly, unbidden, the waters of the Watching Pool darkened to black. A tiny whirlwind appeared at the bottom of the pool. It rose swiftly through the water and burst into the air. It was a vision of black flies! Thousands of them, spinning in a vicious vortex of spite and hate. Atalanta forced herself to stand. Black flies were terrifying to her and to her kind. There had been times — too many times! — when the evil made by the Shifter turned into swarms of stinging flies, filling the unicorns' ears and sensitive noses, blinding their eyes.

For now, the swarm was only an image. No actual harm could come to the herd through the Watching Pool. Just the terror of the visions.

The flies filled the water from edge to edge, then disappeared.

Atalanta took a deep breath and looked into the waters.

She saw an iron gate, spikes reaching to a black and threatening sky. An ominous smear of dark, dirty clouds drifted behind the gate. The smear billowed and shrank, then shifted into a towering pillar of fire and darkness. Sickly yellow-green light wheeled in the center of the pillar. Gradually, the light resolved itself into a lidless eye. There was a face and form behind the Eye, but yellow-green clouds of smoke obscured them. All Atalanta could see was the lidless socket, the pupil blazing red.

The Eye of Entia, the Shifter!

The Shifter was enemy of all humans and animals in the worlds above and below the Celestial Valley. A demon — or worse! — whom no living being had ever seen. A ghastly presence that could shift, change shape, look like friend or foe, and no one could tell the difference. The only safety humans and unicorns had against the Shifter was that he couldn't hold a shape — any shape — for more than a few hours.

No one really knew the nature of the Shifter's Eye. Some said it was a part of the ghoul himself, split off in the time before animals could speak. Others said it was a grisly servant, created by the Shifter to spy on all those that he considered his enemies.

The area around the demon-red pupil was a wounded white, filled with red veins engorged with blood. The fiery pupil rolled in the socket, searching for prey.

And then the voice of the Shifter called for the Princess of Balinor. *"Arianna!"*

It was a huge, hollow voice, with the timbre of dull iron. It filled Atalanta with horror.

"Arianna!"

The Eye rolled as the voice called. Searching, while its Master distracted Atalanta with his calling.

The Shifter's voice echoed a third time, filled with a horrible coaxing.

"Arianna!"

Atalanta shivered. She struck the water sharply, one decisive blow that made the waters part and foam over the Shifter's terrible form. The dreadful Eye winked out. The Shifter's voice sounded farther and farther away, still calling for the bronze-haired girl. Finally, the voice was gone. The waters of the Watching Pool shone clear.

But now Atalanta knew why she hadn't slept last night. She had thought the Princess would be safe in the place where the unicorns had sent her. Instead, the Princess and the Sunchaser were in danger worse than they had been before. They were both wounded. They were separated. And the Shifter's Eye searched on. Atalanta knew that what the Shifter wanted, the Shifter got. He never gave up.

The events in the Pool meant sad news for Numinor, the Golden One, King of the Celestial Valley herd.

Atalanta left the banks of the Imperial River and walked through the meadow to the Crystal

Arch. This was the bridge between the Celestial Valley and the worlds above and below. This was where the rainbow was formed each morning, and where the unicorns sang in the new day.

Hooves whispering in the scented grass, the unicorns lined up under the Crystal Arch, ears alert, tails high, manes waving gently in the light breeze. Their horns shone and their glossy coats gleamed in the tender light of the fresh morning. There were hundreds of unicorns, one for each of all the colors of the Celestial Valley and all the worlds above and below it. Each unicorn made a separate part of the rainbow, from the violet Atalanta herself to the crimson Rednal of the Fiery Coals.

By custom, they faced the east. They waited for Numinor, the Golden One, lead stallion of the Celestial Valley herd. And as the sun's rim cleared the top of the Eastern Ridge, the stallion himself came down the mountain.

Numinor was the color of the sun at high noon. His shining mane fell to his knees. His tail floated like a golden banner. At the base of his golden horn, a diamond sparkled brighter than the sun itself. This jewel — like the jewels at the base of all the unicorns' horns in every part of the Celestial Valley — held a unicorn's personal magic.

Numinor trotted powerfully over the rocks and brush that lay on the side of his mountain. He halted in front of the rainbow ranks and arched his neck.

16

"I greet the rainbow," Numinor said, his voice like a great bronze bell.

"We welcome the sun," the unicorns said in response.

And then they all sang the first part of the Ceremony to Greet the Sun, as they had from the beginning of time:

"Red and yellow, orange and green
Purple, silver, and blue
The rainbow we make defends those we guard
In Balinor's cities and fields."

And Numinor asked, "When will we cross the Crystal Arch, to walk to the earth below?"

"When the dwellers of Balinor need us!" the unicorns responded.

Then they turned to the rising sun, toward the One Who Rules humans and animals alike. They pledged in a mighty chorus: *"We guard life! We guard freedom! We guard peace!"*

The Ceremony to Greet the Sun was over. Most of the unicorns dropped their heads abruptly to the grass and began to eat, which was their favorite occupation unless there was work to be done below. Numinor nodded to Atalanta and she approached. It was time to talk.

"Any news?" Numinor's eyes were wise and kind.

"It's very bad," Atalanta said. "With the help

17

of the resistance movement in Balinor, we sent the Princess through the Gap to live in safety at Glacier River Farm. The Sunchaser went with her, of course. But things went wrong. She's hurt. And there's worse."

Numinor's golden eyes widened. There was alarm in his deep voice. "Worse than the Princess's injury? How seriously is she wounded?"

"I can't tell. Not from here. She's alive. But her legs have been broken."

"And the Sunchaser? He is not . . . dead?"

"He has lost his horn, and the jewel that holds his magic. He has lost the ability to speak. I called to him, Numinor. I know he heard me. But he didn't understand me! What's worse, the two of them are separated. She is in a human place, with Anale and Franc to guard her, as we planned. "

"And Sunchaser?"

"He's at the farm. As we had hoped. But he is lost to us."

Numinor closed his eyes and breathed out hard, as a stallion will when he is angry. For a moment, he said nothing. Then he said, "The Sacred Bond between the Princess and Sunchaser? Does the loss of his horn and jewel mean he is deaf and dumb to the Princess, too?"

Atalanta sighed. "I don't know. A great deal depends upon Arianna herself. We've never sent a Bonded Pair through the Gap before, of course. And the Princess and the Sunchaser are more than just a

Bonded Pair, they are the source of bonds between all humans and animals in Balinor."

Numinor tapped his foreleg impatiently. He knew this. What he didn't know was what the consequences would be if the bond between the Sunchaser and the Princess was broken. For generations, the Royal Family of Balinor had dedicated the firstborn Princess to a unicorn from the Celestial Valley. The bond between the two was a unique magic, a magic that created the friendships between humans and animals in the world below.

"Atalanta? Do you know what may happen?"

She shook her head. "I'm worried, Numinor. The very nature of the Shifter's magic seems to be changing! He — or something — snatched the vision right from the waters of the pool! It took me many moments to get it back."

"But you did."

"I did. But I was *not* able to see what happened to Arianna for far too long a time."

"But when you were able to see again?"

"She seemed to be fine." A line of worry appeared between her eyes. "I think."

"Entia the Shifter? Our enemy?" Numinor half reared, his forelegs striking the air as if to strike at the Shifter himself. "Does he dare to attack our own?"

"He has sent his Eye to look for them. As far as I can see, he has not found them yet. I doubt he knows how to get through the Gap. But if we discovered how to get Arianna and the Sunchaser to Glacier River Farm, it won't be long before he figures it out, too."

Atalanta's mane drifted in front of her face, obscuring her violet eyes for a moment. "Who knows what will happen then? Our magic is limited on the other side of the Gap. I thought his evil was, too. Now I am not so sure. The loss of visions from the Watching Pool is not natural. And I have no idea what happened to Arianna between the time I saw her fall asleep in the hospital and when I saw her in the wheelchair. But I do know this: Without Arianna and the Sunchaser, the animals in Balinor will begin to lose their ability to speak. And when that happens, there will be chaos. If the bullocks can't be asked to pull the plow, there will be no crops, and eventually no food. If the Balinor unicorns can't be told where to carry their riders, the army won't be able to fight! Balinor will be in the Shifter's power.

"And then . . ." Atalanta turned to face the sun. Her horn gleamed with a hot, pure light. "The waters of the Watching Pool will go dark. Humans and animals alike will be forced into slavery to serve the Shifter's will. Then, Numinor, the Imperial River will dry up, and the Celestial Valley will wither. The Shifter will attack us here. And if we lose . . ." Her voice trailed away.

Atalanta's deep purple gaze swept the lovely valley. The sapphire willow trees were in full flower.

The meadow was thick and green. Two unicorn colts skipped in the sunshine and sang. She said, so softly that Numinor could barely hear her, "All this will be lost."

The great stallion looked toward the sun. His voice was grim. "It's what the Shifter wants, Atalanta. Chaos. The animals of Balinor used as slaves and worse. So he can rule totally and without opposition. He has already kidnapped the King and Queen. Hidden the Princes. All this before we could act. We thought that sending Arianna and the Sunchaser through the Gap would at least ensure that the humans and animals of Balinor could still speak together. If they cannot, if the two races cannot communicate, there is no way the Shifter can be overthrown."

Atalanta stood close to Numinor. He smelled of fresh grass and clear water. The terrible Eye was gone, but it seemed to her that a faint scent of dead and dying things still drifted in the air. "You know the law, Numinor. I cannot cross into the Gap. Not unless Arianna and the Sunchaser summon me. I can only appear to her in dreams. That's all. If for some reason she cannot bond with the Sunchaser, we are in terrible trouble indeed."

"There must be something we can do, Atalanta."

The Dreamspeaker bowed her head in thought. "There may be one thing, at least. If I can

21

find the Sunchaser's jewel and get it to him, it may help him, and Ari, too. The jewel is a crucial part of the bonding, Numinor."

"I know that," the stallion said testily. "But where is it? And how will you get to the Sunchaser? And how will he know what to do with it when he does have it?"

"Leave that to me."

"I have left it to you. I've left it to you and look what's happened!"

Atalanta looked at him, a long, level look. "Do you wish to quarrel, Numinor? After all these years together? It's to the Shifter's advantage to have us at each other's throats."

"You're right. I'm sorry. But this . . . our whole way of life! It could disappear in war!"

"I will do all I can do. But I have to act now. The Shifter may have thought of it himself. If he has . . ." She closed her eyes. "I won't think about it. Not now. Leave me, Numinor. I have work to do. I have to send someone to help them."

4

Ari jerked from her deep sleep. Was that a sound of bells? She blinked. Time had passed. She didn't know how much. Suddenly, she knew without a doubt there was someone else in the hospital room with her.

Instinctively, she grabbed for the heaviest weapon she could find — her water pitcher. She held her breath. Her hand tightened on the pitcher. Whatever this danger was, she was ready.

A dog trotted around the side of the hospital bed and thrust its cold nose under her hand. Ari breathed out in relief. The dog was friendly. She could tell that right away. It was a male collie with a magnificent gold-and-black coat. The ruff around his neck was creamy white. His head was elegantly narrow, and his ears were up. A white blaze ran down the middle of his tawny nose.

Ari ran her fingers gently over his head, then snuggled them deep in his ruff. If he had a collar, she might be able to find his owner. Yes, there it was, a thin chain wound deep in the fur. Was that what had made the chiming sound? She fumbled for a minute, then tugged it free.

A necklace, not a collar! She held it up. The chain was made of a fine silver and gold metal. Each link in the chain was a curiously twisted spiral. A ruby-colored jewel hung at the end, as large as her thumb. The late afternoon sun struck crimson lights from the jewel. "Well!" Ari said. "Your owner must miss this!"

The dog barked and pawed urgently at her hand.

"Shall I keep it for you? It might get lost if you have it. And we'll give it back when we find your master."

He panted happily at her, then licked her wrist with his pink tongue. Ari slipped the chain over her neck. The ruby nestled against her chest. It was warm, perhaps from being snuggled in the dog's fur.

"Who are you?" Ari asked softly. "And what are you doing here?"

The dog nudged her hand with his head. Suddenly, he turned to face the door to her room. A low rumbling began in his throat. It rose to a growl, then a snarl. The door swung inward, and a nurse Ari didn't know walked into the room. He was pushing a wheelchair. He stopped at the sight of the menacing dog.

"Wow," he said. "Hey." He lifted both hands,

either to keep the dog away, or to show that he didn't mean any harm. "Don't make any sudden moves, Miss Langley. You just keep calm." He edged sideways into the room. The dog swung his head as the nurse came closer. The snarls increased. "Now look, Miss Langley. I know you can't get out of bed, but you can cover your head and chest with the pillows, okay? I'm gonna have to call Security. I can't handle a dog this big by myself. But you're going to be all right. Just stay calm."

"I am calm," Ari said. "I'm just fine." She tapped the dog lightly on the head. "Easy, boy. Easy."

The growls stopped. The collie turned and looked up at her, as if to say, *Are you sure this is okay?*

"I'm sure," Ari said. "Lie down, boy."

The big dog lay down with a thump.

"It's *your* dog?" the nurse said in astonishment. His face turned red with embarrassment and anger. "You can't keep a dog in here!"

The door behind him banged open. Two uniformed men rushed in. Behind them were Ann and a thin man with a worried face and a long brown mustache. The collie leaped to his feet, then backed protectively against the bed, staying between Ari and the others.

"Linc! Lincoln!" Ann said. "There he is! Come here, boy. Come *here*! Frank! Do something!"

The worried-looking man dropped to one knee and began to chirp, "Here, Lincoln. Good doggie. Good doggie."

25

The dog turned to Ari, ignoring them all. There was a question in his deep brown eyes. Ari twined one hand deep in his ruff.

"He jumped in the car when we left the farm," Ann explained to the security guard. "Then he jumped out when we got to the hospital and ran off. I don't know how he knew Ari was here. He's always been her dog, and none of us can do a thing with him. Lincoln!" she added despairingly. "Come HERE!"

"Lincoln," Ari said. "Is that your name?"

He barked. Ari's hand went to the neck of her hospital gown. The ruby lay warm beneath her hand. If the necklace belonged to the collie's owner — then the jewel was hers?

"You don't remember Lincoln?" Ann burst into tears. Frank patted her awkwardly on the back. "Oh, Ari. Oh, Ari!" Ann sobbed.

"I don't care if it belongs to the President of the United States, that dog has got to go," the nurse said. "Here, you two guys are with Security, right? Take him out of here."

Lincoln growled. He rolled his upper lip back, showing his sharp white teeth. The two security men exchanged a nervous look. One of them cleared his throat. "Ah," he said, "I don't think this-here is in my job description. I don't think it is. No-sir."

"It doesn't matter," Ann said impatiently. She wiped her nose with the back of her hand and sniffed. "Ari's coming home with us now, anyway, and the dog goes wherever she goes."

"You know the doctors don't think she's ready to go home," the nurse said in a fussy way. "If you two were responsible foster parents, you'd keep her right here. Where she belongs."

"Responsible foster parents don't run up hospital bills they can't pay," Ann said tartly. "And we've made some arrangements. A friend of ours suddenly showed up this afternoon, and she's going to stay with Ari as long as we need her. She's a medical person, a veterinarian. Her name is Dr. Bohnes. You remember Dr. Bohnes, Ari?"

Ari didn't. She shook her head. All at once, an image of a short, stocky old lady with bright blue eyes and white hair popped into her head. As if someone or something had sent the image to her!

"Well, you will," Ann said in a positive way. "She's a very old friend of yours, milady, I mean Ari." She turned back to the nurse. "So you see? We can take Ari home now. Dr. Bohnes has been given all the instructions needed for her therapy. She'll get the best care we can give her. Come on, Ari. Let's get you *home*."

Ari allowed herself to be helped into the wheelchair. Ann draped a light jacket over her shoulders and a cotton throw over her knees. Then the nurse pushed the wheelchair down the long corridor and out into the sunshine. Lincoln walked gravely by her side.

Free of the hospital at last! Ari blinked in the bright light, at the cars in the parking lot, a plane flying overhead, the smell of gasoline, the crowds of people. Ann explained everything Ari saw. Each time Ari asked and asked again, she felt more desperate. None of this was familiar. None of this was *home*. But she had no idea of what *would* be home. Ann and Frank helped her into the van. They were on their way to Glacier River Farm.

Ari kept a tight hand on Lincoln's ruff and tried to fight her fear.

Frank lifted Ari onto the backseat and folded the wheelchair down to store it. Ari held on to the overhead strap and gazed out the window all the way to the farm. They passed quickly through the city and out onto a huge road that seemed to end at the sky. "The Thruway," Ann explained. "The farm is only twenty minutes from here. Do you remember yet?"

Ari remembered nothing. She held on to the collie as the van went down an exit ramp and turned onto a small deserted road. They passed fields of corn and purple-green alfalfa. Finally, they came to a long stretch of white three-board fence. A sign read GLACIER RIVER FARM, with an arrow pointing away from them toward the east.

Frank turned into a winding driveway made of gravel and stone, and they bumped along toward a large gray farmhouse standing on the crest of the hill. Long gray barns with green roofs spilled down the hillside. Ari could see horses in the pastures, grazing quietly under the sun.

"You'll want to see Chase first, I expect." Ann turned and looked at Ari over the passenger headrest.

CHASE! Ari's heart leaped at the name. Her hand tightened on Linc's ruff. He whined in sympathy. The van bumped to a stop in front of the largest barn. Ari waited patiently while Frank carefully set the wheelchair up on the gravel drive. Then he reached into the van and hoisted Ari into the chair with a grunt of effort.

"Watch her legs, Frank," Ann fussed. "Take it easy, now. And don't push her too fast!"

Frank rolled the chair into the barn. Ari took a deep breath: She loved the barn at once. There was the scent of horses, straw, and the spicy odor of sun-cured hay. Stalls lined the broad gravel aisle. Most of them were empty, but a few curious horses poked their heads over the half doors and watched the little procession roll past. Lincoln trotted beside Ari, his head up, ears tuliped forward in eager attention. His eyes brightened. And as they came to the end of the long aisle, to a large box stall in the corner, he gave a welcoming bark.

Frank rolled the wheelchair to a stop and stepped back. Ari couldn't see anything in the gloom at first. Her heart beating fast, she rolled herself forward, then pushed the half door to the stall aside. It rolled back and daylight flooded in. A great shape lay curled in the corner. The head turned as

29

she rolled farther into the stall, and then the animal got to his feet.

It was a stallion. The light gleamed on his bronze coat. His chest and quarters were heavily muscled, his withers well-shaped. But it was his head and eyes that were the most beautiful to Ari. His forehead was broad, the muzzle well-shaped, with delicately flared nostrils. As he stepped forward, she looked deep into his eyes, large, brown, and full of sorrow.

"Chase," she whispered. "You are Chase. I . . . Ann!" She gasped and bit short a scream. The light hit a great wound in his forehead. She could see the stitches holding the gouge shut.

"The accident," Ann said gloomily. "Hadn't been for Dr. Bohnes, we might have lost him."

"Might have lost Ari as well," a tart voice snapped.

"Oh, Dr. Bohnes." Frank gave his mustache a nervous tug and backed away respectfully. The vet marched into the stall and put her hand on Ari's shoulder. She was small, but sturdily built, with snow-white hair and bright blue eyes. She was wearing high rubber boots, a stethoscope swinging from her neck.

Ari half turned in her wheelchair, reluctant to take her eyes from the stallion. If she gazed at him long enough, if she could touch him . . .

"Do you remember anything?" Dr. Bohnes asked softly.

"I know his name," Ari said sadly. "And that's all. He is mine, isn't he?"

"Till the end of time." Dr. Bohnes clapped her hands together with a competent air. Her sharp blue eyes traveled over Ari's face. "Humph! They didn't feed you too well in that place, I see."

"Please!" Ari said. She stretched her hands out to the stallion. He stepped forward delicately, as if treading on fragile ground. He bent his head and breathed into her hair. "Chase!" Ari cried. She wound her arms around his neck, as far as she could reach. She laid her cheek against his warm chest. She could feel the mighty heart, slow and steady, and his even breathing.

"Do you remember . . . anything?" Dr. Bohnes asked softly.

"I've lost something!" Ari cried. "That's all I know. But I don't know what it is!"

Dr. Bohnes patted her back in brisk sympathy. "I'll tell you what, young lady. We'll get to work on those legs of yours. And I know just what will help strengthen them."

"Riding?" Ann said, her voice alight with satisfaction.

"Riding," Dr. Bohnes confirmed. "As soon as we get you on your feet, my dear, we'll get you on your horse. And as soon as we get you on your horse . . ." The three adults exchanged glances.

"Yes?" Ari prompted. She kept her hand on

31

the stallion's side, as if to make sure they wouldn't be parted again.

"Well. We'll see."

"How soon?" Ari asked. Her eyes met the stallion's, and she smiled. "How soon before I ride?"

Dr. Bohnes screwed up her face. It looked like a potato. "How soon? That, my dear, depends on you. And on how much pain you want to put up with."

Ari set her jaw. "As much as I have to," she said. "I used to ride him? Every day?"

"Never apart," Frank said sadly. He chewed his mustache with a melancholy air. "Well, you slept in the palace, I mean — in the house, of course. Not in his stall. But still!"

"We won't be apart for long," Ari promised. She raised her hands to his face. He bent his head further so that she could examine the wound on his forehead. Whatever had happened, it had been a terrible blow. The stitches had healed well, but the skin was soft over a depression right in the middle of his forehead. She remembered something: Scars like this one healed white. She closed her eyes so that the others wouldn't see the tears. Why could she remember things like this, and nothing about her own past? She felt his breath on her cheek. It was warm and smelled of grass. She looked into his eyes, and he gazed back, his own eyes searching hers.

Horses didn't look directly at humans. No animal did. Ari knew that, just the way she knew how to pull on a pair of jeans or wear a T-shirt. "Dr. Bohnes," Ari said after a moment. "The accident . . . both of us were in it?"

"That's right," Dr. Bohnes said.

"It was a car accident?"

"We don't talk about it," Ann said. "It doesn't do to talk about it. It was terrible. Terrible."

"I just wanted to know — did Chase forget, as I did? Has he lost his memory?" She rubbed her eyes. She was tired. So tired! Not much was making sense right now. "I know that's a silly question, in a way. How would you know if a horse lost his memory? But I can't help feeling that — I don't know. That he's trying to tell me something."

"Perhaps he is," Dr. Bohnes agreed. "The coming weeks will tell, won't they?" She put her hand on Ari's shoulder. "This one needs sleep, Anale. She's practically falling out of her chair. Let's get her up to bed."

"Anale," Ari said drowsily. "Anale. I knew someone by that name, once."

"You will again, milady," Ann said, tucking the blanket around her knees. Frank began to push the wheelchair down the barn aisle.

Ari could barely keep her eyes open. "Chase," she whispered. "Chase."

The stallion whinnied, a loud, trumpeting call that jerked her back from the shores of sleep. "I'll be back soon, Chase," she said. "I promise."

33

5

The sun sank below the Western Ridge of the Celestial Valley. A few stars shone at the edge of the twilight sky. Atalanta backed away from the Watching Pool. She was disturbed by what she'd seen. No. She was afraid. Arianna had no memory of who she was. Chase was deaf to his Bonded Mistress. And there was the dog. What was she going to do about the dog?

The Imperial River reflected the stars and the line of rainbow-shower trees that grew at the north side of the Watching Pool, but tonight the waters would not reflect the moon. This was the first night of the Shifter's Moon, when the Silver Traveler's Dark Side faced the Celestial Valley. For four nights in a row, no magic would work at all.

The Dreamspeaker cantered up the hillside. There would be no sleep again for her tonight, nor for any of the Celestial Valley herd. On Dark Side nights, the unicorns stayed awake. Mares with colts and fillies took shelter on the lee side of the valley, out of the evening wind. The others, mares and stallions alike, were supposed to pace the valley in a guardian circle, alert for sights or sounds of the Shifter's forces. There had never been an invasion of the Celestial Valley, not within Atalanta's memory. So the Ritual of the Shifter's Moon had become an excuse for staying up all night, singing, dancing, and telling stories and tales unicorns loved to hear.

It was different tonight. Because of what Atalanta had just seen, the Ritual of the Shifter's Moon was a grim necessity.

Atalanta jumped gracefully over a log, then picked her way through a fall of rocks to the place where the brood mares stood with their young. She came to a halt on an outcrop of rock. Just below her, the unicorns cropped grass and exchanged gossip. The colts and fillies jumped and rolled, excited to be up this late. Nobody, Atalanta thought sadly, had a thought of war. Only Ash, a silver-gray unicorn close to Atalanta's own color, and a leader in the Rainbow Army, knew anything at all about fighting. Ash was practicing attack. But then, Ash spent all of his free time practicing fighting, because he liked the exercise. He dove forward, forelegs extended, head down, ears flattened against his skull. His steel-gray horn pierced the night air. This movement was called the "Otter," after the sleek river creature. Then Ash darted sideways, head moving back and forth, back and forth, snapping his teeth. This was called the "Snake." Atalanta watched him for a few moments. Then she tapped her foreleg on the rock shelf.

"Friends!" she called. Her voice was low and sweet. But somehow, the call attracted the attention of the entire herd. In silence, they gathered in front of her, the rainbow colors of their coats invisible in the dim light thrown by the stars. "Friends! You must guard in pairs tonight. And tell me if you find any of these things in our valley:

"A smell of dead and dying things. This is an odor like none you've encountered before. Once you smell it, you will not mistake it.

"The sight of a black unicorn, or one with eyes of fire.

"Any human or animal unknown to us." She paused for a long moment. "Especially a dog."

"A dog, Dreamspeaker?" Rednal, the crimson unicorn, spoke. "But I thought . . . we had heard that the Princess has the Sunchaser's jewel, and that the jewel was brought to her by —"

"Be quiet!" Atalanta said, not quite angry, but close. "There are ears and eyes abroad tonight that are no friends of ours. You will not speak, or guess at what events are occurring in the world below, in Balinor, or on the other side of the Gap. We can't take the chance that it will give the enemy information that he could use. Just remember that the

36

Shifter can take the form of anything. Anything at all."

"We know that, Dreamspeaker," Rednal said cheerfully. "But even Entia himself can't hold the shape of another for very long. So if we, say, stare at a tree for more than a few minutes, and it turns into, um . . . alfalfa, we'll know immediately . . ."

"To eat it!" another unicorn called out. "Alfalfa's my favorite food!"

There were some giggles from the herd. Atalanta frowned to herself. How would they react to what she had just learned? "The nature of magic changes," she said. "We no longer know how long the Shifter can maintain a shape that is not his own. Now, I'd like three or four of you to take the colts and fillies below. Down to the windbreak by the river."

"But, Dreamspeaker." A portly mare with a very young colt by her side spoke up in protest. The colt's horn was barely the length of Atalanta's hoof, which meant he wasn't more than a few days old. "We were all going to tell stories tonight. It will be the first time for my young one here."

"Please," Atalanta said. The word was mild, but her tone wasn't. Several of the unicorns exchanged significant looks. They were a little afraid of the Dreamspeaker. There had been rumors that she went beyond the usual use of magic to . . . what, no one really knew.

There wasn't any more discussion. Two

mares herded the colts and fillies into a small circle and led them out of the grove. Atalanta waited until she was sure they couldn't hear her. Then, since there was no way to soften her news, she said it straight out.

"I did not send the dog to Arianna. I did not find the jewel." A soft breeze picked up her forelock and stirred her mane. "I don't know who did. There is other magic abroad in Balinor and beyond the Gap. I don't know where this magic is from."

"But what shall we do?" Rednal was bewildered.

"We wait. She will heal, in time. And as she does, I will send her dreams. I can do no more. Except one thing. I can hope. I shall hope. I hope that Arianna remembers who and what she is. And that she puts the Sunchaser's jewel to its proper use."

6

The first month at Glacier River Farm, Ari was confined to her room. She slept a lot, her dreams frequent and puzzling. She had no idea what they meant.

She lived for the mornings. Each morning, Frank brought Chase out to pasture and stopped beneath her window. She waved and called to him, fighting the intense longing to be up and with him. Her legs wouldn't heal fast enough. It seemed to take forever.

"You're coming along quite nicely," Dr. Bohnes said. It was a fresh summer morning. Ari's window was open. The smell of new-mown grass drifted into her room. Six weeks before, she had come home from the hospital. Her days had been an endless round of doctor's visits, and X rays, and casts.

She was tired of it all. And even the memory of the tunnel had faded.

Dr. Bohnes picked up another gob of salve from the jar and dug her fingers into Ari's right calf.

Ari winced, but she didn't cry out. The massage therapy worked. She'd walked outside on the lawn every day this week, hardly using the crutches at all. "But when can I ride Chase?"

Dr. Bohnes's old fingers were strong. She worked the salve all the way down to Ari's ankle, then took an elastic bandage and wrapped her leg all the way to the knee. "Get up," she said.

Ari swung her legs over the side of the bed. Linc was asleep on the floor and she nudged him gently with her toe. He opened one eye and yawned, then rolled out of the way. She stood up, determined not to use the cane. Pain slammed her right leg like a hot iron brand. She bit her lip and shifted her weight to her left side. That at least was only an ache. "It's fine," she said with a gasp. "Just fine."

"Hmph." Dr. Bohnes drew her eyebrows together in a skeptical way. "You're going down to dinner tonight? With Frank and Ann?"

"Yes."

"You ask your foster parents about riding Chase."

"They'll want to know if it's okay with you."

"It's okay with me."

"Then is there a problem? Chase is mine, isn't he." She didn't say this as a question. She'd asked questions for two months. Where are my real parents? How long have I lived here? Where did I live before? Why are my dreams so weird? And Dr. Bohnes didn't have any answers. None that Ari believed, at any rate. But Ari didn't have to ask who owned Chase, she *knew* it: Chase was hers. Forever.

Dr. Bohnes narrowed her eyes. They were a sharp, clear blue. Ari thought they saw everything. "Your memory any better?"

Ari shook her head.

"Well. You'll remember how to ride. It's like breathing, to somebody like you, anyhow."

"I rode? Was I . . ." Ari was shy of this particular question, but she had to ask. "Was I any good?"

"You were very good." Dr. Bohnes sniffed disapprovingly. Ari blushed. Being conceited was the worst crime ever in Dr. Bohnes's mind. Um . . . no, Ari thought. The second worst crime. Abusing an animal was worse. Dr. Bohnes rapped her knuckles with the stethoscope. "Are you listening to me? I'm giving you your riding program. Don't blink those big blue eyes at me, miss. I know how excited you are. Now. You ride twenty minutes *once* a day for a week. Hot baths every day and more massage. Then you can ride twenty minutes *twice* a day for a week. All at the walk. Then divide the time in the saddle between the walk and the trot. We'll extend the time, twenty minutes at a time, until you're up to an hour. Once you're up to an hour, you can try cantering. No jumping for a month."

41

"No jumping for a month," Ari concluded at dinner. She was so excited, she hardly noticed what she was eating. "So if it's fine with Dr. Bohnes, it's fine with you?"

Ann poked her fork into her mashed potatoes. "You tell her, Frank."

"Me!" Frank twisted his mustache. Then he ran his hands through his hair. He'd been eating peas, and one of them was stuck in his thin, wispy beard. "Why me?"

Ann put her fork down and glared at him. "Because *I'm* not gonna do it."

"Tell me what?" Ari asked.

"There's a problem with Chase."

Ari's heart went cold in her chest. "He's not sick. If he were sick, I'd know about it. I can almost feel him think. And that wound in his forehead is almost healed. Isn't it?"

"He's just fine, honey." Frank patted her hand. "But we have these bills from the hospital . . ."

Ari ignored this. "If Chase is healthy, it's okay. You can tell me anything."

Ann cleared her throat. "You know the Carmichaels."

"That rich guy and his daughter? You've told me about them."

"We — she's taken a shine to Chase."

"Anyone would," Ari said lovingly.

"And they've offered us a lot of money to lease him for a year."

"What?" Ari was aware that her voice was soft and her tone mild. "You said no, of course."

"We're not selling him, or anything like that, of course!" Frank said in a shocked way. "This lease is just like rent. He'll be right here at Glacier River Farm. They won't own him, or anything like that. I mean, he's not ours to sell."

"He's *mine!*" Ari burst out.

"He's not yours to sell, either, milady," Ann said gently. "But we need the cash bad, Ari."

"Lease her another horse," Ari said.

"She doesn't want another horse," Frank said. He wriggled in his chair. He was very upset, Ari could see. She could also see that no one would want another horse if Chase were around.

"Well, she can't have him," Ari said flatly. "He's special. He's *mine!*"

Frank shrugged. "He's just another horse now, Ari, without his . . ."

"Frank!" Ann said warningly. "You know Dr. Bohnes said she has to remember all by herself. Or it won't stick." She leaned over and patted Ari's hand. "I'm sorry. I'm real sorry. But we don't know what else to do. We gotta eat, Ari. And this is the only way we know how to make money. Please, honey. Please. You've got a month more. Then they take him."

The bills. The hospital bills. They were her fault. But she had a month. Four weeks when she didn't have to think about it. And, holding back hot tears, Ari said, "All right."

She thought the words would choke her.

7

The sun rose over Glacier River Farm, washing pale color over the green pastures and turning the white fences to butter-yellow. Linc walked down the gravel path to the stream that bordered the woods surrounding the barns and old gray house.

"Linc! Lincoln!" Ari's voice had wisdom and a warm authority in it. The dog turned eagerly. The call came from a thick stand of pines that stood just beyond the small waterfall that fed Glacier Brook. He cocked his head, and his ears tuliped forward.

"L-i-i-incoln!" Ari and Chase cantered out of the trees and into the sunlight. She drew in the reins, stopped, and smiled at the collie. "Where have you been?" she teased him. "Chase and I have been out for miles. And you missed it all, Linc."

The dog raised his muzzle and barked happily. Ari snapped her fingers lightly, and the dog pranced to her side.

Ari wore breeches, high black boots, and a faded T-shirt. The sun glanced off the ruby jewel suspended from a gold chain at her throat. She had left her hair unbound this morning, and it swept past her waist and just touched the back of her saddle. The great horse she rode bent his neck and danced as the collie approached. Ari swayed gracefully in the saddle and flexed the reins. "Easy now, Chase," she said. Amusement colored her tones. "You know Linc."

The horse snorted and pawed the ground, arrogance in the set of his head and neck. *Ah, yes, I know him,* he seemed to say. *But will he obey the Great Me?*

Ari settled into the saddle and quieted Chase to a full halt. She patted her left thigh. Linc rose on his hindquarters, resting his front paws against thickly padded girth. Chase shook his head irritably but stayed quiet under her hands. Ari scratched the collie's nose affectionately. "I want you both to be good today," she said softly. "I know neither of you is going to understand what will happen. But you have to bear it. You have to bear it for my sake." Linc dropped to the ground and cocked his head to one side. His forehead wrinkled with a question. "Our month is up. And we've got a problem. It's a girl who takes riding lessons here. Her name is Lori Carmichael."

Linc growled a little. Chase shifted on his hooves.

"She met Chase while I was laid up with these stupid legs of mine. She really . . . likes him." Ari took a deep breath and fought back tears. She had to act normally, for her animals' sake. "Her parents have taken out a lease on you, Chase. They're paying a lot of money so that she can ride you for a year. And the farm needs the money. This . . ." She swallowed hard, the tears she'd sworn she'd never shed now rising in her throat. She stroked the horse's neck. "This is our last ride, Chase. Just for a while, that is. This morning, Lori's coming over and I'm going to give her a lesson, to show her how to ride you." She sat a little straighter in the saddle. "So. I still own you, Chase. I've just had to lend you out a bit. Frank and Ann need the money for my medical bills, and there's no other way for me to raise it. I'm so sorry. I'm so dreadfully sorry. But there's no other way around it. Now, both of you are going to behave, aren't you? Linc? Chase?"

The collie barked. Chase flicked one ear back. Ari waited a moment for her voice to come under control. "We'll be late for morning chores," Ari said to the both of them. "Let's ride!" She touched her heels lightly to Chase's side, and they cantered toward the big barn that formed the heart of Glacier River Farm. Chase jumped the three-board fence that bordered the south pasture with careless ease, but the fence was too high for Linc. The collie grumbled softly under his breath, then wriggled through between the two lowest boards. Ari glanced over

47

her shoulder and grinned to herself. The big dog was fastidious, and he hated to get his coat rumpled. She'd brush him after she cooled Chase out.

As horse and girl swept through the pasture, Ari kept a keen eye on the ground ahead. Here, the grass was knee-high, due to be mowed for hay. The heavy growth disguised the earth and would conceal any woodchuck holes that might trip the great chestnut stallion up. But more than that, there was something about this spot that suddenly disturbed her. She didn't know why, just that this place, a mile or more from the safety of the farm itself, was eerily quiet. No birds sang here, and the wildflowers were scarce.

She flexed Chase to a walk. She wasn't anxious to get back on this, her last free morning on her stallion.

At first, the sound was no more than a breath on the wind sailing past her ears:

Arianna, Arianna, Arianna.

She drove her back lightly into the saddle and flexed the reins to check Chase's forward stride. Yes, there it was again. Her name, sailing the breeze.

Arianna!

"Yes?" she said. She came to a full halt and turned in the saddle. The pasture was quiet under the morning sun. Unnaturally quiet for this already spooky place. Even the breeze was stilled. It was as if the world held its breath.

48

Chase curvetted under her hand. She sat easily erect as he turned in a circle.

Nothing stirred. Nothing at all. Then, to her astonishment, she heard a quarrel: two voices — one low, angry, and hissing, the other high and panicked. Ari's throat tightened. The grass here was high, but not high enough to conceal a person, not even a small child. Where were the voices coming from? And what was the quarrel about? She couldn't distinguish the words, just the pitch of the two speakers. She guessed the fight was over something that the high-voiced one had, which the hisser wanted badly.

Suddenly, Lincoln dashed forward, barking furiously. He leaped into a stand of taller grass that grew just in front of them. The high-pitched voice shrieked. Lincoln's deep barks turned to angry growls.

"Lincoln!" Ari swung out of the saddle, wincing a little as her bad leg hit the ground. She held Chase's reins in one hand and walked forward. Her heart was hammering in her chest, but she said calmly, "Hello? Is anyone there?"

Lincoln's barks stopped abruptly, as if a brutal hand had closed around his throat. Fear for her pet drove Ari forward. "Lincoln," she called firmly. "Here, boy."

There was no movement in the clump of grass, just a flash of Lincoln's gold-and-black coat.

And something else. A shadow slipped through the grass. Quietly. Slyly.

She took a deep breath. A terrible odor hit her like a blow. Dark, fetid, and bloody. Chase shrilled a high, warning whinny. He threw his great bronze body in front of hers and she reeled backward, landing on the ground with a painful thud.

"Whoa, Chase," she said, in an I-really-mean-it voice. "You *stand*."

The horse flung his head up and down, up and down, the odd white scar on his forehead catching the sunlight like a prism. But he obeyed her and stood trembling as she dropped the reins and walked forward to the brush that concealed her dog.

She knelt and parted the grass with both hands. Lincoln bolted out of the grass, his jaws speckled with a dark, oily liquid that gave off that hideous smell, his barks splitting the air like a hammer. Behind him, the hissing voice rose in a frustrated wail: *Give it back!*

The dog snarled, almost if he were saying, *No!*

Ari grabbed Linc's ruff with both hands. "You *sit*," she told him.

He sat, his brown eyes desperate. He raised one white forepaw and clawed urgently at her knees.

"It's okay," she soothed him. "It's *okay*." Gently, she pushed him aside and bent forward. She parted the long grass. Whatever it was lay coiled in a stinking puddle just beneath her searching hand. She held back a scream and took a deep breath. She narrowed her eyes, trying to bring whatever it was into focus, but the black and oily substance shifted, twisted, and coiled like a snake. Impossible to make out the shape.

She bent lower, her hair falling around her cheeks. The blackness spun in a whirlpool that burrowed deep into the earth. And at the bottom of the pool was a red-rimmed, fiery eye. The eye turned, rolled, searched the air above her. Saw her. And fastened its hideous gaze on her face.

Fear hit Ari like a tidal wave. It engulfed her: cold, relentless, unimaginable. She struggled with the fear like a rabbit in the jaws of a snake. She forced her hands over her own eyes, to shut out that terrible searching gaze.

Then a whisper came out of the air over her shoulder, from the first speaker. An older man, perhaps? *Come back, Arianna. Come back.*

Ari straightened her shoulders and took her hands from her face. Whatever was going on, it was better to face it than to hide. She spun around. Her dog and her horse looked back at her. There was nothing else in the meadow. She forced herself to turn to the terrible pool and the red-rimmed eye in its depths. Ari swallowed the sickness rising in her throat and said, too loudly, "Get out of here. Go on. GET! Both of you!"

The eye blinked and disappeared. Nothing

51

remained of the oily pool. No scent. No sound. And the voice on the breeze was gone. Her fear receded. Just like a wave at the beach, it ebbed and flowed away.

Ari sat back on her heels, frowning. Her heartbeats slowed to normal. She got up and ran swift hands over Chase's back and legs: He was okay at least. She turned to Linc, who waited patiently as she explored his fur with quick fingers. No cuts. No bruises. If that *thing* had been trapped somehow, it hadn't hurt the dog. Then she felt something deep in the fur at Linc's throat. She tugged it carefully free and turned it over in her palm.

"What's this?!" she said. "Look at this!" She held it up so that the sun struck white light from it. A twisted shell of silver, the size of charms on a necklace. The charm was about an inch and a half long and no more than an eighth of an inch wide. It was the long, pointy sort of shell that might have held a very thin snail. Ari held it up and admired it.

Chase whinnied. Ari jumped a little at the sound. Chase whinnied again, more urgently. Ari looked at her watch. "Uh-oh. You're right, Chase. We *are* going to be late!" She tucked the tiny shell in her shirt pocket and scrambled to her feet. If she was very late, poor Ann would be as mad as fire. Ari knew how hard it was, making a living on a horse farm, even one as beautiful and big as Glacier River.

Ari remounted, and the three of them headed home.

8

Just a few minutes later, Ari and Chase leaped the five-bar gate in the fence that bordered the farmyard. Ann came out of the barn at the sound of hooves on the driveway.

"You were gone awhile," she said. Ari noticed that Ann had patched her jeans with duct tape. No wonder Ann and Frank hadn't been able to resist the huge amount of money Lori's parents were willing to pay the farm to lease Chase for Lori's private use.

Ari closed her eyes briefly against the familiar stab of pain: Chase being leased, *used*, by a stranger. She shoved the thoughts out of her head and smiled down at Ann.

"Thought you might have fallen off." Ann's eyes were bright and curious.

"Off Chase?" Ari kept her voice warm. "Never." She hesitated. Should she tell Ann about the strange incident in the pasture?

Ann shot a swift, secretive glance toward Ari's legs in their breeches and high black boots. "A person never knows what you're up to,"she said. Her mouth thinned in affectionate annoyance. "And I worry about you." Then Ann asked, "How are your legs? The hospital called about getting a new set of X rays."

Oh, my, Ari thought. X rays were expensive. It's a bad day for her already. She doesn't need to hear about that creepy eye. "My legs feel fine this morning," Ari lied. "I don't need any more X rays." She swung out of the saddle and dropped to the ground. It was an effort, but she kept the pain out of her face. "A few more weeks of riding, and you'll never know that I've been in an accident."

That strange, flickering glance at her legs again. Ann ducked her head. Ari knew Ann didn't believe her. "Well," she said with a brave smile, "I'm sure we all hope so. But you must be careful, my . . ." She stopped herself. "Ari," she added.

Ari wished for the thousandth time that she could remember her life before the accident that broke her legs and gave her a concussion. That she could recall her mother and her father. That she knew why, out of all the foster parents that the county social services department could have chosen, she'd been placed here with Ann and Frank, who never seemed to know how to deal with her. Who had treated her with a weird mixture of love

54

and respect in the three slow, painful months of recovery she had spent here already.

"I think the orthopedist will be pleased when he sees me next week, Ann. We managed to jump five fences this morning, Chase and I. And we galloped for a good twenty minutes."

"Cool him out really well before the Carmichaels get here," Ann suggested. Then she said with mock bossiness, "And you get to cleaning those stalls quick, you hear?"

"You bet," Ari said cheerfully. She looped Chase's reins into one hand and walked him into the barn.

She took Chase down the aisle to the wash racks, past the stalls lining either side. She didn't remember anything about her life before the accident, but she knew she must have loved this place. Each stall was made of varnished oak, with black iron hayracks and black barred doors. Most of the horses were turned out to pasture. They'd been in their stalls all night. Ari had volunteered to clean out the manure and put fresh bedding in for them before they came in from pasture. Their names were on brass plates over the doors: MAX, SCOOTER, SHY-NO-MORE, BEECHER, and CINNAMON — the names went on and on.

She led Chase to the cool-water wash rack and took off his saddle and bridle. She hooked him into the cross ties and turned the shower on. Lincoln curled into the corner with a heavy sigh. Ari suppressed a giggle. Lincoln was resigned to what the rest of the morning would bring: the routine that went on day after day, cooling down, mucking out, training the young horses on the longe line. It'd be hours before she'd have time to brush Linc and clean his white forepaws. And Lori Carmichael would be coming this morning for her first lesson on Chase.

Ari frowned at that and stroked the great horse's neck. She was going to do her best to talk Lori out of using a harsh bit on Chase. Frank had admitted Lori wasn't a very good rider. Lori would want to use the harshest bit she could, since that was an easy way for a bad rider to get control of a horse that knew more than the rider did.

Chase turned and looked at her, a question in his deep brown eyes.

"It'll be a short lesson, Chase. I promise." He was a huge horse, close to seventeen hands high, and she had to stand on tiptoe to whisper in his ear. She ignored the spray of water down her back. "And I'll make sure she uses a snaffle today. You know that if it were up to me, I'd throw all the Carmichaels off the farm, don't you?"

He nodded, as if he understood. Ari ran her hands down his satiny neck, then over the white scar in the center of his forehead. That was the thing about Chase. He always understood.

In the months she'd spent recovering, Ari

had relearned Glacier River Farm and how it worked. Ann and Frank boarded and trained more than forty horses at the farm. Frank said that the farm had everything a horse owner could want, and more. The pastures were green and smooth, with triple-barred white fences all around. The buildings — barns, house, and indoor arena — were built of a warm red brick that glowed in the sun and was softened by rain. The farm veterinarian, Dr. Bohnes, had her own special office with a little clinic for injured horses in the boarder barn. There was even a small restaurant that was open for lunch and dinner for horse shows.

And, of course, there were trails. Miles and miles of trails. Ari and Dr. Bohnes had explored the strange, twisting roads that wound through the woods and valleys of the farm one afternoon. Dr. Bohnes had pushed Ari in a wheelchair. Some of the trails seemed to lead nowhere. At other times they seemed to lead everywhere. Ari had asked Dr. Bohnes about the unexpected caves and tunnels that filled the woods. She told the vet how they pulled at her — especially the cave in the south pasture.

Remembering now, she paused, one hand on Chase's neck. The south pasture. Where she'd seen that awful eye.

The old vet hadn't seemed surprised. But she'd warned Ari away from the tunnels. Millions of years ago, the glaciers moved through the land here like titanic ghost ships. As they moved, the land swelled under the glaciers like ocean waves, rising, falling, and folding itself to help smooth the glaciers' path to the sea beyond. The huge icebergs had long gone, but they'd left caves and tunnels under the softly swelling hills.

Ari was drawn to them in a way she couldn't explain. She'd told Frank about her need to explore, to find her way through them, and he'd given her an alarmed look. He was a mild-mannered man, and anxious. Worry lines creased his forehead, drew deep grooves on either side of his mouth. They got even more prominent when she'd told him about the way the caves seem to draw her in, beckoning.

"You can't!" he'd said, leaning forward, so close she could feel his breath. "You *stay away from them*!"

"Lincoln wouldn't let me get lost," she'd replied, frowning at the strangeness of his reaction. "He'd lead me home. And so would Chase."

Except that Chase wasn't hers anymore. You've got to remember that, she told herself.

"I remember that," Ari said aloud, softly. "I may not remember anything else, but I remember that." She wiped the water away from Chase's neck. His mane was long and gleaming. "How could I forget you belong to someone else now?" She touched the silver shell in her pocket. It lay there, warm under her hand. "Oh, Chase," she said sadly. "How can I remember if I belong anywhere? Or to anyone?"

She rolled the shell in her hand. It felt warm, almost hot.

"There's something," she murmured aloud. "There's something I'm supposed to do! Somewhere I'm supposed to go! Chase. Help me!"

The big horse rested his muzzle on her shoulder and breathed softly into her hair. But he didn't have an answer.

9

"Just take it easy, Princess," Mr. Carmichael shouted across the arena. "And if the horse gives you any trouble, give him the whip."

Lori Carmichael scowled and said, "For goodness *sake*, Dad," and bent to brush her spotless riding boots with a towel. She was shorter than Ari, and sturdily built. Her hair was white-blond and drawn back in a tight bun low on her neck. "Aren't you ready yet?" she snapped at Ari.

Ari hated her on sight.

The three of them, Chase, Ari, and Lori, were in the middle of the huge indoor arena, the center of all the riding activities at Glacier River Farm. Six inches of sand covered the floor. This made a cushioned footing for the horses. The building itself was huge. The rafters soared thirty feet high at the peak. They dropped to twenty feet at the walls to meet the bleachers that surrounded the arena on three sides. Mr. Carmichael, his wife, and Lori's older brother sat in the judge's box, where celebrities gathered at official horse shows when the prizes were given out.

"Let's *go*," Lori demanded. "Give me a leg up, will you?"

"You'll remember not to pull at his mouth," Ari said quietly. "And keep your weight off his back unless you want him to turn or stop."

"Excuse me?" Lori said. She lifted one eyebrow. Her eyes narrowed in sarcasm. "My father turned the check over to Frank five minutes ago. Which means this horse is *mine*."

Ari couldn't stop herself. All her good resolutions about accepting the lease agreement with courage went flying. "It's just for a year," she said. "And the agreement was that he's yours only when you come to the farm." She was angry, but she kept her gestures calm and her expression unexcited. "Could you wait a second, please? I'll just check the length of the stirrup leathers." Ari gave Lori a polite smile and moved closer to Chase. She slid one hand over his sleek withers and murmured so that only the horse could hear. "Please, Chase. Listen to me when she gets on. Listen to *me*."

She stepped back, handed the reins to Lori, and cupped her hands together to give Lori a leg up. The girl planted one black-booted foot in Ari's palm and heaved herself onto Chase's back. A short whip dangled from one wrist. She dropped into the saddle with a thump. She clutched the reins and pulled. Chase tossed his head and backed up.

"Whoa, now," Ari said. "Walk on, Chase."

The bronze horse shook his head from side to side, the harsh bit Lori's father had insisted on jingling in his mouth. Lori gave a small shriek and clapped both heels against his sides. Chase raised his muzzle and rolled his eye back so that the whites showed.

"Just sit still," Ari said, more loudly than she'd meant to. "He's never had anyone on his back but me. And he's not used to . . ."

"He'll just have to *get* used to it," Lori snarled. She sawed the reins back and forth, back and forth, a technique good riders use in only the most extreme circumstances. Ari had never used it on Chase. Even with the mild snaffle bit in his mouth, it would have hurt to have cold iron drawn harshly over his teeth. This cruel copper bit was much, much worse. If Lori kept it up, his mouth would bleed.

"Easy," Ari said. "Please, Chase."

Sweat patched the great animal's shoulders. He shuddered, his ears turned to Ari's voice. He danced on the tips of his hooves.

"What's *wrong* with him?" Lori yelled. "You've done something to him!" She jounced uncomfortably, her legs banging against Chase's side. Ari saw she was beginning to panic. In the stands, Linc began to bark.

"You keep that blasted animal under control," Mr. Carmichael shouted. "Give him the whip, Princess. Give him the whip!"

Chase whinnied, a low, urgent, what's-happening-here sort of noise.

Ari bit her lip and walked toward them, hand outstretched. "Why don't you slide off, and we'll try again tomorrow, Lori?" she suggested. "It might be a good idea if you helped groom him and saddle him, for instance. It'll give him a chance to get to know you bet —" She stopped in midsentence. Chase gathered himself together. His muscled haunches bulged. His chest expanded with the effort of keeping his forelegs safely on the ground. Ari knew what those signs meant. "Easy. Please, Chase. Listen to me."

Lori raised her right arm, the crop in her hand. Ari stiffened and shouted out, "NO!"

The whip descended onto Chase's back.

Chase went berserk. He put his nose to the ground. His hind legs flew out and up. Lori slid forward over his neck, screaming. He reared back, forelegs reaching to the roof. Lori slid back in the saddle, both hands clutching his mane, her feet dangling free from the stirrups. Ari heard the *thump* of running feet from the stands, Linc's deep barks, and Mr. Carmichael shouting, "Lori. *Lori*. LORI!"

Lori sawed frantically at the reins. Chase's jaws were wide open, blood-flecked foam spraying over his neck, spotting the strange white scar on his forehead. He pitched up and down, eyes furious, the breath exploding from his nostrils. His ears lay flat against his skull.

Ari moved fast. She came to a stop directly in front of the giant horse. She raised both hands, ignoring the pain in her legs, her voice level. "Whoa, boy. You *stand*!"

Chase's ears flicked forward.

"You hear me, don't you?" Ari commanded. "Stand, please!"

Chase stood. He dropped his head, sighing. A little blood trickled over his muzzle.

Lori slumped over his neck, crying in a loud way. Ari stepped up to Chase, looped the reins in one hand, and stroked his chest with the other. She could feel him trembling. She soothed him gently as Frank and Mr. Carmichael ran across the arena and up to them.

"Outta the way, girl!" Mr. Carmichael shoved Ari aside and grabbed Lori. "Lori! Lori, baby! Are you all right?" He pulled his daughter from the saddle and set her on the ground. Then he hugged her, his back to Ari. Lori glared at Ari over her father's shoulder.

"Well!" Frank said. One thin hand tugged nervously at his long brown mustache. The other twisted the top button of his denim shirt. "Doesn't seem as though anyone was hurt. Does it?"

Mr. Carmichael whirled, holding Lori tight to his side. "How dare you put my daughter on that horse! It's unsafe! He could have killed her!" His fat face grew dark with rage. "I want him shot!"

Ari clutched the reins. Chase's head went up. His ears went forward. He stared straight at Mr. Carmichael.

And a voice bellowed angrily in Ari's mind: *Little man!*

She looked at Chase, hardly believing what the voice in her head must mean.

The horse pawed at the arena floor. Again, Ari heard his voice inside her head:

You shall be dirt beneath my hooves, little man.

"Chase?" she wondered aloud. "Chase?!"

He turned to her, his gaze direct and angry. His nostrils flared red. He reared, pulling the reins from Ari's hands. Then he dropped his head low to the ground and swung his head from side to side, the way a stallion will when he is ready to strike at an enemy. He pawed at the ground with his iron hooves. *I will crush his bones with the Snake!*

"But they'll shoot you!" she said. And then to herself, *I can't believe this. I won't believe this. Is Chase talking to me?* She put her hands over her eyes, to quiet her thoughts. She dropped them abruptly when Mr. Carmichael stormed, "I'm getting the gun. Where's the gun, Frank? I want the darn *gun.*"

Lori shrieked, "Shoot him, Daddy. Shoot him!"

"No one is going to shoot anyone here," Ari said with quiet authority. "Chase. You stand, please. Please, boy. For my sake!"

For a long, agonizing moment, she didn't think the command would work. Then the great stallion took a shuddering breath and stood still.

Ari kept her eyes on his every move. Moving slowly, she picked up the reins and walked toward him. "Are you all right now?"

Chase looked down, his eyes calm, his flanks moving in and out with regular, easy breaths.

"Chase?"

No answer in her mind. Perhaps she had been dreaming. Ari shook her head briefly to clear it. She'd been nuts to think that he had spoken to her. She ran her hand down Chase's neck, then turned to walk him back to his stall.

"Just a minute there, young lady." Mr. Carmichael folded his arms across his chest and glared at her. Lori leaned against him, her cheek pushed into the shoulder of his sport coat. She gave Ari a measuring kind of look.

"Oh. Of course. The check. You'll want that back." Ari fumbled in her jeans pocket, then remembered Mr. Carmichael had given the check to Frank. She looked at him. "I'm sorry the lease didn't work out."

Lori pushed herself away from her father and whined, "But I want to ride Chase, Daddy. And I *can* ride him. That horse isn't going to listen to me with

66

her around." She jerked her chin at Ari. "She made Chase throw me off."

"He didn't throw you off," Ari said. "You fell off. There's a big difference."

"She did it on purpose, Daddy. I know she did. She wouldn't let me ride him with the right kind of bit. He can't stand that copper bit. Look how his mouth is bleeding."

"*You* made me put that bit in his mouth!" Ari said, astonished. "Why are you lying?"

"I'm not lying. You're the one who's lying. You're the one that trained that horse to make me look like a jerk. It's because you don't want me to have him! You want to have him all to yourself."

"That's not true," Ari said.

"Now, Ari. Now, Ari." Frank put his hand on her shoulder. "I know you're unhappy with this leasing agreement, but we've talked about it. Remember? With your legs so busted up right now, it isn't really possible for you to ride the horse as much as he needs to be ridden to keep fit. If you look at it one way, the Carmichaels are doing us a big favor."

Ari stared at him. She knew Frank was embarrassed by needing the money from the lease to keep Glacier River Farm up and running. But to blame Lori's bad riding on her!

"Here." Mr. Carmichael shoved Frank with one finger. "We'll keep the horse. But my little girl here is right. The horse hasn't been trained properly. Give him here." He snatched the reins from Ari's hand before she could move. "We'll call around, Princess. And we'll find a real trainer to knock some sense into this animal." He jerked hard on the reins. "Come on, you."

Chase dug both front hooves into the sand and pulled his head back. He wasn't upset, Ari saw, just wondering what the heck was going on.

"Make him come with you, Daddy," Lori whined. "Wait! I'll get back on. You hold him!" She remounted, smiling angelically at her father.

"Move, darn you!" Mr. Carmichael jerked again. Chase didn't budge. He stood looking down at all of them, splendid head held high. Mr. Carmichael took the lower part of the reins in one hand then swung them around. The loose reins came down hard. The blow raised a thin welt on Chase's glossy neck and he jumped back, snorting. He was still puzzled, Ari saw.

And she knew why he was confused.

Ari didn't remember anything about her life before the accident that crippled her legs. Not her mother; not her father. Not even if she had any brothers or sisters. But she did know that she had always owned Chase. He was as much a part of her as her heart, or her lungs, or her hands. And she knew that she had never, ever laid a hand or a whip on him. Which was why he was calm now. He didn't believe anyone would hurt him deliberately. She could almost hear his thoughts — not in the way she had heard his voice a few moments ago, but because

68

she loved him. And that love let her understand him the way she could understand no one else. His expression told her: *The pain from the slashing reins was an accident. Wasn't it?*

Mr. Carmichael jerked on the reins to make Chase come forward. Obediently, the big horse stepped closer. With the horse directly in front of him now, Mr. Carmichael swung the reins and struck. Blood welled against Chase's golden neck in a thin trickle. It was only a matter of seconds before he lost his temper. Mr. Carmichael was a fool to think he could control an angry fourteen-hundred-pound stallion with anything but a gun. What might happen after Chase exploded was unthinkable. Lori, her face pale, jumped off.

Ari thought fast. There was only one thing she could do.

Suddenly, Ari shouted, "Linc!" Lincoln bounded down from the bleachers in three giant leaps and flew toward her, a gold-and-black blur. She pointed at Mr. Carmichael. Linc laid his ears back and growled. Mr. Carmichael dropped the reins with a yelp. Ari sprang forward, scooped up Chase's reins, and leaped into the saddle. She urged Chase into a hand gallop. With Lincoln streaking beside them, Ari guided the horse to the south end of the arena, which was open to the soft summer air.

Ari galloped to the clinic. Then she pulled Chase up and sat quietly. Lincoln settled gravely on the gravel drive, forepaws extended. He cocked his head and looked at her. She sighed and ran one hand through her long hair. "I hated to do that, Chase."

Chase shifted underneath her. Lincoln lifted his head to look at her.

"I know. I know. It's a terrible thing I did. Ann and Frank are going to be really upset. But what else could I do? You saw how Mr. Carmichael was beating Chase."

Lincoln rumbled — a cross between a growl and a low bark. He curled his upper lip a little so that she could see the point of one ivory-colored eyetooth.

Ari added hopefully, "Maybe Lori and her father will be so upset they'll forget all about the lease."

The collie sneezed. It was more of a snort than a sneeze, the kind of snort that meant *yeah, right!* in a very sarcastic way. Ari slipped out of the saddle and knelt beside her dog. She ran her hands lovingly through his creamy ruff. "Are you talking to me, too, now?" She laughed a little sadly. "I don't know, guys. The both of you talking to me? Phooey. Maybe I'm just going flat-out crazy." She bent and kissed the tawny spot right in the middle of Linc's forehead. Chase nudged her shoulder with his nose. Behind her, she could hear loud, angry voices: Mr. Carmichael shouting at Frank, Lori shouting at her father.

Ari stood up a little straighter and looped

Chase's reins over her arm. She'd have to take Chase back into the arena and face them all. But not now. The scars on her legs throbbed with a fierce pain. She closed her eyes and bit her lip to keep from crying out.

Everything was going totally wrong.

10

❧

"Just stand there a bit," a fussy voice said at her elbow. "I've told you before. Those are just muscle spasms. It hurts now, but it shows your legs are healing."

Ari opened her eyes and smiled. Dr. Bohnes had come out of the clinic, attracted by the noise and the shouting. "Hi, Dr. Bohnes."

The little vet jigged back and forth from one foot to the other. Ari would never say it aloud, but the way Dr. Bohnes dressed made her want to laugh. She liked bright-colored shirts, leather sandals, and long, baggy skirts. Her hair was pure, brilliant white, cut short. It curled over her pink skull like a wispy cloud. Ari hadn't seen Dr. Bohnes yet today, what with one thing and another. This morning's shirt was a bright, tie-dyed orange, yellow, and red. Ari didn't know how old she was. But she would be Ari's grandmother's age, at least. Ari blinked back tears.

She couldn't even remember if she had a grand-mother.

"Older than that, milady," Dr. Bohnes said cheerfully.

"That makes three of you today," Ari said with surprise. She smiled. She didn't mind Dr. Bohnes calling her milady. She always did. And it made her feel less alone somehow.

"Three of us what?" Dr. Bohnes demanded.

"Reading my thoughts."

"Oh?" Her bright blue eyes sharpened. She looked at Lincoln and then at Chase. "And what kind of thoughts were you having, that the animals could read them?"

"Never mind." Ari nodded toward the arena. Ann had joined the quarrel, and the voices were even louder. "There's been kind of an upset this morning. Maybe I just imagined it."

"Hah! I told Frank and Ann not to lease Chase out. Especially to those dratted Carmichaels." She snorted, with far more gruffness than Lincoln had. "That horse never tolerated anyone on his back but you. And he never will."

"I thought he would if I asked him," Ari said simply. "And we need the money, Dr. Bohnes."

"We wouldn't if —" She bit off what she was going to say.

"If what?"

"Never mind. Come along. It's past time to massage your legs."

73

"But . . ." Ari looked toward the arena build-ing. The argument had drifted outside. Mr. Car-michael and Lori were gathered around Frank. Mr. Carmichael was waving his arms and yelling about how dangerous Chase was. "I should . . ."

"Nothing you can do there," Dr. Bohnes said briskly. "And if you ask me, it's better to get Chase out of sight."

This made sense. Dr. Bohnes almost always made sense. Ari took Chase and followed her color-ful, tiny figure past the round pen and to the back of the big barn, where the elderly vet kept her little clinic.

Although Dr. Bohnes was a horse vet, injured or sick animals from miles around eventually found their way to the bright blue door of her clinic. There was a short line there today: the little boy from the Peterson farm up the road with a fat calico cat; a sorry-looking yellow dog with a sore paw; a moth-erly lady with a parakeet perched on her shoulder. The parakeet squawked angrily at the cat, who opened its golden eyes once, snarled, then went back to sleep in its owner's arms.

"Huh!" Dr. Bohnes grumbled. This meant she was irritated at all the work in front of her. "Sponge Chase down, Ari, and put some of that sticky salve on the cuts in his mouth. You know, it's the same stuff I use on your legs. Then turn him out, won't you? By the time you've finished with that, I'll get through this lot here."

Ari gave her a quick hug, smiled at the little Peterson boy, and took Chase to the small paddock where Dr. Bohnes treated the larger animals. She removed his bridle and haltered him, then asked him to stand while she fetched warm water and the sticky salve. Ari didn't know of any other horse that would obey the "stand" command as well as Chase did. She'd never known him once to break it.

Lincoln followed Ari into the storeroom, where the vet kept her medicines. Ari loved the scents of the storeroom. Dr. Bohnes mixed many of her own salves and poultices from herbs, nuts, and berries that she grew in a special garden. The air was filled with the sharp scent of arrowroot, a lingering odor of lavender, and something roselike.

Ari inhaled with delight. Linc took a breath and sneezed. Ari grinned to herself and searched the shelves for the midnight-colored cream that Dr. Bohnes used to heal her scars from the accident. Her hands were quick, sorting through the jars and herb bags on the shelves. She picked up a small ceramic pot so that she could reach for the large canister of salve against the back wall.

A horrible smell hit her like a fist. Her hand loosened and the pot fell. Ari made a hasty grab to catch it before it smashed onto the flagstone floor. Behind her, the dog growled, then barked. Ari caught the jar just in time and looked at it, puzzled. She'd never seen anything like it on the vet's shelves before. The closer she looked at it, the harder it was

75

to see just what color the pot was: flame-red? Sickly yellow-green? And was that where the terrible stink came from? Curious, Ari tugged at the cork stopper.

Lincoln leaped to her side and pushed his nose against her wrist. His snarls twisted like snakes, if snakes had been sounds.

"Just a minute, Linc," she said. "Easy, now." She hesitated. She was pretty sure that the vet had nothing truly dangerous out in the open. But maybe she'd had this curious thing locked up somewhere and forgotten to put it back.

The urge to open the pot was powerful. Something, *something* twisted her fingers around the top, as if . . . as if a huge, clawed hand — invisible, powerful, mean — were forcing her to open it.

Ari pulled off the stopper and looked in.

At first, she saw nothing but dark. Then a thin coil of acid smoke rose from the depths of the jar. There were shapes in the smoke. Ari was sure of it. She held the jar up and watched the shapes spiral toward the low ceiling. Lincoln barked and barked. The smoke curled around her face, slid past her nose, poured into her eyes.

And she saw . . . she heard . . .

She was in the center of nighttime, in a place she'd never been before. The sky was dark and starless. At her feet was a humped mound, blacker than the black night sky. The mound shifted, moved, then screamed with the sound of a million hornets. Ari jumped and shouted with surprise. The mound at her feet swelled, grew, unfolded like an evil flower. And an eye formed in the center of the hooded blackness, a green-and-yellow eye, multifaceted, like some grotesque and terrible insect. The same terrible vision she'd seen in the meadow!

Where are you? a thousand voices whispered. The eye rolled in its bloodied socket, searching, searching. . . .

It was all Ari could do to hold onto the pot. She was dimly aware of Linc's excited barking, the dashes he was making to get out of the range of that terrible eye. The rest of her world faded, leaving her to this terrifying encounter. She took a deep breath, then another . . .

And fainted.

11

"Tell me what you saw," Dr. Bohnes demanded. "Everything." She peered into Ari's face. Ari was lying on the old leather couch in the vet's office.

"Chase?" she said aloud. Her voice was foggy. She cleared her throat.

"He's fine," Dr. Bohnes said impatiently. Her strong old hand closed around Ari's wrist. Her grip was warm.

Ari focused on the fierce blue eyes. "What happened? It wasn't —" She forced the words out. "I haven't been in another accident?"

Were there tears in those wise eyes? Dr. Bohnes blinked hard. "Nonsense," she said briskly. "You're as fit as a fiddle." She pointed at the collie, sitting anxiously next to the couch. "Lincoln here was barking fit to raise the . . . that is, fit to bust. When I came into the storeroom, I found you on the floor."

"The pot," Ari said.

"What about the pot?"

"Did it break? There was something awful in it, and something terrible was after me. . . ." Ari trailed off. She tried to concentrate. She remembered the eye. The yellow-green eye that was searching, searching. The feeling that if it saw her, it would pierce her to the heart. And the buzzing of angry hornets. She shivered. "I opened the ceramic pot. The one with the funny smell. It was an awful smell, to tell you the truth. I can't imagine what that kind of medicine would be for."

"There was no ceramic pot." The vet's voice was firm. "Nothing like that at all on my shelves. Ari, *you must tell me* what you saw."

Ari ran her hands through her hair. The back of her neck was sweaty. "Insects," she said in a small voice. "Hornets, or maybe wasps. It was dark. Really dark. And this horrible yellow-green . . ."

"Yellow-green what?" Dr. Bohnes commanded.

Ari opened her mouth to tell her. She couldn't get the words out. It was as if they were stuck in molasses. She knew — somehow she knew — that if she could tell Dr. Bohnes about the hideous eye, she would be safe, safe from it, because . . .

"It . . ." she struggled. "It was . . . looking . . ." Her brain felt as if it were wading through hip-deep mud. Suddenly, she broke free of the strange lock on her tongue and gasped, "Look . . . looking FOR ME!"

Dr. Bohnes turned pale and started to speak.

"Ari!" Ann opened the clinic door with a bang and thudded into the room. She wore green rubber boots plastered with manure. Her hair was sticking to her skull with sweat. "There you are! It's past time for four o'clock chores, so I started without you. Have you been here all this time?"

Ari struggled to sit up. The whole afternoon gone? Fear clutched her heart. In the days after the accident, there had been many days like that, when she had drifted in and out of consciousness, not knowing where the time had gone. She buried one hand in Lincoln's soft fur. He whined and licked her wrist with his warm pink tongue. She couldn't, wouldn't tell either Ann or Dr. Bohnes that she'd lost all that time. She couldn't face going back to more doctors. They would question her, probe her, ask her things she couldn't answer. "I'm sorry," she said, a little surprised to find her voice so normal. "I guess I got wrapped up in taking care of Chase."

The thought of her great stallion alone in the paddock drove her to get off the couch. She sighed with relief; she was steady on her feet. She wasn't dizzy. And the dark thoughts of the eye drifted away from her like a leaf on Glacier River Brook.

"He's okay, isn't he?" Ann was anxious, Ari

80

could tell. "His, um, mouth is okay?" Her glance shifted nervously away from Ari's.

"Yes," Ari said. "Lori's not all that strong, thank goodness. He has two scrapes on each corner of his mouth, but they should heal."

"That's all right, then." Ann twisted her hands together. "She'll do better next time, I'm sure. With the . . . ah . . . new trainer, I mean."

Ari stared at Ann, astonished. "What?"

"Now, it's not that you aren't a wonderful trainer, but Mr. Carmichael's right. You're only thirteen, and you and the . . . um . . . horse have spent just too much time together. Far too much time. He said it isn't natural . . ." She paused, a peculiar look on her face. ". . . Not natural for that kind of bond to exist between horse and rider. And you know, he may be right. So, it will be good for both of you to have Chase handled by someone else for a change. Just for the year's lease."

Ari swallowed hard. Lincoln pressed against her knees, growling softly.

"You do understand, Ari. Don't you?"

Ari kept her eyes steadily on Ann's face. She controlled her rage with a terrific effort of will. She could feel the red in her cheeks, and her heart pound. After a long moment she said, "Do we really need the money that badly, Ann?"

Ann's eyes shifted. A long look passed between her and Dr. Bohnes. The vet said, "Pah!"

and stamped angrily to her desk. She sat down, slammed open a drawer, took out some papers, and pretended to read. Then she shouted, "I am NOT taking part in this discussion!"

Ari tried again. "Maybe I could work on the Peterson Farm, after school starts. I could earn money there. They need a stable hand."

"You have your duties here."

"I can do two jobs," Ari said stubbornly.

Neither woman looked at her legs, but Ari knew what they were thinking. She pressed on, "The healing's coming along really well, isn't it, Dr. Bohnes?"

"It is," the vet said shortly. She peered at Ann over the rim of her spectacles.

"I don't think it's a good idea for you to go off the farm just yet, Ari." Ann rubbed her neck. Her hand was muddy; it left a streak of mud between the folds of fat. "And as for school —"

"Of course I'll go to school," Ari said, astonished. "Why ever wouldn't I?"

Ann gestured vaguely. "The farm . . . the work. We were thinking of Dr. Bohnes home-schooling you."

Lincoln's growls deepened. "You make it sound as if I'm a prisoner here," she said quietly. "I haven't been off the farm since the accident except to go to the hospital. Not to the mall, not to the movies. Nowhere."

"Don't be silly!" Ann said. She chewed her lip

nervously. "Of course you can leave the farm. Not just now, of course. But soon."

"It's for your own safety," Dr. Bohnes said at the same time.

Ari looked from one to the other. Something was going on here. Something weird, and a little scary. "I'm going to check on Chase," she said. "And then I'll be in for dinner. Sorry I missed afternoon chores, Ann. I'll make it up to you tomorrow."

"That'll be fine," Ann mumbled. "I didn't mind. I didn't mind doing them at all."

Outside the clinic, Chase was standing with his muzzle to the air, ears up, his deep chocolate eyes gazing far into the distance. The sun was setting over Glacier River Farm. Streaks of red, pink, and gold flowed from the setting sun like water from a fountain. The green of the fields was shadowed almost to black. A few stars poked white light through the oncoming night. The white scar on Chase's forehead glowed briefly, like a firefly, and then dimmed as the sun sank in the pink ocean of light. Something . . . an animal perhaps, scrabbled briefly in the bushes planted against the grain shed at the rear of the paddock.

Ari held her breath and listened hard. She heard the slight scrape of something — feet? — on gravel. Then silence.

"Rabbit?" Ari said to Linc.

He brought his head up at that, ears tuliped forward. He grinned and wagged his tail.

"No rabbits, huh?" Ari asked.

Linc dropped his head with a disappointed sigh. Ari chuckled and let herself into the paddock. She stood beside Chase, one hand on his mighty side. Lincoln panted softly as he stood next to them. For a minute, she stood there and thought of absolutely nothing

"It's been a strange day, Chase," she said.

He whinnied.

"You seem to agree." She paused, then sent him an urgent thought with all the force of her mind. *Do you remember today? How you spoke to me in the arena?*

Chase shook himself, then dropped his muzzle to the earth and began to graze. Ari gazed at him a long moment. He seemed larger than usual, as he stood in the half dark. The twilight shadowed his haunches, traced the muscles in his broad chest. He fed quietly.

So she'd dreamed it, imagined it, maybe even had a delusion. Maybe Ann was right, and it wasn't safe for her to go away from the farm. No, that was stupid. Stupid. She wouldn't let them — any of them — talk her into questioning her own mind. She was as sane as she'd ever been. She knew it. She was as sure of that as she was of her love for her horse and her dog.

"Would you like to stay here for the night, Chase?" she asked aloud. There was a tank of clean water in the corner of the paddock, and she could bring him his hay and grain. It was pleasant here, in the evening air. And, if she had to do what she *thought* she had to do, it would be easier with him here, instead of in the big barn.

She took two flakes of hay from the stack Dr. Bohnes kept for the clinic animals and scattered them on the ground. It was good hay, timothy and clover, with a little alfalfa mixed in for flavor. Chase examined the hay with a pleased air. Ari knew he was happy because his lower lip softened, and the wrinkles above his eyes deepened. He snorted happily and stuck his nose in the pile, searching for the purple-green alfalfa blossoms before the others. Alfalfa to horses was like chocolate to people; a little was delicious, but too much meant a stomachache.

"Now, how did I know that, Linc?" she said to the collie. Perhaps her memory was coming back, in bits and pieces. Her heart lightened, and she hummed to herself as she went in search of grain for Chase's dinner.

Dr. Bohnes kept the grain locked in the shed at the back of the paddock. Ari remembered something else that she must have known before her accident: Too much grain could colic a horse. And colic could be a killer. She was careful to measure three scoops of oats and a half scoop of corn into the feed bucket. She liked the warm, cereal smell of the grain, and she ran both hands through the kernels, partly to mix the corn and oats together and partly because she liked the feel of it between her palms.

Except that grain was soft and giving. What she'd found in the middle of the oats was not. Curious, Ari stepped under the light over the back door.

Another spiraled stone. This one was creamy violet, much thicker and heavier. It was twice as long and wide as Ari's thumb. She patted her shirt pocket. Yes, there was the other stone. She took it out and laid the two together in her hand. They appeared to be made of the same stuff, but the colors of each stone were totally different: one rose, one violet. A wisp of a melody came to her and without thinking, she sang:

> *"Yellow, silver, blue*
> *The rainbow we make . . .*

— and something-something something," she muttered. Darn! She'd almost had it. The song chimed softly in the back of her mind, like a car radio set too low. She shook her head impatiently. Don't push it, Dr. Bohnes had said. Memory's like a spiderweb; push too hard and it will break. Breathe softly, and the web will hold.

A wind rose and died again, chilling the back of her neck. Suddenly, she desperately wanted the warmth and light in the farmhouse. She didn't want her memory to come back if it brought her horrible-looking eyes and strange spiraled stones and bits of songs that she couldn't complete.

She ran her hands through Chase's grain again, to make sure that no more mysterious stones lay in the bucket, and set it down for him. He looked up from the hay and hurried to the bucket, plunging his nose into the bottom. She watched him for a long moment, wrapping her arms around her body to shake off that sudden chill. She whistled to Linc, then climbed over the paddock fence and set off at a jog across the graveled drive to the house. The lights were on, and she could see Ann through the kitchen window, moving between the stove and the table. She slid her boots off by the back door, checked Linc's coat and paws for burrs, and let herself in. Frank sat in the rocking chair by the fireplace. He held a large red book in his lap, and he was frowning. Ari knew that this was the account book for the farm. It recorded all the money that Glacier River Farm took in and paid out. It was a bad sign when Frank scowled.

Ari smiled at Ann and washed her hands at the tap. "Shall I set the table?" Ann nodded abruptly. Ari had no idea why it embarrassed Ann to have her set the table, but it did. The dinner table sat in the center of the kitchen. It was made of a shiny wood that was chipped in places to reveal spongy orange wood beneath. Ari set out the cornflower blue tablecloth and the plates with the blue ladies on the rims.

She liked these plates. The center was white, but the figures circling the center were blue. Each lady was different, some slim and lovely, with long dresses and windblown hair, some curvy and smiling, with violets, roses, and silver wands in their hands. Each woman danced beneath a delicately carved arch. Above the arch was a soft drift of clouds. . . .

Ari stopped and stared at the plates, the knives, forks, and spoons for the table clutched in one hand. Crystal arch. Violet, rose, and . . . it was the song.

Had she made the song up?

She frowned. She'd seen these plates every day of her life. At least, every day of her life that she could remember. Which was the last three months. So she could imagine that she had made up a song to go with the images she'd seen.

But the melody?

The melody was like nothing she'd ever heard before.

"Ari?"

She was dimly aware that Ann was speaking to her. Lincoln nudged her urgently with his nose.

"Ari!"

She focused on Ann with a start of surprise. "Yes, Ann. Sorry. I was daydreaming, I guess."

"Are you sure you're all right?" Ann came closer and reached one hand out to smooth Ari's hair. "Dr. Bohnes didn't know how long you'd been asleep on the floor in the storeroom, but she didn't think it was too long."

Just all afternoon, Ari thought. *She'd go wild if I told her I fell asleep for hours and that I had night-mares every minute and then I heard this strange song. Not to mention the eye. What's happening to me? Did the accident scramble my brains and my legs, both?* Aloud, she merely said, "I'm fine, Ann." She set the knives, forks, and spoons in place and sat down at the table.

"Well, we're not." Frank closed the red book with a thump. There were deep purple smudges beneath his tired eyes. He rubbed the back of his hand over his mouth. "We're broke."

Ari looked down at her plate. Ann put a ladle full of macaroni and cheese in the center. The yellow cheese oozed onto a blue lady with a sweet, sad expression. Frank thumped heavily across the wooden floor and sat at Ari's right. Ann took her place across from her. Ari said, "We have to lease Chase, then. There's no way out."

"I'm sorry, Ari, I really am. But the money we can get from Mr. Carmichael is money to feed the other animals." He smiled, a tired, sad smile. "And us, of course." He reached over and touched her sleeve lightly. "I know you mind. I know you mind a lot."

"They're going to take him away? To another trainer?"

Neither Ann nor Frank said anything. It was,

Ari thought with a sudden spurt of rage, because they were too cowardly.

"Don't look like that," Frank said nervously. "If there was any other way, you know we'd take it."

"You could sell that necklace Lincoln had around his neck." Ari set her fork carefully across her plate. Then she drew the fine chain over her head and held the ruby up. It caught the firelight. Its glow was like the heart of the fire itself.

Ann looked away, as if the sight of the jewel were too much to bear. Frank put his hands before his eyes.

"No!" Ann's voice was hoarse. "You must never, ever let that out of your sight. Do you understand?" She leaned forward. Her breath smelled of peppermint.

"We could sell it," Ari said. "Where's it from, anyway? And what was a valuable thing like this doing around Linc's neck?"

"We don't know," Frank said uneasily. He cast a sidelong glance at Lincoln, curled as usual at Ari's feet. "But we can't sell it. You can't sell it."

"If it's mine, I can." Ari twirled the necklace carelessly around one finger.

Horror spread over Frank's face slowly like a stain spreading in water. "Put it away," he said in the grimmest voice she had ever heard from him. "And we'll have no more talk of that, Ari. Do you understand?"

"Frank," Ann said in a low voice. "Maybe

she's right. Maybe here, it doesn't matter. After all, here he's a horse. He doesn't look anything like . . ."

"What doesn't matter?" Ari asked. "And he doesn't look like what?"

"Nothing." Frank sighed. "Nothing. It's safer for you not to know. Eat your dinner, Ari. Please. And don't think about it anymore."

"You won't change your mind? About Chase?"

"I can't, Ari. I'm sorry."

Ari drew the necklace back over her head. She tucked the ruby inside her shirt next to her heart.

Ari helped with the dishes and went up to bed early. She kissed Ann and Frank good night and smiled when Ann drew back in surprise at the intensity of her hug. She whistled lightly at Lincoln. The big dog uncurled himself from the corner and padded up the stairs after her.

She went into her room and snapped on the light. It was strange, she thought. She only remembered three months of being in this room. She had no memory of what her bedroom had been like before. But she felt so cozy here; her room "before" (as she thought of the time when she had two whole legs) must have been a lot like this one. Pale green walls, and a flowered bedspread to match. White wicker dresser and nightstand. The desk where she'd thought she'd do homework when she started school in the fall. Except, according to Ann and Dr.

91

Bohnes, she wouldn't be starting school at all. Well, she could have done the homework Dr. Bohnes would have given her here. If she was going to stay.

"I can't, Linc. I can't stay here and let Chase go to someone else." The horse wouldn't stand for it. And when Chase didn't want to do something — the only person to stop him was Ari herself. If she didn't take him away in the morning, terrible things would happen. Mr. Carmichael meant his threat. If Chase did hurt Lori — and the way Lori rode, he would hurt Lori, even if he didn't mean to — Ari had heard Mr. Carmichael say it:

Chase would be shot.

Ari stripped off her breeches and T-shirt, then grabbed her pajamas. She put one bare leg into the bottoms and stopped, looking at the twisted muscle, the scars that the accident had left. She finished putting her nightclothes on and got into bed. She switched the bedside lamp off, then heard Linc settle heavily onto the rug at the side of the bed. She slept.

And as she slept, she dreamed.

12

The moon sailed high and white over Glacier River Farm. It shone through Ari's open window and turned the patchwork on her quilt to pale shadows. To Linc, who lay beside Ari's bed, the moon was known as the Silver Traveler. He watched it now, head on forepaws, dark eyes shining, as it bobbed along the river of sky until it reached the giant pines that guarded the forest. Then the Silver Traveler floated there, as if caught in the net of the trees.

Lincoln raised his head, eyes suddenly alert. A ray of moonlight passed through the window and touched Ari's sleeping form. She stirred in her sleep and sighed.

The moonlight grew stronger, harder, turning from heavenly light to earthly substance, until a solid arch appeared. One end rested at the foot of Ari's bed. The other rose to the Silver Traveler at the top of the pines. There was a distant sound of bells, as if some celestial harness jingled. A light brighter than the moon appeared at the top of the arch and moved swiftly down the path. The jingling of the harness bells grew sweeter, not louder.

Lincoln whined, deep in his throat.

The bright light stopped at the window's ledge, as if hesitating to enter or considering where to go. Then it passed into Ari's bedroom and stopped at the arch's end.

Lincoln rose to his feet. The light dimmed for a second, or perhaps less, then flowered to a brilliant rose. A unicorn stood in the center, her horn a crystal spear, her coat a burnished violet. Her white mane flowed like spun silver, reaching her knees, covering her withers, so that she appeared to be wrapped in moonlight.

Atalanta. Goddess to All the Animals. Atalanta, the Bearer of Legends and the Keeper of Stories. The Dreamspeaker! She had come! Lincoln lowered his head and sighed, contented.

"And, you," she said to the dog, a steely note in her silvery voice. "Who are you, dog?"

Linc raised his eyes at her and thumped his tail.

"What? You cannot speak? Or will not?"

Linc whined, then rolled over on his back, white belly exposed to the unicorn's sharp horn.

Atalanta tilted her head to one side, considering the collie. Whatever had sent him seemed to bear the Princess no ill will. And there were limits to what she would be allowed to do. She, too, sighed deeply. She gazed at the sleeping Ari, her eyes a tender purple. She moved nearer, hovering over the bed, carried by the arch of moonlight. Gently, she lowered her crystal horn until the very tip touched the ruby at Ari's throat. The jewel warmed slowly to a deep red flame.

"I will tell you the Story, little one," Atalanta said in her gentle voice. "But you must come to me to hear it."

Ari stirred and murmured in her sleep. The ruby necklace shimmered as she turned.

"If you come to me, Ari, I may tell you everything."

"Mother?" Ari said sleepily. "No. Where are you? Who are you?"

"Ah, Ari, I live where the Arch meets the Imperial River. That is my home. But I will meet you elsewhere, if you will come."

"It isn't you, Mother, is it?" Ari's eyes fluttered. She yawned. Atalanta raised her head. As soon as her horn left the jewel, the fiery light in it died away. The silver Arch beneath her hooves began to dim.

"Remember, Ari. Come to me. Because you love the Sunchaser. Because you love me. Ari, the most important thing of all? You must use the jewel to save the Sunchaser. It is his, and his alone. Help him! He cannot be who he is without it!" She turned and began to walk the arch to go back to the Silver Traveler in the sky. She left the scent of flowers behind her.

When Ari came fully awake, the only memento of Atalanta's visit was a faint silver shimmer in the air and a smell of roses. But that could have been only the moonlight and the air from the open window.

"Linc!" Ari sat up in bed. She rubbed her eyes and yawned again. She reached over the side of the bed to the floor, her hand fumbling for the dog. She felt the silken triangle of his head and then his warm tongue on her fingers. She scratched his ears a little, the way he liked best, then swung her feet onto the floor and switched on the bedside light. "I had the strangest dream," she said. He looked back at her, tongue hanging out, a grin on his face.

"You silly dog." She bent over and hugged him. "It was a nice dream," she said quietly into his ear. "A beautiful dream." She inhaled happily. "I believe I can still smell the flowers from that dream, Linc. Do you know what I saw?"

I do, his eyes seemed to say.

"Of course you don't, silly. So I'll tell you. But we have to tell Chase first. Okay?"

Lincoln cocked his head. Ari pulled on a heavy sweater and prepared to tiptoe as quietly as possible down the stairs and out to the barn. "But first," she whispered to the dog, "I'm going to put this in a really safe place." She tucked the ruby necklace carefully into her top drawer, under a pile of riding socks. "Just imagine what would happen if I lost it now!"

Linc followed her out of the house and to the back of the clinic, where Chase was stabled with Max the buckskin for company. Max stirred as she approached, and nickered. Ari smiled to herself. Hoping for a handout. She slipped through the fence rails and walked to her horse. Chase stood dreaming his own dreams. She slid her hand along his satiny sides. He turned to her with a look of surprise.

Ari wrapped her arms around his neck and whispered in his ear. "I dreamed of a magical creature. A unicorn. And it was so funny, Chase. I just know I've had this dream before." She frowned to herself. "Or maybe it wasn't a dream. Maybe it was from my time before the accident." She laughed. "Except there aren't any unicorns, are there, Chase?"

He blew out once.

Ari rubbed his ears tenderly, her expression thoughtful. "You know, Chase, I was getting just a little bit scared to take you and Linc away from here. I was thinking we could leave the farm here and find another farm, where they don't know us. I could work for our room and board, cleaning stalls and grooming the horses, and maybe we could sleep in the hayloft. It would be warm there, even in winter."

Chase whinnied. Ari knew what that whinny meant. "You think that's a bad idea? It has its disadvantages. Frank would plaster my photograph all over the television stations, and whoever took us in would take us right back. That is, if we didn't get hurt by some horrible person first. But you know — that dream gave me a fabulous idea."

Chase's eyes were mysterious in the dark of the barn. Ari rubbed his muzzle affectionately. "I'm going to start by talking nicely to Lori and her father in the morning. She can't possibly want a horse that doesn't want her. Once she sees that he'll never listen to another trainer, she's got to give it up." She hugged Chase hard. "I know. You think that she and her father are so selfish, they'll never let you go. I've thought about how to fix that, too." She frowned. "I've been thinking about money. Lori and her father like money more than anything, I think. Well, I've had an absolute brainstorm. I'm going to use the jewel to save you! That's what came to me in the dream. I think. Anyway, I'm going to get Dr. Bohnes to sell the ruby necklace for me! She's the only one who will really understand about you and me. And she knows that the necklace is mine to sell. She won't feel as *responsible* as Ann does." She laughed. "And that necklace has to be worth a huge amount. I'll give part of the cash to Lori and her father in return for breaking that lease agreement. The other part of the cash will pay off the debts we've got. This is going to work, Chase. I just know it will."

Ari fed him a handful of sweet feed, then limped barefooted through the damp grass and back into her room. She fell asleep and dreamed no more dreams.

13

Ari was up with the sun. She dressed quickly. There is always more work than time to do it in on a horse farm. Ari felt guilty about missing her assigned chores from the day before. So she was determined to do twice as much work this morning. She owed it to Ann and Frank. She'd tried to thank Frank once. He'd given her the warmest smile she'd ever seen. "It's nothing, mila . . . my dear. We'd spend twice as much if we had to."

"But it doesn't mean they should," she said to Linc. The jewel was still in her sock drawer. She drew it out and held it tight for a moment. How much was it worth? A hundred thousand dollars? She didn't know. But Dr. Bohnes would. She tucked it carefully away again. She wore her blue denim shirt and her breeches and patted her breast pocket to make sure that the stones she'd found the day before were still safely there. Maybe she'd find more of them today. And maybe, like the ruby necklace, they'd be worth some money. Heck! She could be rich and not even know it!

The morning air was fresh, the sun a narrow orange slice above the eastern horizon. Ari was happy. Her legs were achy this morning, but not too cramped. With luck, she'd have all her problems solved by lunchtime. Dr. Bohnes would sell the ruby necklace for a pile of money. Lori and her father would want the money instead of Chase. And all the bills would be paid off. She was sure of it.

Maybe she and the great stallion could take a long ride this afternoon!

She fed and watered all the horses — taking care of Chase first. Then she turned all the horses in the big barn out to pasture and began to clean the stalls. Lincoln helped her by staying out of the way.

Mucking out was hard work, but Ari enjoyed it. She worked hard this morning. She wanted to get every chore finished before breakfast. Lori had scheduled a lesson on Chase at nine o'clock, and so far she hadn't canceled it.

Ari used a large plastic manure fork that let her lift the piles neatly into the manure wagon. After the piles were dumped, she turned the fork over, pointy side down, and raked the sawdust bedding away from the damp spots. The air dried out the dirt floor.

Then she raked all the sawdust neatly to the sides of all the stalls and put the manure fork away.

She surveyed her work with satisfaction. She was a heck of a good barn rat, if she said so herself. She'd be employable anywhere. "Because," she reminded Linc, "you just never know when you're going to need a good job. You know? I can see it all. I'll have a job, a little money in the bank, and life will be wonderful. And all because of that necklace."

She checked the large clock over the barn office door. It was seven-forty-five. She had just enough time before breakfast to drive the tractor and wagon out to the manure pile and dump it.

She settled into the tractor seat, shifted the gear into drive, and drove slowly out of the barn. She put on the brake when she saw the Carmichaels' big red Cadillac pull into the parking lot. A pickup truck pulling a horse trailer came into the lot right behind them.

She took a deep breath. They were early. Way too early.

Mr. Carmichael got out of the car. He looked fatter and angrier than ever. Lori jumped out of the passenger side. She was wearing a new pair of breeches and shiny new paddock boots. The Cadillac had turned up dust when Mr. Carmichael pulled in. It settled on Lori's boots. She scowled, bent over, and fussily wiped them off. The driver of the pickup truck got out, too. Ari knew him. She'd seen him with his students at a farm horse show just two weeks ago. David Greer Smith. So that was the trainer the Carmichaels had hired with all their money. And he was a good trainer, too.

Mr. Carmichael waved his arms and jabbered at Mr. Smith. Lori stood next to her father, arms folded, the scowl still on her face. Suddenly, the three of them turned and walked off to the clinic, where Chase still stood in the paddock. Ari's heart quickened. How did the Carmichaels know where to find Chase? His usual stall was in the front of the barn. Who told them where Chase was?

"Morning, Ari."

Ari jumped. "Frank! Sorry. I didn't hear you come up."

He put his hand on her shoulder. "You did a lot of work this morning."

"Frank, what are they doing here so early?"

"The Carmichaels?" He turned and looked after them. The trainer walked in front of the other two. He was swinging a long lead line in one hand. "Smith called about half an hour ago. You were just starting to muck out. Said they wanted to take Chase bright and early. It's a long ride to his new stable, I guess."

"But you *can't*!" Ari burst out.

"He said they'd sue us if we didn't let him take Chase to a new stable! We'd lose everything, Ari. And our first duty is to you. Ann and I talked and talked about it this morning. We have no choice! This guy's backed us into a corner."

Ari remained calm. "I have this plan. We'll get lots of money, Frank. Truly we will. You have to stop them."

His hand lightened on her shoulder. "Honey, I just ca —"

"Won't, you mean," Ari said furiously. She ran to the clinic, Lincoln barking at her heels. She could hear Frank shout, "Stop! Stop!" She didn't care.

By the time she reached the paddock, she was out of breath. David Greer Smith was a tall man in cowboy boots, jeans, and a denim jacket. He was already inside the fence. Chase was backed into one corner. The stallion looked at the trainer out of the corner of his eye. Ari couldn't read Chase's expression. But she didn't think he was happy. Not upset, yet, she thought. Just curious. And a little annoyed.

"Sir!" she called out.

The trainer turned around. He had a nice face, Ari thought. But nice or not, he wasn't going to get her horse.

"What are you doing here?" Lori demanded.

"What are you doing here?" Ari shot back. "I've come to tell you the deal's off."

The door to the clinic opened and Dr. Bohnes came out. She was wearing a plastic rain hat and rubber boots over a screaming-loud green shirt and black pants. She looked ridiculous, but Ari was happy to see her. "Well," Dr. Bohnes said. She raised her scraggly white eyebrows to her hairline. "What's going on here?"

"We've come to get the horse, as agreed," Mr. Carmichael said in a curt way. "Get this kid out of the way, Frank. She could get hurt."

Ari bit her lip. She didn't have much time. She had to get to Dr. Bohnes alone — with no one else around. She knew Dr. Bohnes would help her sell the necklace. But how could she get all these people out of here?

She looked at Chase. The trainer was advancing on him, the lead line held behind his back. Chase snorted and flung his head up. Then he backed away. The trainer made soft clucking noises with his tongue. Chase danced a little on the tips of his hooves. When the trainer got close, the horse jumped away, just out of reach.

"Good," Ari said under her breath. Then aloud, "Dr. Bohnes?"

"What is it, my dear?"

"Could I talk to you? For just a second?"

"Whoa!" The trainer roared.

Everybody jumped. Except for Chase, who danced away again, just out of reach. The trainer's face was getting red.

"Maybe now's not the time, dear." Dr. Bohnes tied the plastic rain hat more firmly on her white hair. Frank looked up at the sky, which was clear and cloudless, but he didn't say anything. Ari ignored them both. Fine. So the little vet wouldn't help her. She'd just have to help herself. Get Chase away from here, just for a few hours, while she tried to settle things. Quietly, she moved away from the Carmichaels and the others and up to the paddock fence. Chase rolled his eye at her. She lifted her hand to make him whoa.

He stopped obediently at her signal.

"Jeez," said the trainer. He spat on the ground in a disgusted way. Then he grabbed Chase's halter and snapped the lead line onto the ring under his chin.

Ari moved her hand sideways, in a swift, abrupt motion. Chase jerked sharply to the left. The lead line tore out of the surprised trainer's hands. Ari raised her palm. Chase reared, forelegs pawing the air. He was having a good time.

The trainer swore angrily, leaped in the air, and grabbed the lead line. He gave one powerful tug on the line and jerked the horse forward. Then he grabbed the free end of the line and swung it viciously at the stallion's face. The horse roared in anger.

"NO!" Ari said.

I will trample you, little man!

Ari gasped. There it was again. Chase's voice. In her head. As though he was speaking to her. She jumped onto the fence and clung to the top board, her fingers digging into the rough wood. Chase was furious at the insult of the blow. He pawed at the

106

ground, clouds of dirt flying from beneath his iron hooves. The trainer backed up, his face a mask of fear. Chase whinnied, a high, trumpeting challenge.

Get him out of here, milady. Or he will die!

"Sir!" Ari called. "Please! Sir! Just back up. Please just back up. Don't make him any madder."

OUT! shouted the voice in her head.

"You stop, Chase," she ordered aloud.

For a breathless moment, she wasn't sure it would work. It was crazy anyway, a part of her brain whispered. Talking to your horse?

Chase reared once more, black against the bright blue sky and the brilliant sun. Then he came to earth with a crash and stood still.

"You made him do that!" Lori shrieked. "You made him run away from the trainer. Daddy, I'm *telling* you, if we can just get him away from her, that horse will be just fine. She's just jealous, Daddy, because he likes me better or he would if he got half a chance!" Furious, she shoved her elbow into Ari's stomach. Ari fell backward with a gasp. There was a swirl of coffee-colored fur, a snarl, a scream. Linc jumped across her and barreled full tilt into Lori. He knocked her facedown, then settled all his eighty pounds right onto her back. Lori drummed her heels and yelled, but the big dog didn't turn a hair.

"That's enough out of everyone," Dr. Bohnes said briskly. To the trainer she said, "You, come out of that paddock and talk to me like a sensible man. And you," she turned to Mr. Carmichael, "pick up that spoiled little brat of yours and come into my office. All of you. You, too, Frank. We're going to settle this once and for all." She turned her back, marched into the clinic, and left the door wide open.

The trainer picked up his hat, dusted it off, and settled it firmly on his head. "I'll tell you what that horse needs," he said to no one in particular. "He needs a good whipping." He followed Dr. Bohnes into her office.

"Ari!" Frank tugged her arm. "Ari? Can you get that darn dog off of Ms. Carmichael?"

Ari turned around and bit her lip to keep from laughing. Mr. Carmichael was tugging like anything at the big collie's thick ruff. Linc wasn't budging. He sat on Lori's backside with a grin on his face, completely ignoring the infuriated man. Ari whistled. Linc pricked up his ears, hopped off Lori, and walked over to Ari, his tail wagging happily.

Lori picked herself up. Her new boots were smudged and her perfect blond hair didn't look anywhere near perfect anymore. Her face was redder than her father's.

"You two stay here," Mr. Carmichael ordered. "Come on, Frank. We'll settle this with the old bat inside."

"She is not," Ari said clearly, "an old bat."

"Just shut up," Lori muttered.

"Both of you keep quiet. Please?" Frank said. "I'll be with you in a minute, Mr. Carmichael." He waited until the other man had disappeared into Dr.

Bohnes's office. Then he came over to Ari and crouched in front of her. "Ari," he said.

"Yes, Frank?"

"You've got to let the horse go."

Ari shook her head. "I'm going to sell that necklace. Dr. Bohnes will do it for me."

"No, she won't. She can't."

"It's mine, isn't it?"

He hesitated. "Well, yes."

"Then I can sell it."

"Even if you do sell it, Ari, the Carmichaels don't have to take the money back. We have a contract." His thin face was lined with worry and distress. "Do you know what that means?"

"It means you signed my horse away."

"I signed your horse away. But it's just for a year. And then he'll be home, I promise." He stood up and ran his hands through his hair. Ari suddenly felt very sorry for him. "My gosh, this sure got mixed up," he said under his breath. "You two wait right here. I'll be back in a few minutes."

Ari watched as he went into the clinic and shut the door. Lori stood a little apart from her, arms folded defiantly over her chest. Finally she said, "That stupid dog of yours should be shot, too."

Ari decided not to respond to this. Lori was a horrible mess of a human being, and that was that. There wasn't a thing she could say to her. The best thing was to totally ignore her.

She gathered her long hair up into a knot,

109

fished a rubber band out of her jeans pocket, and wound it into a ponytail. Then she went into the paddock.

"Where are you going?"

"None of your business," Ari said shortly. She took the lead line the trainer had left in the dust and clipped it on the left ring of Chase's halter. Then she tied the free end to the ring on the other side. She looked up at her horse. Her legs were still too mangled to jump on him from the ground. She'd have to get a box. "You stand," she said softly. She left him there, still as a statue and as good as gold.

"I'm getting a step stool from the shed!" she said loudly.

Lori shrugged: *Who cares?*

Once in the shed, Ari peeked out. Lori was staring after her, but she was pretty sure she couldn't see what she was doing. She just hoped that Dr. Bohnes hadn't gotten a sudden (and rare) cleaning fit. The old vet hadn't. The windows were still as filthy as ever. Ari wrote on the dirty pane with one finger:

Sell the "DOG LEASH" in my sock drawer!

PLEASE!

Love, Ari.

"And I hope," Ari said fiercely to herself, "she remembers how the necklace came here. Linc was wearing it around his neck."

Then she picked up the step stool and marched out of the shed. She set it on the ground next to Chase.

"What are you *doing*?" Lori demanded.

"Leaving," Ari said briefly. She leaped neatly onto the stallion's back and settled her long legs just behind his withers. His chest and barrel were so powerful that the spot between them made a perfect place to keep a good grip. She squeezed her left leg, and he responded by turning in a circle. Max, the buckskin gave a startled squeal and jumped out of the way.

Ari spread the makeshift reins wide, tapped both heels lightly against his sides, and he backed up a few steps. Then she gathered the lead line in, tapped more firmly, and he sprang forward. They flew up and over the fence.

"You can't do that!" Lori screamed. "You come back here!"

"Linc!" Ari called. "Come on, boy!"

But Lori moved with astonishing speed. She grabbed the dog's ruff with both hands and held on. Linc wriggled in her grip. He looked at her. Ari looked back. Lori wasn't about to let go, unless Linc bit her. And Linc would bite only if she gave him permission. "Linc!" she called. "You find me when you can. Got that? Find me."

He barked. Ari prayed that he did understand. That, like Chase, when emotions were high he could somehow figure out what she needed.

She raised a hand in farewell and galloped Chase into the woods.

14

Atalanta splashed one cloven hoof in the water and watched the ripples drift away. She stood under a sapphire willow tree at the edge of the Imperial River, watching the world of Glacier River Farm in the magic waters of the Watching Pool. The vision was of Arianna and the Sunchaser fleeing the only security they had.

The willow branches dropped gracefully into the crystal-clear stream. Whenever a breeze came up, blossoms fell, blurring the images of Arianna and the Sunchaser. Then the flowers swirled away like little blue boats carried on the current. Sapphire willows grew only in the Valley of the Unicorns, as far as Atalanta knew. And Atalanta was the wisest unicorn in the Celestial Valley herd.

She raised her head and looked across the fields to rest her eyes from the visions. It had been a long, long night. A month had come and gone, and the Shifter's Moon was back. There'd been no attack from the Shifter — at least not yet. And Atalanta had walked the Path from the Moon and across the Gap to warn Arianna in a dream. But there were still three nights left of the Shifter's Moon, when her personal magic would not work — and Arianna was racing toward — what?

Atalanta sighed. Her crystal horn scattered splintered light on the grass.

It was so beautiful, her world! Unicorns stood peacefully throughout the Celestial Valley, as bright as the colors of the rainbow: Blue, scarlet, bronze, emerald, each a jewel of light in the already light-filled land. A sunstruck golden unicorn — brighter than the others — grazed on the hillside at Valley's end. Numinor, the Golden One.

All this beauty. All this could pass away in the next few days.

"What news at Glacier River?" Tobiano marched heavily through the grass, curious as always about matters that didn't concern him.

Atalanta nodded her greetings. The black-and-white-spotted unicorn was as rude as he was nosy. Atalanta's clear violet eyes softened with amusement. Tobiano had a good heart, in spite of himself. "Come and see."

He came and stood by her. Together, they watched Arianna and the Sunchaser take the paddock fence and gallop to freedom in the woods. The collie wasn't with them.

"She isn't wearing the jewel?" Tobiano asked.

Atalanta closed her eyes for a long moment. "No," she said sadly. "She is not wearing the jewel. And the dog isn't there. I still don't know what to make of the dog, Toby."

"Huh!" Tobiano's horn was short, but the noise he made through it was loud and brassy enough for a unicorn with a much longer one. "And what are you going to do about that?"

"I did what I could, Toby." She lifted her head and looked at him. Her silvery mane stirred in the soft breeze. "I have already broken the laws of our kind by visiting her on that side of the Gap. That's all I could do. I can't tell her the rest. Not yet. Not unless she crosses the Gap. And if she crosses the Gap, she will be in grave, grave danger. . . . We have no power over the humans at Glacier River, other than the power of dreams. What more could I do?"

Toby looked cross. "You could have told her straight out what's going on," he grumped. "I would have."

"Perhaps," Atalanta said, with a slight edge to her soft voice, "that is why I am Dreamspeaker and you are not. The laws are there for a reason."

"Huh!" Toby said again. "If you ask me —"

"Well, I haven't asked you," Atalanta said, reasonably enough.

"Certain unicorns I know ought to do a little more than just stand around looking into the Watch-Pool when there's this much trouble afoot."

"If she crosses the Gap, I can do a little more than just visit her, Toby. But she has to cross first. You know that."

"Blah, blah," he said grouchily.

A slight frown appeared between Atalanta's violet eyes. Toby ducked his head, embarrassed. Apparently even he had limits to his rudeness. He muttered a quick, "Sorry!" Then, "We're all doin' our best. I mean, I know you're doin' your best. You lemme know if I can help."

She looked at him steadily. "Would you be willing to walk the Path from the Moon with me to join them? Into Balinor? I have a job for you. Your colors are very . . . usual, Toby. With a little care, you could look just like a unicorn of Balinor. We can disguise your jewel. If you were clever, and I know you can be, no one would guess that you are a celestial unicorn."

Toby looked as if he didn't know whether this was a compliment or not.

"It is very important," Atalanta assured him. "I need to have you tell me what's going on in Balinor. I see only what I ask to see in the Watching Pool. And, Toby, if I don't know what to ask, we could all be in very serious trouble. I want you to walk among the unicorns of Balinor as one of them and tell me of events that I do not know." She leaned close to him and bent her head to his ear. "There is no one else in the herd that could do it."

Toby rubbed his black-and-white horn

against the trunk of the sapphire willow tree. He brought his left hind hoof up and scratched his left ear. He yawned carelessly, as if what Atalanta said had been an ordinary, everyday kind of thing. Instead of what it really was. A challenge. An adventure. Leave the Celestial Valley? Walk the Path from the Moon to the earth below? He, Tobiano, the rudest unicorn in the celestial herd? A chance to be . . . a hero?

Atalanta may have smiled a little. It was hard to tell. She said in her gentle voice, "I'd have to check with Numinor, the Golden One, of course. But he would allow you to leave the herd. If you are willing to go."

Toby hummed a careless little tune through his horn to hide his excitement and said, "Sure. Heck. Why not?" And he turned and marched off, rolling through the meadow like a little barrel.

Atalanta turned back to the Watching Pool and watched as Arianna tried to lose herself and her horse in the woods outside Glacier River Farm. She leaned closer to the water, her silvery mane trailing in the starflowers on the bank . . . and watched.

15

Ari raced along, her body swaying comfortably. Chase's hand gallop was smooth and swift. She felt as if she wasn't really sitting on his great bronze back, it was as if she were floating. She kept a sharp lookout for woodchuck holes and stones. The stallion was agile and quick, but at this speed even he could trip and fall. She would go to the cave created by the long-ago glaciers in their path to the sea. The cave in the south pasture. Near the meadow where she'd found the first of the strange spiral stones. The south pasture was large enough to hide Chase and her during the day.

It called to her now, stronger than ever.

She shook her head, as if to free it from dreams. Linc knew where the cave was. As soon as he got away from Lori and her father, he would find them. So it was a sensible thing to do.

Wasn't it?

She pulled Chase to a half-halt at the edge of the south pasture. It was peaceful under the sun, the uncut hay shifting slightly with the breeze. The cave lay on the far side. The entrance was concealed because the meadow dropped off to a deep ravine, but she could see it with her mind's eye, as clear as anything.

Ari guided Chase through the grass with her knees, the lead line loose over his neck. She listened carefully. Were there shouts in the distance? And was that the sound of another horse?

She felt Chase tense between her knees. His head came up. He whinnied, the call of a stallion to a member of the herd. Someone was after them. Ari leaned over his neck and whispered urgently, "Hush. Hush now, Chase."

She urged him to a swift trot. They reached the meadow's edge, and she slid to the ground. She walked carefully down the slope to the cave, urging the horse along with small murmurs of encouragement. He slid, caught himself, then flattened his ears. This meant he was cross with her, and despite the urgency of her search for the cave, Ari felt laughter bubble up in her throat. "Well, I'm sorry," she muttered. "I know you don't like it when the footing's rough. But this is an emergency, Chase."

He snorted and even seemed to nod his head. Ari wondered again about her ability to catch his thoughts. Was it true that he could speak with her in moments of great stress? Or was it just her imagination?

"There it is, Chase. The cave." She pulled on the lead line. He caught sight of the dark entrance, barely taller that his head. He balked, pulling her backward.

."No, Chase." She kept her voice low, but put all the urgency she could into it. "I know you don't like small, dark places. No horse does. But we have to hide. Just for a while." She stopped herself and listened hard.

Arianna! That whisper on the breeze! She rubbed her hands through her hair. Was the voice coming from the cave?

Ari cocked her head. The voice — if it had been a voice — faded with the wind. And now there was no doubt about it. There was a horse coming through the woods after them. Somewhere north of where they were now, which meant it or they were coming from the farm itself. "Come on, Chase." She tugged at the lead line. Chase backed up, swinging his head back and forth, back and forth. He dug his hind hooves into the ground and pulled away. So it was serious then, his refusal to go into that deep dark place. She loosened the line; Dr. Bohnes always said in a tug-of-war between a fourteen-hundred-pound horse and a one-hundred-and-three-pound human, it should be obvious who would win.

She made her voice firm and low. "Please, Chase. *Please*. For me."

The faraway hoofbeats grew nearer. Then stopped. Good. He or she or whoever was up there wasn't sure which way to go. But she had so little time!

Ari quickly freed the makeshift reins from the knot she'd made and turned the rope into a lead line again. She clipped the line to the ring in Chase's halter and backed herself into the cave, not pulling, just letting him stand. She would let him make his own decision. "See, Chase. Come on, boy. Walk in. It's just a nice hiding place. There's nothing in here."

She stopped herself in midsentence. There *was* something in here. She could feel it. And there was an odor. Faint. Horrible. Just like the stink she had run into the day before, in the meadow and then again in the vet's room. Still holding the lead line, she turned and searched the darkness with her eyes. It had rock walls and a dirt and gravel floor. There was slight trickle of damp from an underground water source.

Was that a low buzzing? A whine? Flies, black flies? Yes! She could just make out a mass of them against the north wall. No wonder Chase didn't want to come in. Horses hated black flies. She backstepped out into daylight. If she soothed him, explained to him, maybe she could ride him in.

Chase's ears pricked forward and he turned his head, listening to something behind him. There was a familiar scrabbling through the brush above. Lincoln poked his head over the lip of the rise and looked down on them. He had escaped the Carmichaels! He barked once. Ari knew that bark: It was a warning. The dog bounded down the slope. He came directly to her, bumped her knee with his head, then whirled and faced the rise. He barked again, and again Ari knew what it meant: Stay away! *Stay away!*

The thrumming of hooves grew nearer. Ari took a deep breath. She would face them, whoever they were. She heard a horse breathing hard and heavy, and a grunt from the animal as the rider pulled him up. His feet scrabbled in the gravel at the lip of the rise, just as Chase's had done. Then Max, the buckskin, fell over the edge. He slid down on his haunches. The rider on his back pulled hard on the reins. The gelding's mouth gaped wide and he twisted his head with the effort to get away from the bit.

Horse and rider tumbled straight toward them. Lincoln threw himself in front of Ari, trying to protect her. Still holding the lead line, Ari leaped backward into the cave. Max made a massive effort to avoid sliding into them. He gave a great heave with his front legs. The rider flew off and crashed into Chase. The stallion leaped forward, startled at the impact. His great chest smashed into Ari. She fell flat on her back, her head hitting the stone wall.

There was an immense, terrifying buzz of a million flies.

She heard Lincoln's snarl of rage.

There was a flash of bright violet, the scent of flowers.

And then . . . she heard nothing at all.

16

ri woke up. She had wakened like this once before. After the accident. After the terrible crash that had twisted her legs and wiped her memory as clean as a blackboard eraser.

But then, she had awakened to pain worse than fire. Now she woke to sky that was a different blue from any blue she had seen before. To the smells of a forest that wasn't pine — but what?

Cautiously, she sat up. The ache in her legs was familiar: a dull throb in her calves where the scars were, an ache in her right knee. No different, then. No new injuries.

She sighed in relief. A wave of dizziness swept over her and she fell on her back. She fought the blackness. Chase! Where was Chase? A cold nose poked her neck, a warm tongue licked her cheek. She smiled gratefully and wound her hands in Lincoln's ruff. He stepped back and she held on to pull herself upright again. She blinked the dizziness away and looked. Chase stood near. So near that she reached out one hand and steadied herself against his iron-muscled foreleg. He bent his head and whiffed gently into her hair. She got up and dusted off her breeches.

Are you all right, milady?

His voice in her head! Tentatively, she spoke to him. "Chase? Is that you? Or am I dreaming?" She bit her lip and said to herself more than to the others, "Or maybe I'm crazy? The doctors told me they weren't sure why my memory's gone. Maybe I'm just plain nuts."

Chase looked back at her. The nice little wrinkles over each eye were sharply cut with worry. His nostrils flared red and his lower lip was tightly closed. She knew he was upset. She stroked his neck, then quickly checked him over. She remembered falling down, the horse and the dog rolling after her. If either one were hurt, she'd have to run back to the farm for help.

I have no hurt, no wound. But she may be injured. Go to her.

"She? Who?" A groan answered her. Ari looked around.

And she felt as if a giant hand squeezed all the breath out of her. Wherever Ari was, she wasn't at Glacier River Farm anymore.

The sky she'd wakened to not moments before was a purple-blue, unlike any she'd seen before.

She was in a meadow. At least, she was pretty sure it was a meadow. The grass was thick, knee-high, and of a bluish-green that reminded her more of water than anything else. The broad-bladed blue-green grass was as thick and uniform as a carpet.

The meadow itself was an irregularly shaped circle surrounded by dense trees. But the trees weren't any more normal than the grass or the sky. They were tall, with thickly gnarled branches that bent and twisted.

Had she been here before? A second groan, louder than the first, jerked her back to her companions. Lincoln, his tail waving, danced through the strange thick-bladed grass and bent his head to look at whatever was lying there. Ari hesitated. Should she run away?

"I will not," she said aloud. Chase snorted in approval. She cautiously approached Lincoln and whatever he was looking at. She wished she had a heavy branch.

The third groan made Ari stand up straight and march over to the hump in the grass. She knew that voice. And she was well acquainted with the crossness in it. She put her hands on her hips and looked down. "Lori Carmichael! What are you doing here?"

Lori's hair was tangled with bits of twigs and gravel. She wasn't hurt: Ari saw that right away. She was sitting cross-legged, with her head on her knees. And that last groan was exasperated, angry even, but not wounded. The blond girl blinked up at her. Her face was scratched and muddy. "What have you done now?" she grumbled.

"What have I done? You were the one who came chasing after me. And Max. Poor Max. You rode him too hard, as you always do. When you came crashing down that . . ."

"He *slipped*," Lori said furiously. "Can I help it if that dumb horse slipped!?"

Chase walked gracefully through the grass and stood next to Ari, watching Lori with courteous interest. Lori glared at him and got to her feet. Ari suppressed a giggle. Lori's breeches were torn right across the seat. And her underwear was green with little flowers on it.

"What did you do with him?" Lori demanded in a nasty voice.

"With Max, you mean?"

"With Max, you mean?" Lori mimicked furiously. "Who else, stupid? Godzilla? If you think I'm walking back to the farm all bumped up like this, you've got another think coming."

Chase lowered his head and nudged Ari gently. *He did not cross the Gap with us.*

"Gap?" Ari put her hand on Chase's mane. It was silky under her hand. "Chase, what's the . . . Gap?"

I do not . . . I do not . . . recall.

"What are you doing now! Talking to your horse? Great. Just *great*. I told Daddy that accident

126

made you loony, and I was right." Lori took a couple of steps toward them, then looked down to shove Lincoln out of the way. He growled, deep in his throat, but moved aside.

Lori looked around angrily, then gasped. Her face turned white. For the first time she seemed to realize that she — they — were in a place so strange it might have been another planet. "What's going on here?" Her voice quivered. She looked at the trees, with their bizarre branches bent and curled like hair after a bad perm. She glanced up at the purple-blue sky and looked past the trees to the horizon beyond. She flushed bright red and pointed, her eyes so wide Ari could see the whites all around them. "Ari! Ari! *What is that?*"

Ari shaded her eyes with her hands and looked at the sun. It was in the same position in the sky it had been at home, about halfway between the eastern horizon and straight overhead. Which meant Lori was pointing west. Ari wheeled around slowly, almost afraid to look beyond the trees. "Why, it's a village!" she said in amazement.

"What do you mean, a village, Miss Know-It-All? That's not like any village I've ever seen. A village!" Lori was making a huge effort not to cry. She was shaking so hard Ari wondered if she'd shake herself right out of her riding boots.

Ari kept her voice gentle, the way she did when she handled a scared horse. "Those are buildings, don't you think?"

"With grass on the roofs? Don't be an idiot."

"Sure. You've seen pictures. Those are thatched roofs. You know, long grass that's dried and then put on top of a house to keep the rain out."

"I don't like it here. I want to go home. You take me home. Right now! If you don't, I'm going to tell Daddy to buy Chase and you'll never see him again."

Ari ignored her. "Where do you suppose we came out?" she asked thoughtfully.

"Came out? Came out?"

"Well, we're on the other side of the cave, aren't we?" Something Dr. Bohnes had told her about Glacier River came back to her now. "The land here folded and folded again when the glaciers came through millions of years ago."

Chase nodded. *The Gap.*

"So that's the Gap, Chase?"

"Stop that!" Lori shrieked. "Stop that right now!"

"Stop what?"

"Pretending that horse is talking to you!"

"Well, he is talking to me," Ari said reasonably.

"Don't be an idiot!"

Ari walked up to her horse and put her hands on either side of his muzzle. She pulled his head down and laid her cheek against the strange white scar on his forehead. It felt cool, cooler than the rest of him. "Can we go back the way we came?"

He nickered, low in his throat. *No.*

"Do you know where we are?"

On the other side of the Gap.

"Do you know what place this is?"

The wrinkles over his eyes grew deeper. *I . . . I perhaps have dreamed of this place.*

"But you don't know where we are."

Before he could answer, Lori screamed, "Cut it out, cut it out, CUT IT OUT!" She fairly danced up and down in rage. "I want to go home RIGHT NOW!"

"I don't know how to go home, and Chase doesn't, either."

Lincoln whined, lay down on the grass, and put his paws over his eyes. Did he understand what she'd just said? Ari thought she truly would go crazy if he started to talk to her, too. She found herself hoping that the dog hadn't really understood what she'd just said, but that he was tired. Or the sun was hurting his eyes. Or something.

I want to go home, too.

Ari stared at him, her mouth open. *O-kay.* The dog was talking, too. Lincoln's voice was different from Chase's. For one thing, he had an accent. He sounded just like Mrs. Broadbent, the dressage teacher. She came to the farm once a week to teach first level to the riding students.

"Hel-lo," Lori said in an incredibly sarcastic voice, jerking Ari's attention away from Lincoln's newfound ability to chatter. "Earth to Ari. Let's get it

129

straight. You do know what's happened here, don't you?" The tears welled up in her eyes. "We've been abducted by aliens."

"We haven't been abducted by aliens. For one thing, the sun's in the same position it was when we fell through the cave."

"So?"

"So I think we're on the other side."

"The other side of what?"

"Of the farm. A different side. A side . . ." Ari hesitated, "that maybe was here all the time, but the glaciers folded it away. I mean, we can breathe the air and everything, Lori. And I've seen pictures of those thatched roofs in books. I know I have. If we were on another planet, everything would be weird."

"Oh?" Lori's eyebrows rose to her hairline. "You don't think this is weird? *Excuse* me, but this is weird enough for me, thank you very much. Now, let's get out of here."

Ari looked at Chase, standing regally alert, and at Lincoln, sitting majestically, if a little forlornly, on the grass. If they went home, would she be able to speak with them again?

"You do want to get out of here, don't you?" Lori's voice was quavering again.

"Sure. So let's go up to the village and ask how to get back."

"Are you crazy?"

"I don't think so."

Lori grabbed her by the shoulders and shook her. "What if they attack us?"

"Why should they?" Ari removed Lori's hands from her shoulders. "Here's what we'll do. Those trees are pretty thick. And the village is on the other side of the forest. So we'll go through the trees and wait until we see some people walking around and see how normal they look. If they look pretty normal, we'll . . ." Ari stopped. "We'll ask for the police station. Then we'll go to the police station and ask our way home."

"Finally, a plan that doesn't sound stupid." Lori folded her arms across her chest and tapped her foot.

"Good." Ari picked up Chase's lead line, whistled to Lincoln, and set off for the forest. "Are you coming?"

"I'm not walking all that way. I'm hot. I'm hungry. And I'm tired. I'm going to ride Chase."

Ari debated. She could drag Lori whining all the way through the woods, or she could put her on Chase and get some peace and quiet. She patted Chase's neck. "Do you mind?"

She sits like a sack of potatoes.

"Just don't dump her off, okay? We've had enough physical stuff this morning." She nodded to Lori. "He doesn't mind. Much. I'll give you a leg up." She crouched and cupped her hands together. Lori put her left foot into Ari's cupped hands. Ari counted "one, two, three" and on the count of three, pushed her hands up. Lori pushed off the ground with her right foot, then swung her right leg over Chase's back. The stallion snorted, tossed his head, and rolled his eyes. Ari raised her hand quietly, and Chase settled down with a grumble. Then Ari crouched down in front of Lincoln.

"You have a pretty good nose, boy?"

We collies have excellent noses.

"That's great. Can you lead us to the village? By scenting the people and . . ." Ari sighed. She'd missed breakfast this morning and she realized she was starved. "And the food?"

Of course. Lincoln's mental tone was lofty. *No problem at all. Of course,* he hesitated, *collies are not bloodhounds, you know.*

"I know."

Nor are we terriers. Terriers have excellent noses. However, a nose isn't everything, you know. There are more important issues for dogs than a great sense of smell. Beauty, for example. We collies are —

"Lincoln?"

— among the most handsome of breeds. . . .

"LINC!"

Yes?

Ari put her hands on her hips and regarded him with exasperated affection. My goodness. Who would have thought her beloved dog was as gabby as this? "Quiet, please. Just find us the village."

132

Right you are. He trotted ahead, plumed tail waving gaily. Ari walked behind him, not so much leading Chase as walking companionably side by side. They crossed the meadow. Linc's gold-and-black back almost disappeared in the tall grass, but the way was soft-going. The blades grew straight and tall. Despite how thick the grass was, it bent easily with their passage.

And the way was almost silent.

It was not as easy once they got to the woods. Inside the forest, the branches intertwined overhead to make a canopy that kept out the sun. The golden leaves held the light, much as a glass holds water.

Ari could see where they walked, but the close-growing trees made their forward progress almost blind. Thank goodness the branches started growing a third of the way up the trunks and the ground underfoot was thickly padded with leaves and not much else. At least they didn't have brush to wade through.

Lincoln's progress was erratic, just as it was when he and Ari went out for walks at home. He stopped and sniffed at piles of leaves, investigated mysterious holes, and occasionally marked the trunk of a tree with his scent, lifting one leg with an intent, faraway expression. The chief difference was that Ari heard all the dog's chatter in her mind, which was addressed as much to himself as to her:

Now that would be a woodchuck hole on the other side of the Gap, but Canis alone knows what animal den this would be. And that trail up the trunk, could have been a squirrel, but are there squirrels here on the other side of the Gap?

She became almost happy with the constant chatter the deeper they went into the woods. The leaves were darker here, the gold deepening to a dull brown. The forest was quiet and alternately dim and dark. Really quiet. And Lincoln's cheerful comments kept her mind from wondering what that dark hump really was at the foot of an especially large tree, or if she'd actually seen a shadow slip between the trunks of two slender saplings.

Lincoln came to an abrupt halt and growled. Ari froze in place. That was Lincoln's "stranger!" growl. The hair along the dog's creamy ruff rippled and stood up.

Chase stopped, ears forward. He curled his upper lip over his teeth.

Lori, a sob of fear in her throat, cried, "What! What is it?"

"Hush!" Ari strained her ears to hear. Flies. Black flies. And that horrible, dead animal odor that she'd smelled three times before.

Lincoln whirled to them, teeth snapping. *BACK! BEHIND THE TREE!*

To her astonishment, Ari heard Chase respond.

What? Chase demanded. *I hide from no thing nor beast, dog!*

Lincoln's tone was grim. *You'll hide from this! Quickly now!*

Ari couldn't stop to think about this new phenomenon. Her dog and her horse could talk to each other.

There was a quiver in the air, just like the beating of a drum. Ari counted under her breath, almost without realizing she was doing it. "One. Two. Three. Four."

"What is it?" Lori was so scared, she almost whispered with terror. Lincoln, cold determination in his eyes, nudged them behind the trunk of the largest tree near them.

The sound in the air grew closer:

"One. Two. Three. Four."

"Something's marching," Ari whispered. She looked up at Lori. The blond girl's face was white. Ari could hear the quick shallow breaths she took. "Easy, now," she said, just as she would to a frightened horse. "Deep breaths. Take very deep breaths."

"ONE! TWO! THREE! FOUR!"

There were voices in the beating of the air. Deep voices, many of them, and all of them marking time together.

Ari flattened herself against the tree, not daring to look around. Lori bent her head into Chase's mane and sobbed silently, her shoulders shaking.

Chase kept his head up, his nostrils flared. He was confused and angry. *Horses, milady. And yet, not horses.*

Ari was afraid to answer. Suddenly, Chase started forward, snorting. Lincoln flung himself in the way, pressing the great stallion's body out of sight of the oncoming marchers. Ari huddled between Chase's legs. The ground shook.

She had to see! Ari crawled forward, peering around the huge tree trunk, almost hidden in the leaves piled at its base.

The marchers came through the woods.

Ari stuffed her fist in her mouth to keep from screaming.

There were so many of them — perhaps a hundred. Each was coal black with red eyes, demon eyes. Each had an iron horn springing from the middle of its forehead.

Black unicorns.

An army of them.

They carried fear with them — and terror. It was in the air they breathed, the ground they marched upon. They passed the tree where the companions lay hidden, in pairs. Their flaming eyes stared straight ahead. Their coats were blacker than coal, blacker than the bottom of the night itself.

Ari's mouth was dry. Her breath was short. She may have fainted, just a little, from the utter horror of it.

When she opened her eyes, they were gone. The air was clean and sweet, the ground firm. It was as if they had never been.

"Lori?" Ari was surprised at how calm she sounded. "You okay?"

"I guess." Lori's voice was a mere squeak. "Did you look?"

"I looked."

"What *was* it?"

"Did you look?"

"No." Lori paused. "I mean, yes."

"Well, so you know what it was." Ari knew that Lori had been too scared to raise her head from Chase's mane. If she told Lori that'd she'd seen a herd of black and fire-eyed unicorns, evil in every step they took, the blond girl would dissolve in a sticky puddle of tears. And they'd never get out of this forest.

"I didn't exactly see, I guess. So what was it?"

"Just some . . . ah . . . bears."

"Bears!" Lori sat up with a squall.

Lincoln looked at Ari reproachfully, *Now you've done it. She won't stop shrieking until we get to the village.*

"BEARS!" Lori drummed her heels into Chase's sides. The stallion cocked his head at Ari. *May I dump her, milady?*

"You may not. We will just . . ." Ari sighed, "march on. Maybe she'll shut up when she sees we're close to safety."

None of them spoke again. The fear was still with them.

Half an hour later, Lincoln led them to the edge of the woods, and they gazed upon the village for the first time. Ari looked. She couldn't tell if it was safe or not. But there was a sign. And the sign said:

WELCOME TO BALINOR

Ari stopped. Stared. And a cold, cold wind blew over her heart. What was this? *What was this!*

More than a village lay ahead.

She took one step forward. Then another.

About the Author

Mary Stanton loves adventure. She has lived in Japan, Hawaii, and all over the United States. She has held many different jobs, including singing in a nightclub, working for an advertising agency, and writing for a TV cartoon series. Mary lives on a farm in upstate New York with some of the horses who inspire her to write adventure stories like the UNICORNS OF BALINOR.

The
Princess School

If the Shoe Fits

Jane B. Mason ☙ Sarah Hines Stephens

For David and Anica, with thanks for the royal treatment.

—JBM & SHS

Copyright © 2004 by Jane B. Mason and Sarah Hines Stephens

All rights reserved.
Published by Scholastic Inc.
SCHOLASTIC and associated logos are trademarks
and/or registered trademarks of Scholastic Inc.

ISBN 0-439-54532-3

12   11   10   9   8   7   6   5   4   3   2   1   4 5 6 7 8 9/0

Printed in the U.S.A.   40

First printing, February 2004

Chapter One
Ella

"Ouch!" Ten-year-old Ella Brown's bare foot came down on a sharp rock. Lifting the skirts of her hand-me-down gown, she hopped on her left foot to inspect her right. No damage, just dirt.

I should be used to dirt, she thought grimly.

With a sigh, she continued gingerly down the lane, picking the least muddy path. She wished yet again that she had a decent pair of shoes for her first day of Princess School.

Her old shoes were full of holes and blackened with soot — too shabby to wear, even with a secondhand dress. They were fine for chores, but not for Princess School. At Princess School the right pair of shoes could make all the difference. Ella ought to know.

Biting her lip, Ella remembered the mysterious shoes that had arrived the night before her Princess School entrance interview — the grueling interrogation every prospective princess faced in order to gain

143

admittance. The shoes sparkled in their velvet-lined box. A small bow shimmered on each curved toe. They were perfect! Until she put them on. As soon as they were on her feet, Ella realized they were much too big.

Of course she had worn them to the interview anyway. Even though they were made of glass, too big, and *really* uncomfortable, they were better than the grubby slippers she had. Ella would rather go barefoot than be seen entering Princess School in *those*.

She stepped over a small puddle in her path and sighed again. It was, quite simply, a miracle that she had been accepted at Princess School at all. And Ella was pretty sure she knew who to thank for it. The telltale sparkle on those new shoes, and the fact that her fairy godmother had recently accepted a job in the Princess School administrative chambers, could only mean one thing. Somebody had been up to a little bobbity-boo.

Ella smiled. Her fairy godmother, Lurlina, looked out for Ella when no one else did. She didn't always get things exactly right . . . like the time she was trying to help clean and decided to banish all of the dust and pet hair from the house. The poor cat was bald for months. But Lurlina *almost* always made things better. And this morning Ella was counting on that.

She hoped Lurlina could make her some new shoes with a quick wave of her wand (and get the size right this time). All Ella had to do was get to Princess School early enough to find her fairy godmother without anyone noticing she was barefoot. That shouldn't be too hard, right?

Looking down, Ella saw her muddy toes peeking out from under her dress. If she bent her knees slightly and walked with her back straight, her hem brushed the ground (gathering *more* dirt), but it hid her feet completely.

"This just might work," Ella said to herself, half smiling.

Then she rounded the corner and the gleaming towers of Princess School came into view. They pierced the sky like jeweled points on a crown. Beneath the stone spires, the enormous arched entrance was swarming with gilded carriages, teams of horses, coachmen, servants, and dozens of novice princesses.

Ella's bent knees suddenly felt weak.

For the first time in her life, Ella wished she were sitting in the kitchen peeling potatoes or sweeping cinders back into the fireplace. At least there she knew what she was doing. It was awful to admit, but she felt more at home in front of the hearth than in a school full of girls in gowns.

How will I ever fit in here? Ella wondered. Doubt swept over her as she realized she wasn't at all sure she would. As she gazed at the fanciful scene before her, she felt the urge to turn and run.

Suddenly the pounding of hooves and rattling of wheels jolted her out of her thoughts. Just in time she dove out of the way of a speeding coach. By pressing against the bushes on the side of the road she only barely managed to keep from being run down.

The coach whizzed past in a blur of blue and gold. One of the large, spoked wheels bumped into a rut in the road and a shower of mud splashed onto Ella's skirts.

With her heart beating fast and her fists clenched in anger, Ella peered after the racing carriage. It was her father's coach! And the piercing cackles and disgusting, snorting laughs echoing out of the windows were all too familiar. Her lying stepsisters!

What were Hagatha and Prunilla doing in her father's coach? Ella fumed. That morning, after Ella served them breakfast, Hag and Prune told their mother they were getting a ride to Princess School with Prince Hargood.

"Such a waste to send the whole coach for just one girl," Ella's stepmother, Kastrid, had said. She flashed a crooked smile as Ella cleared the breakfast dishes and hurried downstairs to finish pressing Hagatha's gown and Prunilla's hair ribbons. "Ella, you can walk."

Ella knew Hag and Prune had lied on purpose. She swiped at her skirts angrily. They couldn't get over the fact that Ella was starting at *their* school — and heaven forbid they should all arrive together! The older girls didn't think Ella could make it at Princess School.

Ella had hoped that starting Princess School would change things at home. That her stepsisters would stop ordering her around and insulting her. That her stepmother would stop treating her like hired help. That her father would stand up to his new wife. But if today's start was any indication, nothing had changed, and nothing ever would.

"There's no way I'm going to spend the rest of my life in my stepmother's kitchen," Ella said out loud, giving her skirts a final swipe. She would show her awful stepsisters she was as good as they were, even with a muddy dress and bare feet.

Bent knees wobbling, Ella headed for the draw-bridge that led up to the school's entrance. Several long-necked white swans glided in the moat beneath the bridge.

They look more regal than I do, Ella thought. She held her head a little higher. If she was going to get in unnoticed, she had to look like she belonged. Luckily most of the other students were too excited to pay attention to a shabbily dressed new girl. But Ella found it difficult not to stare at them. They were lovely, with fancily braided and coiled hair. They wore gowns of every color — in silk and velvet and brocade. The fine fabrics glimmered in the sun. Clustered in small groups, the girls chatted animatedly with one another, making polite princess gestures with delicate fingers.

Ella looked past them toward the school entrance and her heart jumped. The white marble steps up to the school were so polished, the sun glinted off them. The carved wooden doors were as ornate as any gilded picture frame, and when a princess or member of the faculty stepped up to them, the heavy doors opened with a quiet *whoosh*. It sounded as if the castle itself were drawing a breath.

On either side of the doors, trumpeters raised long golden instruments to their lips. Then, with a few short blasts, they announced that the first day of the new school year was about to begin.

As she gazed at the castle that was to be her new school, Ella was filled with awe . . . and dread. Her stepsisters were right: She would never make it at Princess School.

You can't think like that, she scolded herself. *Be confident. You can do this.*

Ella squinched up her toes and walked more quickly

toward the steps. She needed to find Lurlina before class started. But with each step, she passed another perfect princess-in-training and her courage began to melt away. It seemed every novice she walked by was more beautiful than the last. They were all so well pressed and dressed!

Here I am in dirty rags, and I don't even have shoes on! Ella thought. *Lurlina* has *to come through.*

At the base of the stairs, Ella stopped in her tracks when she saw the prettiest girl yet. Her hair was the color of wheat in the sun. Her cheeks were like rose blossoms. Her eyes were bluer than the clearest lake.

"Do be careful, dear," the girl's mother cooed while her father wrung his hands nearby.

"Won't you please wear these gloves?" her father begged, holding out a pair of metal gauntlets suitable for a knight.

The beautiful girl smiled kindly at her parents, refusing the hand armor. Tiny fairies buzzed all around her, adjusting her collar, twisting an already-perfect curl, smoothing her delicate eyebrows, draping her skirts more elegantly down the stairs, twittering their advice in her ears.

Ella almost laughed out loud at the bustling fairies. What could they possibly do to make this girl more lovely?

Forgetting all about her own predicament, Ella

lifted her skirts to climb the stairs, the final ascent into Princess School. With a gasp, she saw her own pale naked foot shining like the moon on the stone stair. She quickly dropped her skirts back over it and looked around to see if anyone else had noticed. No one turned in her direction, except the beautiful girl with the fairies.

Ella stared into the other girl's deep blue eyes and waited. She waited for her to say something mean. To laugh and point. She waited to be ridiculed. Exposed as a fake. Thrown out of school! But all she saw in the other girl's eyes was curiosity.

"What is it, Rose?" the girl's mother asked anxiously.

"Are you afraid? Do you want me to come with you?" Rose's father asked, looking around to see what had caught his daughter's eye. "I can call the guards."

"Please, Father, it's nothing." Rose brushed her parents off with a smile. "I'm fine. And I'm going to school now. *Alone*."

Ella watched, shocked and grateful, as the girl strode confidently up the stairs without so much as another glance in her direction. All eyes, it seemed, were on Rose. Ella took a cautious look around to see if anyone else had seen her. She could still make it inside unnoticed. Except . . .

Leaning against a banner pole, another girl peered

at her with an odd smile. The girl had an unbelievably huge coil of auburn hair piled haphazardly on her head, and her navy dress was strange — shorter than Ella's and looser. But before Ella could decipher the look on her face, the girl turned away and waved, not very royally, to a prince on the other side of the rose garden.

The prince returned the wave with a grin and then ducked inside an enormous manor house. Ella squinted into the distance. The sign over the door read THE CHARM SCHOOL FOR BOYS.

Ella's stomach gave a lurch. The Charm School! Every prince in the kingdom went there! And princes made her almost as nervous as princesses. Ella sighed. Why did *everything* make her so nervous?

With her feet hidden, knees bent, and stomach fluttering, Ella walked up the last few stairs and stepped through the already-open doors of her new school.

She felt her breath catch in her throat. The inside of Princess School was as overwhelming as the outside. The polished stone floor was an ornate pattern of square pink and white stones. The tall, narrow, diamond-paned windows reached from the floor to the ceiling, ending in delicately pointed tops. The ceiling itself was silver leaf, while the alabaster pillars between the endless arches were covered with carved roses and ivy.

Excited voices echoed loudly off the tall arches. Teachers stood in the glittering foyer, directing new students to class. For a moment Ella couldn't even move. Prospective princesses swarmed past her. Which way was her fairy godmother's chamber?

A woman in a red velvet gown approached Ella. "Your name?" she asked, eyeing Ella's mud-strewn gown warily.

"Cinderella Brown," Ella replied, her heart sinking. Out of the corner of her eye she could see the girl who'd been waving excitedly to the Charm School boy outside. She seemed to be watching Ella with renewed interest. A trumpet blast echoed down the hall, interrupting Ella's thoughts and distracting the other girl. There would not be enough time to find Lurlina before class. Ella would have to start Princess School barefoot and filthy.

Chapter Two
Rapunzel

Rapunzel followed the barefoot girl with the filthy gown into the large hearthroom and sat down in a velvet-cushioned, high-backed chair. The hearthroom was big and echoey, like most of the rooms in a castle. A fire burned in the grate of a large fireplace to take away the morning chill. Tapestries depicting kings and queens doing things kings and queens do lined the walls. But Rapunzel wasn't really looking at the furnishings. She was looking at the other girls. And she was scowling.

Okay, maybe she had been locked in a tower for years and years (and years), but she had never seen such a bunch of prissy girls in her life! With the single exception of the girl in the muddy gown, the room was filled with nothing but fancy-pants princesses.

Like Rapunzel, all of the girls in this class were at Princess School for the first time. They were first-years,

Bloomers. Girls returning for their second year were known as Sashes. Third-years were Robes, and the fourth and final-year students were called Crowns.

Rapunzel slouched. This bunch of Bloomers looked a little fidgety. Most of them had not taken their seats. They were introducing themselves with small nods and curtsies, exchanging compliments and pleasantries while Rapunzel sat back and chewed the end of her braid. If this was how Princess School was going to be, Rapunzel wasn't sure she could take it.

Rapunzel turned her narrowed eyes toward one of the prettiest Bloomers in the class, Briar Rose. Dressed in a stunning gown that matched her blue eyes, Rose had shining golden hair and a warm smile. She was completely surrounded by other novice princesses. Already they had a nickname for her: "Beauty." Ugh!

"I'll bet she is just full of herself," Rapunzel muttered to a sour-looking king on the tapestry closest to her. "And I bet she couldn't eat her way out of a gingerbread house."

Rapunzel had no respect for people who couldn't take care of themselves. After all, she had been taking care of herself since she was tiny — since Madame Gothel took her from her parents and put her in a thirty-foot tower.

"Nobody keeps me locked up," Rapunzel mumbled, though she had to admit she'd had some help escaping — at least the first time. She was only seven when Val, short for Prince Valerian, appeared at the base of the tower and called up to her.

Rapunzel's scowl disappeared when she thought about her friend. He might be a prince, but he would always be plain old Val to her. Val was eight when he first stumbled across Rapunzel's tower in the woods. He wasn't trying to save her or anything. He just wanted somebody to play with.

"Come down!" he'd called.

"How?" Rapunzel asked.

"Just climb!" he'd answered.

At first Rapunzel thought he was kidding. The tower was almost ten times her height!

"I bet you can't," Val teased.

So then, of course, she did. He coached her, pointing out places to put her hands and feet.

"I would have climbed up," Val said when Rapunzel finally made it to the bottom, "but heights make me vomit."

Rapunzel smiled as she remembered the incredible sense of freedom she'd felt that first time she'd escaped from the tower. Being cooped up was horrible! As the memory faded, Rapunzel saw a girl with silky brown hair and a pink gown curtsy in her direction. In an instant the scowl was back.

Rapunzel wished she were with Val right now. He wasn't very far away — just across the rose garden. Rapunzel was sure second-year Charm School could beat the pantaloons off of first-year Princess School. But she knew she had a better chance of turning into a frog than of getting into the all-boys' school.

Maybe I should have tried the Grimm School, Rapunzel thought as the first-year girls settled into their chairs with a swish of skirts. Glaring at the back of the perfectly postured princess in front of her, Rapunzel knew that would never have worked out, either. The Grimm School was actually closer to her tower than Princess School, but the students who went there were *spooky*. They were real witches! Not only did they learn to fly on broomsticks, which actually sounded kind of fun, they also practiced magic. They concocted potions and cast spells on anything and everything, from trees to animals to people. It was rumored that a few years ago a Grimm girl had even turned a princess into a lizard! And if you thought the students were bad, the teachers were positively evil. Rapunzel shivered. She'd had her fill of nasty sorceresses living with Madame Gothel.

Just then Madame Garabaldi, the Bloomers' hearthroom instructor, strode importantly into the room and held her arms wide for the pages to take her robe. Her silver-streaked hair was pulled into a tight bun, and her hazel eyes gazed sharply over her half-spectacles at the students. Madame Garabaldi cleared her throat as a scribe hurriedly passed scrolls to all the girls. Then, with a final horn blast, class began.

Rapunzel scanned the list of classes written on the silver-leaf-trimmed scroll she'd just received.

Fine Art of Self-defense

That sounded okay.

Frog Identification

Not too terrible.

History: Princesses Past and Present

Well, all right.

Stitchery: Needlework, Spinning, and Embroidery Basics

Were they serious?

Rapunzel gazed down at the scroll to read the final class:

Looking Glass Class — Hairdo How-to and Essential Self-reflection

With a moan, Rapunzel dropped the scroll on her desk and glanced around to see her classmates' reactions. The other Bloomers were gazing politely at Madame Garabaldi, who strode around the chamber, reading from an enormous scroll all of the rules the girls were expected to follow.

"Proper attire is to be worn at all times," Madame

157

Garabaldi enunciated. Her gaze left the list and settled on the barefoot girl who Rapunzel had noticed on the bridge. The girl's face reddened. It didn't look like much got past Madame G.

"Politeness must be observed," Madame Garabaldi rapped out. "Continuously maintain a regal countenance. Homework will be carefully completed. And you must *always* be prompt." Madame Garabaldi laid down the scroll.

"You will find," she continued, "that the punishments we serve here at Princess School are not nearly as harsh as those realities you will encounter once you graduate." Pausing for effect, Madame Garabaldi breathed a puff of air out her nose. She almost looked like a dragon. "Or perhaps you'd have a vine time living the rest of your days as a ridiculously colored squash?" She finished by gazing around the room, smiling at her own joke. But the smile was not exactly warm or welcoming.

Rapunzel stuffed her braid back in her mouth and chewed. Was this what it felt like to be nervous?

Suddenly the heavy classroom doors swung open with a *whoosh*, and the palest princess Rapunzel had ever seen stumbled in.

"Pardon the interruption, Madame Garabaldi," a page said, skirting the girl and bowing low several times before the stern teacher. His hands were shaking slightly. "May I present Snow White?" He gestured toward the pale girl with black hair before backing quickly out of the room, flourishing his pointy hat.

Snow White stood alone at the front of the room. All eyes were on her, and her too-short, high-collared, old-fashioned dress.

Madame Garabaldi was too angry to speak. Her lips quivered and she looked like she wanted to turn Snow White into a pumpkin. Everyone waited for her to say something.

But it was Snow White who spoke first.

Her berry-red lips turned up into a silly grin, and she gave a little wave to all the girls staring at her.

"Hi-ho, everyone!" she chirped.

Rapunzel let her braid drop from her mouth. *Things could be worse*, she thought. *I could be* her.

Chapter Three
Snow White

Snow White smiled at her new classmates. In spite of the scowling woman next to her, her heart was full of joy. She was at Princess School! And she was sure that each and every one of the girls looking at her would become a good friend.

"As it is your first day of Princess School, your tardiness will be excused," Madame Garabaldi said in a carefully controlled voice. It sounded as if her teeth were clenched. "But should it happen again, you will receive double tower detention. Be warned: Tardiness has been the demise of many a princess." The instructor looked pointedly at each girl in the class before turning back to Snow. "Please take your seat," she said in a low tone. "Now."

Snow shivered. The look on Madame Garabaldi's face reminded her of the way her stepmother, easily the most horrible person Snow had ever met, used to look at her over the dinner table. Snow's smile returned. *I don't miss that!* she thought. Surely her new teacher couldn't be as bad as her stepmother.

Snow hummed a little on the way to her seat — a new tune the birds had taught her just that morning. As she turned to sit she caught Madame Garabaldi's eye and the song quickly died in her throat.

Snow did not miss withering looks. Ever since she'd gone to live with her seven surrogates, the dwarves, she hadn't seen anything close to a glare. Until now.

Tomorrow, she told herself, *I'll just have to get up earlier.*

Snow hadn't meant to be late. But she'd needed to help pack seven lunches and see the dwarves off to work. Then she had stopped for a quick visit with Mother Sparrow, whose injured wing Snow was tending. It was almost healed. Snow swung her feet under her desk, thinking of her happy home in the forest.

Behind her, other Bloomers were starting to whisper.

"She doesn't look a thing like a princess! How did she get in?"

"And where did she get that outfit? Look at that collar!"

"I heard she was raised by gnomes."

Snow's feet swung more slowly under her desk. She would not let her good mood be ruined by gossip. She had come too far. She'd even walked past the

Grimm School *by herself* on the way here. She had been looking forward to this for months.

Life with the dwarves was good. Wonderful, even. They worked together to keep their small house tidy. Snow did most of the cooking (though the dwarves often offered to prepare the food, they *all* preferred her delicious soups and pies to their gray gruels and goulashes), but as she worked, the dwarves entertained her with music. And they were constantly doing nice things for Snow, like picking her flowers or bringing her an empty bird's nest. The only bad thing about her cottage life was that the dwarves worked a lot, and Snow got lonely while they were gone . . . even with the company of the woodland animals.

Snow smiled at a few of the girls seated close to her. *They'll like me once they get to know me*, she thought.

A couple of the girls turned away from Snow, but one or two returned her smile, including the friendly-looking, dirty-gowned girl just behind her.

Snow felt better already. Nothing kept her down for long. And look, at the front of the room Madame Garabaldi was reading the school announcements and looking a lot less stern.

"By decree, the Royal Coronation Ball will be held at the end of your second week at Princess School!" she announced. "At the ball, one student — the most elegant and graceful of all — will be crowned Princess of the Ball!" Madame Garabaldi practically beamed. She gazed into the distance and swayed back and forth to imaginary music.

The mood in the room changed at once as everyone pictured herself at the Coronation Ball. The girls began to murmur with excitement. Many of the Bloomers, like Snow White, were born princesses, but lots of them were merely princess hopefuls waiting for an opportunity to wear a crown. This could be their chance.

"The honor of being the Princess of the Ball is great," Madame Garabaldi went on, still smiling and swaying. "It cannot be won by birth or marriage. Indeed not. It is an honor bestowed by one's peers. Every girl in the school will get to cast a vote, and she who is most admired will be crowned."

A few of the princesses glanced expectantly at the beautiful princess with shining, wheat-colored hair and striking blue eyes.

"Of course," Madame Garabaldi continued with a mild look of disdain, "a Bloomer has not received such an honor in more than four dozen years. I certainly would not recommend getting your hopes up."

The excitement in the room faded as quickly as it had grown. Only Snow did not notice the change in the atmosphere. The room was silent when she clapped her hands together, unable to contain her enthusiasm.

"Oh my great golly goodness," she exclaimed. "My very first ball!"

Chapter Four
A Single Slipper

Ella slipped out of hearthroom the moment class ended. It was easy to go unnoticed now. The whole school was abuzz with talk of the ball. Ella made her way through the pink-and-white mazelike hallways, past the gilded, velvet-lined trunks where girls kept their books and supplies, and toward the flower-carved winding staircases leading to other wings of the castle. Around her she heard girls planning what they should wear.

"Do you think rubies go with silk?" a second-year Sash asked her friend as they strolled by, arm in arm.

"Oh, Arabelle! You *have* to wear your tiara," another girl said loudly to a group of her friends. "Have any of you seen it? It is royally gorgeous!"

Talk of ribbons, gowns, and jewels spilled off everyone's tongues. Ella wished she could stop and talk to the other girls. But what would she say? She didn't have a fancy hair ribbon to her name, let alone a gown suitable for a ball.

"At least I can finally get some shoes," Ella consoled herself. Maybe Lurlina could help her out with something to wear to the ball, too. Ella stopped in front of a heavy wooden door and slowly pushed it open. An ornately carved sign over her hand read PRINCESS SCHOOL ROYAL ADMINISTRATIVE CHAMBER.

"I'm looking for Lurlina Busybustle, if you please," Ella said with a curtsy to the woman behind the gilded desk.

"Oh, you must be Ella. Lurly left something for you," the woman said kindly. Then she began pawing through an enormous velvet bag filled with scrolls.

"You mean she's not here?" Ella asked. She felt a lump growing in her throat.

"Oh, no, dear," came the muffled reply from inside the bag. "Aha!" she said, emerging with a small scroll in her hand and a very disheveled hairdo. "Here we are. This should explain everything."

Ella was reaching for the scroll when a rather short page she hadn't even noticed leaped up and grabbed it. He gave the trumpeter by the door a sharp jab with his elbow, and after a few sour notes were played, the page cleared his throat to read.

After a moment of panic Ella calmed herself. "If

you don't mind," she said, putting out her hand, "I'd rather read it myself."

The page handed Ella the note sheepishly. "Of course, your nearly royalness, of course. My mistake," he said with a bow. "It's been such a long summer. I guess I'm anxious to read some decrees."

The page sat back down in the far corner and tilted his hat so it covered his eyes, and Ella began to read.

Halloo Dearie,

I forgot to tell you I am going to a fairy convention in Afaraway Land. I'll be back in three weeks. Sorry I'll miss the Coronation Ball. Have fun in Princess School. I knew you'd get in!

Love,
LB

P.S. Hope you are enjoying the shoes.

Ella's heart sank as she read. Three weeks! She couldn't possibly go barefoot for that long! What was she going to do? Bending her knees so her skirt touched the floor, Ella turned slowly toward the door.

"I have something else for you, too, dear. I think you left this at your interview." The woman behind the desk handed Ella a box. Inside it was one lovely, but oversized, glass shoe.

"Thank you." Ella smiled weakly, remembering the awful interview. She'd had to sit in a much-too-tall chair across from the Dean of Admissions, Miss Prim. And she'd had a terrible time answering the questions because all she could think about the whole time was how to keep her shoes from slipping off and breaking on the stone floor.

When Miss Prim had finally told her she could go, Ella was so anxious to get out of there she accidentally stepped out of one of her shoes. At first she was too embarrassed to go back for it. When she had summoned up her courage to reenter the dean's office, Miss Prim was holding the shoe in her hand, turning it this way and that and gazing at it with what looked like . . . admiration.

Ella couldn't ask for it back after that. Instead, with burning cheeks, she'd pulled off the other shoe, run all the way home, and received a serious lecture from her stepmother for being late. And of course, merciless teasing from Hagatha and Prunilla. Only her father had told her everything would be okay — but he'd told her in a whisper so his wife wouldn't hear. It wasn't particularly reassuring.

Ella gazed at the shoe in her hand. After her interview she'd been certain that the fancy footwear would keep her out of Princess School. Now she wondered if it had gotten her in.

Ella sighed. Little good the shoe would do her now without Lurlina to resize the pair. Ella tried not to think about how she was going to survive for three weeks without her fairy godmother — or what she would wear to the ball.

"Head down, feet covered," she mumbled to herself as she hurried toward her next class. Except for a large group of girls farther down the corridor, the halls were empty and the trunks were closed.

Ella did not want to be late and call attention to herself. But as she approached the group of girls, something made her slow. *Hungch-henh-henh-henh-hungch.* That laugh! Only Prunilla snorted like that when she laughed. And Hagatha's nasal cackle was echoing in the corridor as well.

Hagatha and Prunilla were standing in the center of a bunch of Bloomers Ella recognized from Madame Garabaldi's hearthroom. Ella backed into a doorway. She wasn't ready to deal with her stepsisters at school. Not with Lurlina gone. And not when they were laughing. Only one thing amused Hag and Prune: cruelty.

Ella carefully peeked around the corner to see what they were up to.

"It happens every year," Hagatha hissed at the big-eyed Bloomers. Prunilla nodded beside her sister. "Sometimes the wolf eats the princesses alive and they have to be chopped out. Sometimes he doesn't eat them at all, just chews up their limbs and spits out their bones!"

"Oh, no!" one of the first-years cried.

"How awful!" another shrieked.

The Bloomers pressed closer together. Some of them glanced over their shoulders. Only the girl with the massive, sloppily braided bun — Rapunzel — stood by herself. Her arms were folded across her chest. She didn't look scared but she was definitely listening.

"They come out of the woods and swim the moat." Prunilla made swimming motions with her arms. "They can smell Bloomer blood for miles, you know."

"I've never heard of a wolf that eats young girls!" a cheery voice from the Bloomer crowd protested. It was Snow White.

"These wolves do," Hagatha snapped back. "They're enchanted. The Grimm School sends them." Snow did not protest again.

"But you don't have to take our word for it," Prunilla said in singsong. "You'll see for yourselves soon enough!"

Hagatha and Prunilla pushed their way out of the crowd and sauntered down the hall. Then Hagatha turned quickly and snarled with her teeth bared, looking every bit as awful as a rabid wolf.

The shaken Bloomers screamed in terror and jumped back. All except Rapunzel, who followed the older girls down the hall, watching them with narrowed eyes.

Ella was dumbstruck. She didn't believe Hagatha and Prunilla's stories — not for a second. It was just like them to try to make the new girls scared. What shocked Ella the most was that Hag and Prune were being so terrible to, well, everyone! She always thought they saved their awfulness for her.

The thought of her stepsisters terrorizing her whole class made Ella furious. She wished like never before that she could stand up to them.

Then Ella had a terrible thought. What if everyone at Princess School found out Hagatha and Prunilla were her stepsisters? They might assume she was awful, just like them!

She would have to show the other Bloomers she was on their side. To do that she was going to have to stop going unnoticed. Ignoring her bare feet, Ella strode quickly down the hall. She beckoned to the still-cowering girls.

"Come on!" she called encouragingly. "We don't want to be late for class!"

One of the Bloomers, Snow White, smiled warmly at Ella. The rest of the girls were somber as they pressed together and shakily made their way down the hall.

Chapter Five
Rose

Madame Taffeta's skirts rustled as she gently took Rose's square of muslin and held it up for the rest of the princesses to see. "Note how the stitches are perfectly spaced and sized," she said, her gray eyes wide with admiration. Her round face was rosy from excitement. "Even the choice of thread color is perfect. The mossy green looks positively elegant against the cream muslin! And it's only our second day of classes!"

The girls were in Stitchery class, practicing basic threadwork. They sat in a large circle, each on a comfortable chair with a velvet cushion. Squares of plain muslin, spools of thread, needles, and shiny silver scissors sat on an ornately carved table in the center of the circle. A fire crackled cheerily at one end of the chamber.

Some of the Bloomers looked admiringly at Rose as the teacher held her muslin aloft. But others, including

Rapunzel, openly glared at her. Rose sighed and let her threaded needle fall to her lap, being careful not to let the sharp end touch her finger. Her stitches were straight, even, and perfectly sized, it was true.

Rose had been sewing for as long as she could remember, and with a disadvantage. Whenever Rose went near a needle, her parents forced her to wear a thimble on every finger, for fear she would prick herself. Rose didn't know why. It wasn't easy learning to sew with metal fingertips, but over time Rose had gotten good at it. So now, without those annoying thimbles, her stitching was even better — and she was faster at it. But she wished Madame Taffeta would stop making a fuss.

There was another girl who was fast — the friendly girl who'd been barefoot yesterday — Ella. She moved the needle and thread through the fabric so quickly, it was as if she desperately wanted the task to be done. She had already gone to the table to get a second and a third piece of muslin. Her stitches were almost as even as Rose's, and she had chosen a color that was almost identical to the mossy green. Why didn't Madame Taffeta compliment her?

As if deciding to squash any hope Rose had of ever being normal, Madame Taffeta began to speak again. "Briar Rose, would you like to demonstrate your perfect stitching technique? I'm sure the other girls would benefit greatly from an illustration of your talent."

Rose had no desire to demonstrate anything. For a moment she thought of pointing out Ella's fine stitches. But something stopped her. That first morning on the stairs, Ella had seemed terrified of being noticed. Standing up in front of the whole class might be even worse for her.

Rose stood and quickly ran her needle and thread through the muslin, making a straight line of even stitches.

"Perfect!" Madame Taffeta exclaimed. She snatched up the fabric and held it next to the window so the light shone behind it, making the stitches more visible.

Rose barely glanced at the muslin as she took her seat, but something outside the window caught her eye.

Oh my gosh! she thought, feeling her face flush with embarrassment. Was that Dahlia, one of her guardian fairies, hovering in midair?

The winged pest was spying on her! Rose quickly looked away, hoping Dahlia would disappear before anyone else saw her. That's when she noticed that Rapunzel was glaring at her for the second time in ten minutes. This time, Rose was ready. She glared right back. It wasn't as if she *asked* for this attention. Rapunzel's eyes widened in surprise before she lowered them back to her stitching.

Rose blew out her breath. Being so blessed and so protected was driving her crazy!

I wouldn't even mind being teased by the older girls! Rose thought desperately. Most of the Bloomers were miserable and terrified, and for good reason. The first day and a half of school had been grueling, and not just because of the rules and coursework. Terrible things had been happening to them!

First there was that horrible story about a cursed Grimm wolf eating the first-years. Rose wasn't sure she believed it, but the idea was enough to make anyone shiver. Then there were the trippings. An innocent Bloomer would be hurrying off to class when — *WHAM!* — she would suddenly find herself and whatever she was carrying sprawled across the cold stone floor. A few of the third-year Robes forced the new girls to guess their names, not letting them pass in the hall until they did so successfully. This usually made the Bloomers late for class, which got them in big trouble. But even tower detention (the punishment for being tardy) was not as humiliating as the drenchings. Some nasty Crowns rigged buckets of icy water over the trunks of unsuspecting Bloomers, soaking the girls as soon as the lids were lifted. Wet and shivering, the Bloomers would have to maintain their composure and dignity while they dried off as best they could and rushed off to wherever they had to go next.

Rose shuddered as she remembered that morning's drenching. It was early, and the sun had not yet peeked out from behind the clouds to warm the castle. The girl was small and had shivered uncontrollably as she made her way to class. Rose had wanted to go over and help the girl, but just then a group of Bloomers had come over to ask Rose what she was going to wear to the ball. Before she could break away, the cold and dripping girl was gone.

I'd like to do something about those cruel tricks, Rose thought. *Why can't the older girls just leave us alone?*

Except, of course, they *were* leaving Rose alone. She was getting the usual special treatment. And that was part of the problem!

The Self-defense class chamber was a giant room nearly as big as the school's stables. Thick, woven wool rugs covered the floor. There was no furniture, but today the room was decorated with large wooden props painted to look like trees and shrubs. The chamber looked like a forest.

The Bloomers stood in small groups waiting for Madame Lightfoot to give them instructions. Madame

Lightfoot was famous, the first princess in the land trained in the art of royal self-defense. Though she was the oldest teacher at Princess School, her braided gray hair was the only sign of her age. She was tall and stood so straight that her presence alone was intimidating. She was strict and did not tolerate students who did not work hard on their defense skills but her smile was never far below the surface.

Rose was eyeing the clusters of girls sprinkled throughout the room when Snow White skipped over. "I just loved your stitches!" Snow exclaimed. "If I could sew like that, the dwarves' clothes would almost never need mending. I swear I spend half my days restitching the same tears!" She let out a small giggle.

Rose had to smile. At least the pale girl's compliments were unique! "Do you really live with dwarves?" she asked, intrigued.

"Oh, yes!" Snow answered. "Seven of them! They are the funniest little men — a little strange at first, but really lovable once you get to know them. They bring me flowers and sing merry songs. Oh, and they protect me from —"

Just then Madame Lightfoot clapped her hands to get the girls' attention.

"Today we will be practicing the woodland-path-skip-trip," she announced. She moved swiftly around the room, pairing up the princesses. Rose was hoping she would be paired with Snow so she could learn more about the dwarves (like, how small were they? And would they be interested in meeting a bunch of fairies with too much free time?) but was not so lucky. Snow was paired with Ella. And Rose was paired with Rapunzel — the girl with the ridiculously long auburn hair and the mean stare.

Rapunzel gave a little snort when Madame Lightfoot pulled her and Rose together. The gleam in her eye was mischievous.

She looks like she wants to make a noose out of that hair and string me up, Rose thought. But she didn't care, and she wasn't afraid. It actually felt kind of nice to be scoffed at!

Madame Lightfoot went on, "This tactic is especially good when you find a devilish witch, wolf, or other beast of no-good nature sneaking up to devour you."

There was a chorus of shrieks, doubtless because of the rumored Grimm School wolf. Did Madame Lightfoot know about it? Rose wondered. Was that why she was teaching this skill during the first week of class?

"Ladies," the instructor said sternly, "we are here to learn to defend ourselves. Not to squeal and shriek like helpless children!"

The Bloomers quieted, and Madame Lightfoot continued. "Now, to begin the skip-trip, you must get into a good skipping rhythm. Whenever you are skipping through the forest, of course, you must continuously look from side to side for potential attackers. Keep your basket pushed back to your elbow so your hands are free. Then, when you see someone or something suspicious approaching you, throw out your forward skipping foot to knock the perpetrator off balance. That accomplished, grab your attacker around the neck and toss the scoundrel to the ground. It's really quite simple."

"It sounds mean!" Rose overheard Snow whispering to Ella. She watched as the shabbily dressed girl patted Snow's arm reassuringly. They had to be the nicest pair in the class!

Madame Lightfoot gazed around the chamber at the faces of the confused princesses. "Perhaps a demonstration," she said. "May I have a volunteer to be the scoundrel I am to trip?"

Rose was about to volunteer — maybe it would show the other girls that she didn't think she was too good to land flat on her face — when Rapunzel stepped forward. Madame Lightfoot immediately began to skip in slow motion. Rapunzel assumed a skulking pose and half-hid behind one of the wooden trees. She looked like she was just about to lunge at Madame Lightfoot when the teacher kicked her right foot to the side, knocking Rapunzel's left foot and throwing her off balance. An instant later, Madame Lightfoot tossed

Rapunzel over her shoulder and onto the soft green carpet like a small bale of hay. *Thud!* Rapunzel landed flat on her back.

Rapunzel beamed and leaped to her feet. "Incredible!" she said, not sounding very princesslike. Rose had to admire the girl's attitude. Would she have been as relaxed?

It didn't take long to find out. Madame Lightfoot instructed them to begin working in their pairs at once, and Rapunzel began skipping away. Rose lunged gracefully, but Rapunzel tripped her and tossed her to the ground like a sack of wet wool.

"Are you all right, Princess?" Rapunzel asked. Her voice was not entirely sincere, but Rose pretended not to notice.

"I'm fine," she replied pleasantly, getting to her feet.

Beside them, Snow and Ella were negotiating their own skip-trip. Ella was skipping and Snow was tripping — or, at least, she was trying to. As Ella approached, she slowed down, afraid to trod on Snow's foot. Snow kicked out her leg, but then threw out her hand to keep Ella from falling. Ella grabbed Snow's hand and sat down with a bump.

"Oops!" Ella giggled. "Maybe we should try that again. You don't have to be so nice, you know."

"Sorry," Snow apologized.

Those two are well matched, Rose thought. Then she

looked back at her own partner. She was well matched, too, she decided. Without even dusting herself off, Rose began her own skip, casting her eyes in all directions. Rapunzel came at her from behind a bush, but Rose was ready. She kicked out a leg with lightning speed and hurled Rapunzel to the ground so fast the girl got the wind knocked out of her.

Rose felt a little guilty. She hadn't meant to trip Rapunzel that hard. She was about to apologize when Rapunzel looked up, a wide grin on her face.

"Nice one!" she complimented Rose as she got to her feet and regained her breath. "Can you show me how to do it that fast?"

Rose grinned back. She had a sneaking suspicion she'd just made a friend. And not because she was pretty!

"Of course!" she replied.

Chapter Six
Step-by-step

Ella filled a platter with roasted meat and vegetables and hurried out to the dining room. She didn't want to listen to her stepmother or stepsisters complain about how slow she was. Or how lazy. Or how stupid. She was feeling deflated as it was.

It seemed that in the two days since she'd started Princess School, her stepsisters were more determined than ever to keep her swamped with chores at home. Suddenly the meals she had to prepare had seven courses instead of five. The mending basket was always overflowing. Hagatha and Prunilla had dirtied an extra gown a day, nearly doubling her laundry chores. Just yesterday they put in their winter furs to be aired, and it wasn't even October!

As Ella served the meat and vegetables, she tried not to look too tired. The more tired she appeared, the more her sisters ridiculed her.

"Everyone's talking about the Royal Coronation Ball at school, Mother," Prunilla said as she pecked at a scrap of meat. She looked scornfully at Ella holding the platter of food. "The meat is underseasoned again," she snapped. "Bring me the salt."

"You would think she would learn from her mistakes," Kastrid said coolly. "And yet we have to tell her again and again."

Ella knew the meat was seasoned perfectly. Besides, if she'd added any more salt, her stepsisters would complain that it was oversalted. She just couldn't win. Not since her father had married Kastrid.

"I think the meat is just right," Ella thought she heard her father murmur. She was standing right next to him with the platter. But if anyone else heard, they did not respond. With an aching heart, Ella wished her mother were still alive. How different things would be!

Ella sighed silently and handed Prunilla the glass bowl of salt that sat on the table, well within her reach. Her stepsisters never did anything for themselves if they could make Ella do it for them.

"Anyway," Prunilla said, casting a sideways glance at Ella, "they say the ball is going to be grander than ever this year. The ballroom floor is going to be repolished and the orchestra will have a dozen extra musicians! The fourth-year Crowns are in charge of decorating the ballroom, of course, but Headmistress

Bathilde has asked me to help decorate the ballot box!"

"You!" Hagatha cried, her eyes flashing with envy. "What about me?"

"Well, she asked *me*. But I suppose if you let me borrow your brocade cape I might let you help," Prunilla said coyly.

Hagatha scowled. "I was going to wear that cape, and you know it!" she howled.

"Girls, girls," Ella's stepmother said. "Let's not argue. Of course your sister will let you help with the ballot box," she told Hagatha. "And both of you will be beautifully dressed for the occasion."

"I'm sure all three of you girls will have a wonderful time at the ball," Ella's father added quietly.

The room fell silent, and for a moment Ella was grateful that her father had spoken up for her. But one glance at her stepmother's narrowing eyes told her she shouldn't be. The look on Kastrid's face was so cruel that Ella almost dropped the basket of bread she was holding.

"Ella is lucky to be attending Princess School at all," Kastrid snapped. "It has yet to be seen whether she deserves to go to the ball as well."

Ella looked over at her father, hoping he would say something else. His eyes flitted between his plate of food and his wife's angry face.

185

"But the ball is for all Princess School students, is it not, my sweet?" he said, almost in a whisper.

Kastrid slammed her wine goblet down on the table so hard that the red liquid spilled onto the white lace tablecloth — another stain for Ella to remove.

"We shall discuss this later, *darling*," Ella's stepmother declared, giving Ella's father a withering look. As Ella returned to the kitchen to finish preparing the dessert, her heart went out to her father. Being married to Kastrid could not be any easier than having her for a stepmother. And she knew he had married her because he thought she, his only child, needed a mother.

There was no mention of the ball during the rest of the meal. But as soon as Ella had cleared the dishes and filled the sink with hot water, her stepsisters flounced into the kitchen, talking loudly about the ball.

"I want all of my gowns cleaned and pressed so I can try them on and choose the one that makes me look prettiest," Prunilla announced.

"And I want each and every piece of my gold and silver jewelry polished to a perfect shine so I can choose the ones that bring out my eyes," Hagatha added.

Ella wanted to tell Hagatha that her beady eyes

were not her best asset. Why bring them out? And nothing could make Prunilla pretty, since her heart was as black as coal. But Ella said nothing, only continued washing the giant pile of dishes next to the stone sink.

"We're so sorry you won't be coming to the ball with us," Hagatha said in a sugary-sweet voice.

"Yes," Prunilla agreed. Her face contorted into a sneer. "Who will fetch our refreshments and adjust the skirts of our gowns?"

Ella gritted her teeth. *Politeness must be observed*, she told herself, repeating Madame Garabaldi's words. Somehow they fell flat. Still, Ella said nothing.

Then Hagatha's eyes glimmered, and she leaned back. Before Ella knew what was happening the soup tureen fell to the floor, smashing and splattering soup everywhere, especially all over Ella. Her stepsisters, of course, leaped out of the way just in time.

"What a mess!" Prunilla said. "You are as clumsy as you are slow!"

"You'd better clean it up before Mother finds out you broke her best tureen," Hagatha added.

Cackling like a pair of court jesters, the two left Ella alone in the kitchen with porcelain shards and spattered vegetable soup.

Ella held back tears as she got down on her hands

and knees to begin cleaning up the mess. As she sopped up the soup with a rag, she accidentally cut her hand on a broken tureen shard. In an instant her sadness disappeared, and she was filled with anger.

"I *will* go to the ball," she said aloud between gritted teeth. "And *not* to fetch cakes or adjust skirts!"

Chapter Seven
Mirror, Mirror

Rapunzel sighed. Looking Glass class was turning out to be as awful as she'd feared. Perching on a small velvet stool in front of a dressing table with a huge mirror was bad enough. Rapunzel didn't think she was much to look at, and staring at herself in the mirror only seemed to prove that she was right. Her freckled nose was straight. Her eyes weren't crossed or anything. And Rapunzel had always loved her hair — it was original and incredibly handy.

But in Looking Glass class, in addition to having to look at herself for more than an hour (boring), she was expected to weave fancy braids and twist curls and place hair clips just so. Rapunzel eyed the brush, comb, ribbons, hair clips, and curling iron in front of her. She was sure they would be of no help in tackling her untamable tresses.

Rapunzel held up a thick reddish-brown lock, eyeing it doubtfully. At the dressing table next to her,

Rose smiled encouragingly. "Just divide it into sections and weave them together," she said.

"Easy for you to say," Rapunzel replied, smirking. "Your hair doesn't resemble a ship's riggings!"

Rose giggled and continued to weave her golden tresses into a French braid. She didn't even have to pay attention to what she was doing. Instead, she was listening to the girl on the other side of her prattle on about the ball.

"I hear the crown is made of glittering diamonds!" the girl said, her blue eyes reflecting wide in the looking glass.

"I thought it was made of rubies," Rose replied.

"Someone told me it's made of both!" a third student said. "And sapphires, too!" A chorus of oohs echoed in the chamber.

"I hope a prince asks me to dance!" one of the Bloomers blurted out.

Suddenly the room filled with chatter about the Charm School for Boys. Everyone was giggling, and several girls blushed as well. Besides Rapunzel, only Ella was quiet. She seemed almost sullen as she combed and recombed the same lock of hair.

"I can't wait," said Snow White. "I've been practicing my dancing with the woodland animals."

"I hear the princes at Charm School are majestically cute!" another princess chimed in.

Rapunzel snorted. What was the big deal about boys? They were like girls, really — only different. She and Val had been friends for years, and he didn't make her blush or giggle — more like belly laugh — and he was a boy.

For the millionth time, Rapunzel wished she were with Val instead of stuck at Princess School. Charm School was probably a blast!

While I'm here primping Val gets to fence and gallop on horseback! she thought miserably. *He's right on the other side of the gardens, and I never even see him!*

"Ah, girls," Madame Spiegel said, pulling Rapunzel out of her thoughts. The teacher was standing next to her dressing table at the front of the room, gazing at her own reflection, which was lovely. The young teacher had long, wavy blond hair, strikingly high cheekbones, and wide-set brown eyes.

"You can never be sure what will be reflected back at you when you look in a mirror," she said mysteriously. She caught Rapunzel's eyes in the looking glass. "Can you see your true self?"

Rapunzel made a face at herself and her hopelessly messy hair in the mirror. Of course she saw herself. Who else would she see?

Suddenly one of the girls — the tiny one who had gotten soaked by a bucket of freezing water the day before — leaped up off her stool with a shriek.

191

"Madame Spiegel," she cried. "I think there's something under my seat!" The poor girl had been moaning and twisting uncomfortably on her stool all morning. Rapunzel thought it was because she had caught a chill from the drenching. Now, she realized, it could be much worse.

The room went silent. The princesses' eyes widened. It couldn't be . . .

Without a word, Madame Spiegel went over to the princess's stool. Slowly and carefully she helped the girl remove cushion after cushion from her seat. Since the girl was so small, she had at least half a dozen piled on her chair.

The rest of the Bloomers exchanged silent glances while they held their breath, waiting to see what the lump was. Rapunzel hoped it was just a piece of batting that had gathered together inside one of the cushions. The other possibility was too horrible. Too cruel.

Finally Madame Spiegel lifted the last cushion from the girl's stool. There, slightly squashed but still intact, was a single pea.

At once the chamber was filled with cries of disbelief.

"A pea! A pea!" someone screamed.

"I don't believe it," another girl cried.

The princess who had been sitting on the pea fell to the floor in a faint.

Rapunzel felt sorry for the girl. Personally, she was not afraid of peas — she was pretty confident she could sit on one for hours and barely notice. But peas had sent several princesses into tailspins — robbing them of sleep, making it impossible for them to sit or lie down for days — some pea victims had even needed medical attention. Needless to say, most princesses were terrified of them. Rapunzel would never use the small round vegetable against another princess, not even a princess she didn't like. It was an unspoken rule — a princess pact.

"Who would do such an awful thing?" Rose said aloud as several girls gathered around the fallen princess.

"I have an idea," Rapunzel heard Ella say under her breath so quietly that Rapunzel was quite sure nobody else heard.

"Girls, we must remain calm." Madame Spiegel's voice was steady but strained. "Panic helps no princess." She crouched down over the princess who had fainted and held a small jar of smelling salts under her nose. The girl opened her eyes.

The tiny worry lines that had creased the teacher's flawless skin disappeared. "We must have courage and faith in ourselves," she said. "Without those things we will be defeated by unkind tricks such as these."

Madame Spiegel helped the victimized princess to

her feet, removed the pea from the stool, and set the cushions back on top.

Holding the offending pea at arm's length like a soiled diaper, Madame Spiegel ceremoniously carried the pea to the hearth and threw it directly onto the embers. The flames shot up and the pea exploded into several pieces before sizzling and disappearing into ashes. "Back to our looking glasses, ladies," she called.

Satisfied the offending vegetable had been properly disposed of, the girls sat back down on their stools, many of them checking for peas first.

Rapunzel watched Madame Spiegel stare at herself in a mirror. Then she turned back to her own reflection and wrestled once more with her unwieldy locks. A plain braid would be easy. But a French braid required small sections of hair — at least at first. And none of the clips on the dressing table looked remotely big enough for even a few strands of her thick hair.

Frustrated, Rapunzel grabbed the hot iron and began to wrap a piece of hair around it. But the iron was heavier than she expected, and she nearly burned her neck.

Just then another face appeared in Rapunzel's looking glass. It was Rose. Her hair had been neatly woven into three French braids, the ends of which were twisted into a neat bun at the nape of her slender neck.

"I hate those things," Rose whispered, pointing to the hot iron. "But I can show you a couple of braiding tricks."

"Great," Rapunzel said, smiling. She sat back, letting Rose take over. Obviously the girl knew what she was doing when it came to hair — just like she did in Self-defense. A few minutes later, Rose had half of the hair in a braid that ran partway down Rapunzel's back.

Grateful, Rapunzel turned her head to look at the sides. A beam of sunlight flashed on the mirror's surface. A second later it happened again. And again.

That's weird, Rapunzel thought. She had already put down her hand mirror. She glanced around the chamber and noticed that nobody else was using a small looking glass, either.

Flash. There it was again. She and Rose exchanged a glance in the mirror above her dressing table, and Rapunzel leaned over to look out the window. Halfway across the garden, she saw a boy standing outside the Princess School stables. Val! He was holding a piece of shiny metal, moving it back and forth so it reflected a beam of light into the Looking Glass chamber window!

"Who is that?" Rose whispered, leaning forward to get a better look.

"My friend Val," Rapunzel replied, waving at him. "He goes to the Charm School."

Rose nodded, looking impressed.

Val flashed his metal again and pointed toward the stables. Rapunzel grinned. Val had thought of the perfect meeting spot and signal!

Chapter Eight
Warts and All

Ella walked down the hall lost in thought. She was tired and shaken. The pea incident played again and again in her head. She was certain Hagatha and Prunilla were behind it — even if they didn't carry out the horrible deed alone. And for some reason their cruelties seemed especially harsh to Ella lately. Maybe it was because she had never seen her stepsisters terrorize other girls. Or maybe it was because she had seen true kindness in some of her teachers and classmates.

Ella's thoughts were interrupted as Snow skipped up beside her, humming a little tune. Looping her arm through Ella's, Snow pulled her toward their next class: Frog Identification.

"Aren't you excited?" Snow asked. "This is my favorite class. And today we get to work with real frogs!"

Snow's enthusiasm was infectious. Ella allowed Snow

to pull her along and felt her spirits being slowly lifted by the cheerful chatter.

"Of course I love Princess School," Snow babbled, "but I do miss the forest animals. They visit me every day when I'm home at the cottage. They don't talk much, but they're wonderful company! Have you ever spent time with a toad? I have. Frogs and toads aren't nearly as cuddly as deer and rabbits and squirrels. But I think they're just as cute — in a slippery sort of way! Don't you agree?"

Ella smiled and nodded. She didn't really find frogs appealing, but she did feel better.

They were almost at the Frog ID chamber door when a group of older princesses began to crowd around them and the rest of the Bloomers, shouting taunts. Ella saw her stepsisters in the middle of the hecklers and ducked her head.

"Watch out for warts!" Prunilla called.

"Careful, girls, don't get slime all over your gowns!" a Sash yelled.

"The poor Bloomers," teased Hagatha. "Where else but in frog class would they get dates for the ball?"

The hall was filled with taunting laughter, but Ella ignored it as Snow led her and the Bloomers into the frog chamber. It was the plainest room in the castle. A fireplace stood at each end to warm the rug-free space. A single row of simple wooden tables ran along one wall. Small cages were lined up on the tables, each one containing a captured frog.

"Step inside, girls," Madame Bultad called. "Contrary to Princess School rumor, there's nothing to be afraid of here."

The girls entered the chamber but stood in a group near the door — all except Snow, who immediately went over to the frog cages to say hello.

Madame Bultad, a squat woman with a broad face and almost-black eyes, cleared her throat. Ella thought the sound was remarkably similar to a croak!

"I know Frog ID is the subject of much ridicule," the teacher said. "But as I've told you before, the skills you are acquiring in this room are essential for every princess." She paused for effect. "Unless you would like to find yourself plagued by a frog that you are unable to identify as either a prince under a spell or a green-skinned trickster."

The girls peered nervously at the caged frogs, whispering to one another. Nobody liked to talk about frogs — they generally made princesses nervous. Ella didn't really mind them. She was used to seeing them at the pond near her home and occasionally in the kitchen garden where she grew vegetables.

Madame Bultad continued, "As we discussed, ordinary frogs have become very skilled at disguising themselves as the real thing in the hopes of being kissed by a princess . . . or a princess-in-training." She sprung open the latch of one of the cages and a large, shiny green frog hopped out. Madame Bultad picked it up with a graceful swoop of her arm.

"Notice the golden-hued warts that cover this frog's body."

"He's beautiful!" Snow cried, rushing forward to get a better look.

Ella couldn't help but smile. But Madame Bultad's face grew serious. "Perhaps, but looks can be deceiving. A decade ago these golden warts would have been a sure sign that this creature is actually a prince under an evil spell. But today's amphibians have cleverly adopted these false clues to fool the inexperienced princess. One out of every five ordinary frogs and toads will have golden warts, spots in a crown configuration on its head, or a similar feature. My advice is this: Do not act in haste. Look carefully. Study your subjects. Only then will you find a prince among frogs."

Madame Bultad smiled, and the frogs began to croak loudly.

"And now, ladies, it is time to release the frogs. Each of you shall step forward and open a cage."

While most of the girls looked at one another in disgust, Snow bounded forward and opened a cage, freeing a frog. Ella stepped up behind her and cautiously lifted a latch. She had never touched a frog before, but they couldn't be *that* bad.

"They're not wolves," Rapunzel called, echoing Ella's thoughts and stepping forward herself. "They're frogs!" She sprung a latch and a skinny frog leaped straight to the floor.

Soon the entire chamber was filled with hopping, croaking frogs. Ella had never seen so many amphibians in so many shapes and sizes. And many of them were quite clever. One actually winked at her!

Most of the princesses, though, were not amused — or even interested. Most of them screamed and tried to get away when a slimy green hopper drew near.

Ella studied a frog with a silver circle on top of its head. It was sort of sweet, but . . . slimy.

On the other side of the room, Rose moved graciously away from a dozen frogs that were all trying madly to get close to her.

Rapunzel, for her part, sat on the floor nearby talking very calmly to a particularly large, lumpy frog. "It's nice to see you again, Warty," she said. "And I'm sorry you've been captured. But I don't care how many hopping contests you've won for me — I'm not going to kiss you again!"

Just then, Rose calmly strode over, still being followed by at least twelve frogs. "Yech," she said in a very unprincesslike manner. "I don't care if you *are* under a curse. I'm not going to kiss any of you!" The frogs stopped hopping and croaking and just looked up at Rose, pouting.

Rose looked to Rapunzel for help, but Snow was first to speak. "Don't listen to them," she said, making a hammock in the skirt of her gown to gather up the frogs. "I'll kiss all of you, even if you aren't princes." The frogs hopped excitedly toward her.

"Or will that get me in trouble?" Snow turned to Ella.

Ella abandoned the frog with the silver circle and cautiously reached a finger out to pet one of the frogs in Snow's skirt. "Here, froggy, froggy," she said in a croaky voice. She softly stroked a lumpy frog's back. He actually wasn't as slippery as he looked!

Standing next to them, Rose giggled. The frog Ella was petting croaked loudly, and Ella laughed, too. Warty croaked next and hopped over to Snow. But he was so fat he couldn't jump high enough to get into her skirt-hammock.

"Here you go, Warty," Rapunzel said, giving him a little lift. "You've been putting away the mayflies, haven't you?" The frog flipped right over, letting out a long croak as he landed on the soft fabric of Snow's gown.

"You're welcome," Rapunzel said, laughing.

The next thing they knew, all four girls were giggling hysterically. Across the room, Madame Bultad opened her mouth to tell the girls to be quiet, but began to cough instead.

"Frog in her throat," Rose whispered. Ella and the other girls nearly fell to the floor laughing. They couldn't stop. Ella felt all of her fear and worry slipping away. Frog ID was turning out to be the best class so far!

Then, all of a sudden, the laughter was cut short. Screams from the hall filled the room. "A wolf! A wolf!"

Chapter Nine
Who's Afraid?

A dark-haired Bloomer who had just been to the little princesses' room burst back into Frog ID screaming, "There's a wolf in the hall!"

Leaving the classroom door standing wide open, the girl dashed for the high windows at the back of the room. In a split second her panic spread. Pandemonium broke out.

The loud ribbiting of frightened frogs was overwhelmed by the shrieks of even more frightened princesses. Frogs tripped over one another, trying to get back to the safety of their cages. Bloomers scrambled onto tables, trying to avoid the frogs and reach the high diamond-paned windows. Everyone's worst nightmare had come true. There was a wolf loose in the school.

Strangely, Briar Rose felt calm. She was rarely afraid, but maybe that was because everyone was usually so scared for her she didn't have to be. She moved toward the door, intending to close it and protect the others.

Out in the hall Rose heard another cry. "Help!" A Bloomer in a red cloak dashed past Rose. Chasing after the girl — and moving fast — was a flash of black fur. Rose heard a growl, or maybe a snort, before the chorus of screams behind her drowned out all other noise.

"Is that the wolf?" Snow pushed past Rose into the hallway. The wolf stopped running and stood its ground at the end of the hall. "Oh, isn't he sweet?" Snow crooned, taking a few steps toward the animal with her hand outstretched.

"Shouldn't we grab her?" Rapunzel was suddenly standing behind Rose. Ella was there, too. Madame Bultad, for her part, had hopped up on the tables with the rest of the Bloomers. Her bog-green skirts were hoisted to her knees, showing plenty of yellow stocking.

Before her new friends could pull Snow back inside the room, the wolf turned and ran awkwardly away. It looked as if its two front legs were stunted, and its fur was awfully loose.

A minute later Snow came back into the room. "It's gone!" she called to everyone on the tables, including the teacher. "Poor thing. He looked just awful!"

Rose smiled. Leave it to Snow to be worried about the invader!

Madame Bultad climbed off the table, crossed the room, and cautiously poked her head out the door. Then she cleared her throat. "All clear, girls," she said in her rumbling voice. "Now, stay together and get to your hearthroom while I report this to the administrative chambers!"

The Bloomers held hands and hurried past Rose, looking both ways. Some of them skipped, ready to try their skip-trip if necessary. All of them appeared frazzled. Even Snow.

"I think there was something wrong with that wolf," Snow said, turning back toward her friends, who were still standing by the door. Her voice was full of concern and her eyes were starting to well up with tears.

"I *know* there was," Ella replied over Rose's shoulder. Snow looked like she thought the wolf was hurt, but there was something in Ella's voice that let Rose know Ella was thinking along the same lines she was.

"To start with, that was no wolf," Rose said. She held out her hand to comfort Snow.

Ella nodded. "No. I've seen that fur before, and it doesn't belong to a wolf. It belongs to something worse — my stepmother."

"What do you mean?" Snow's dark eyes sparkled.

Rapunzel pushed a lock of black hair off Snow's porcelain face. Rose had felt like doing the same thing. There was something about Snow. She was so trusting, it made you want to take care of her.

"That was no wolf," Rose announced. "That was a person in a wolf costume."

"Hagatha . . . or Prunilla, one of my stepsisters," Ella added. She wrapped her arm around Snow and glared at the spot where the "wolf" had been. "Those girls live to torture others. I just wish we could prove it was —"

Suddenly Ella stopped talking.

All of the Bloomers had gone, but now a Robe stood in the hallway. She was dressed in a gorgeous sunset-orange dress and her jewels were lovely, but they looked out of place beside the sneer on her face.

"Hey, Cinder Blockhead," Prunilla spat at Ella. "I see you made a new friend." She gestured toward Snow, looking her up and down, obviously disapproving of her old-fashioned dress. "She's perfect for you."

"Leave us alone, Prunilla," Ella said softly.

Prunilla acted like she didn't hear Ella. She slowly walked closer to Snow, staring into her wide eyes. "Do you always look so stupid?" she said with disdain, screwing up her face even more.

"Oh, no," Snow answered sweetly. "I was just so worried about that poor wolf —"

"Never mind," Prunilla cut Snow off and her dark eyes settled on Rose.

Rose watched as Prunilla's whole face changed. She still wasn't what Rose would call beautiful, but the snarl was gone. Now her tiny lips turned up in a smile.

"Briar Rose!" she said in a sickeningly sweet voice. "I'm sure you must have better things to do than to waste your time with this pair of dirty Bloomers! We are reflected in the company we keep, you know. Why don't you come with me, Beauty? I can introduce you to some of the Robes. We usually don't associate with the younger girls, but for you we might make an exception." Prunilla extended her hand limply.

"Thank you. No," Rose replied coolly, stepping closer to Ella, Snow, and Rapunzel and giving Prunilla a steely look. "I don't think I could bear to see myself reflected in *your* shallow eyes."

Prunilla's mouth dropped open into a perfect "O." For a moment she did nothing, then her eyes narrowed into tiny slits. Her mouth closed and opened again. But she was silent as she turned on her heel and stomped away in a huff.

Suddenly Ella bent over, clutching her stomach. Her head bobbed and she gasped for breath. Rose put her hand to her mouth. She hoped she hadn't gotten Ella into trouble! Maybe she shouldn't have said anything to the nasty older girl.

208

"I'm sorry. Was I out of line?" Rose began.

Ella stood up. Her face was red and tears were running down her cheeks. But she was grinning from ear to ear.

"You might live to regret that," Ella gasped, still trying to control her laughter. "But if you ask me, it was worth it!"

Chapter Ten
Rapunzel's Surprise

Rapunzel ran down the hall as fast as she could. It felt good — no, great — not to worry about regal countenance and posture and poise and . . . UGH!

Because of the wolf scare, all of the princesses had been escorted from their hearthrooms to the far court-yard — away from the Grimm School woods — while the royal guards checked the halls. Rapunzel headed to the other side of the castle, toward the stables and Val. It was the perfect opportunity for her to slip away.

Racing out the front of the school, Rapunzel dashed down the steps and hopped the low wall sepa-rating the entrance from the rose garden. She ducked through the prickly bushes and sprinted the last few yards. She hoped Val would still be there. They had arranged to meet in the stables during lunch. The only problem was, Val's lunch ended just as Rapunzel's began.

"Don't worry. Nobody can keep me in," she'd told him. "Just be there." She had sounded confident, but if it hadn't been for this wolf scare, she didn't know how she would have made it in time.

"Val!" Rapunzel called as she flew into the enormous stables. Doves scattered, flying up to the rafters. The horses snorted and pawed the straw at the disturbance. Luckily, none of the stable hands were there. Rapunzel suddenly realized that she could get herself in trouble for being out of school if she was caught.

"Come out, come out, wherever you are," Rapunzel called more quietly. Val *had* to be there. She had stayed up late every night for three nights making him a surprise. She had wanted to give it to him that morning, but he'd left for school early — without her. She simply could not wait another second.

All Rapunzel heard were stomping feet.

Sinking down onto a bale of hay, Rapunzel pulled the surprise out of the pocket she'd stitched into her dress. It was a belt buckle. The buckle had been her father's. Or at least she assumed it had been. It was on the belt Madame Gothel had used to tie up all of her baby things when she whisked Rapunzel away from her parents. Only the buckle had never shone like it did now.

Rapunzel had spent hours polishing and polishing it for Val. She hoped he would wear it every day. That way he would always be ready to flash her messages from the Charm School. Now the buckle was as shiny as her looking glass. Almost. Rapunzel's reflection distorted in the metal and she stuck out her tongue. Wow. And she thought she looked funny in a regular mirror!

"I thought you said you weren't going to turn all prissy and vain on me." Val's laughing voice was muffled in the dim stable. But his smiling green eyes were unmistakable in the shafted light. "And here I find you gazing at yourself in anything that will cast a reflection! Maybe I should start calling *you* 'Beauty.'"

"Oh, stop!" Rapunzel threw the buckle at Val, who stopped teasing long enough to catch it. She felt a pang of guilt for telling Val about Rose's silly nickname, especially now that she really kind of liked the pretty princess. Rose was more than a lovely face. Much more. In fact, she might even be a great friend. But Rapunzel wasn't ready to tell Val about that now. She had other things to tell him about, like the buckle and her plan.

"What's this?" Val asked, turning over the shiny metal object and polishing it a little on his shirt.

"A suit of armor," Rapunzel said dryly. "What do you think?"

Val gave her a look and Rapunzel pulled the rest of her surprise out of her pocket. "*That* is so you can send me light signals when I'm in class on the north side of the building." She pointed at the buckle. "*This*," she said, handing him a small scroll, "is the start of our code."

Rapunzel had come up with several flash sequences that would allow her to communicate with Val. There wasn't too much you could say with light and mirrors. "Hello." "See you later." "Madame Spiegel has a nose like a toadstool." And the most important: "Meet me at the stables — quick!" Rapunzel and Val couldn't exactly have conversations, but it was enough to keep them connected and keep Rapunzel from feeling trapped at Princess School. Besides, once they got good at using it, the code could be expanded.

Val smiled. "What a waste. There you are learning how to do cross-stitch when you would do the most good in King Westerly's Secret Service."

"Hey, I've learned some defensive skills, too." Rapunzel feigned a skip-trip and Val backed away with his hands up.

"Mercy, Your Highness," he said with a bow. "I've heard all about how you can take down pretty girls." Val flopped back in the hay, stretching his long skinny legs. "How *is* Beauty, anyway?" he asked. His eyes twinkled.

"Don't tell me you're stuck on her, too." Rapunzel

knocked the prince's thin crown so it sat askew in his dark curly hair.

"Not stuck, just curious." Val shrugged. "What's she like? Is she just like the stories say?"

It was Rapunzel's turn to shrug. "She's okay." Funny. Last week Rapunzel had been enjoying telling Val all about the fancy frou-frou girls at Princess School and having a good laugh. But now she felt different. Some of the girls weren't so silly. Like when Snow had walked up to that wolf, or whatever it was. That was brave.

Things were changing. Rapunzel didn't feel good about poking fun at the princesses and she didn't know how to explain it to Val. Maybe she was making new friends. Maybe she was fitting in.

Suddenly Rapunzel wanted to get back to school, to see if she was missing anything. The "wolf" could come back at any time!

"So, send me a signal when you're in Chivalry," she said, standing up quickly and backing out of the stables.

"Hey, where are you going? I don't have to be back until the second trumpet blast." Val looked surprised.

"I have to get back before I'm missed. They might be taking scroll call after the wolf alert." Rapunzel ran out of the barn with a quick wave and a smile.

"What alert? What wolf?" Val called after her.

Rapunzel didn't stay to explain. She'd tell him later. Maybe she'd tell him about her new friends later, too.

Thinking about the girls she'd find at the far court-yard, Rapunzel smiled. And as she jumped the wall of the rose garden and hurried up the stone steps to Princess School, Rapunzel felt completely free.

Chapter Eleven
Best-laid Plans

The mood at Princess School was charged. Although the royal guards had declared the school grounds safe and Ella had tried to tell some of the Bloomers that the wolf wasn't really a wolf, everyone was on edge.

The girl who had been chased by the "wolf" had gone home to her grandmother's house. The rest of the Bloomers were so scared that they walked the hallways in groups or pairs, always looking over their shoulders. Ella walked alone, deep in thought.

Aside from the fact that she was used to being harassed, Ella was simply too exhausted to be afraid. She had been staying up later and later every night. After all of the extra chores were done she had important work of her own to attend to.

Ella had been cleaning the parlor when she came up with the idea. *If only my fairy godmother wasn't so far away,* Ella had thought lamentingly. *Her magic could take care of everything!* Running the feather duster over the scrolled backs of the velvet chairs, she remembered how much fabric had been left over after her stepmother had ordered the seats reupholstered. Kastrid had redecorated everything in the house the moment she moved in. Ella knew the changes had cost her father a small fortune. Kastrid adored spending her new husband's money. But Ella was sure her stepmother had done the redecorating for another reason: to destroy every whisper of her mother's memory. Although her stepmother might be able to make her family's riches disappear, she could not take away Ella's memories. They were safely locked in her head and heart forever.

Ella remembered her mother every day. Her mother had taught her so much before she died, like how to cook and sing, how to dance and garden, how to take care of herself and hold onto hope. Her mother was also the reason Ella could sew better than almost anyone in Stitchery. And there were yards and yards of unused velvet just sitting in the attic.

From the first night Ella had started on her gown she'd stayed up late, working by candlelight to keep her project a secret and to get it finished in time. She'd used one of her mother's too-tattered-to-wear gowns as a basis for the pattern. The gown was simple but elegant. The square neckline was high. The long sleeves

217

were snug but not too tight. And the skirt was full, with tiny pleats going all the way around the bodice. After five nights of hard work, the gown was nearly done.

Maybe it was because she was so tired, but as she moved down the hall Ella felt as if she were in a dream. She could barely believe she would actually be going to the Royal Coronation Ball. She knew her father must have said something because just last night Kastrid had informed her through pursed lips that she could go. Ella supposed Kastrid had gone along with it because she knew her stepdaughter had nothing to wear.

"As long as you are keeping up in school," her stepmother had said tightly, "I can't stop you."

Now all Ella needed was to make it through her classes. But that was a little harder than it sounded. Being tired from her housework and her late-night sewing made it difficult to concentrate. During History: Princesses Past and Present, the letters on her scroll swam in front of her eyes. And when Madame Istoria asked her even a simple question, she sat there, speechless, until Rose whispered the answer in her ear. In Stitchery she kept losing her thread. In Looking Glass she barely had the strength to raise her arms over her head and form a braid! But she would do it. Nothing would keep her from going to the ball now.

Lost in a daze of exhaustion and dreaming of the ball, Ella stumbled in her paper-stuffed glass shoes toward Self-defense. She never even saw Prunilla coming.

"Cin-der-el-la," Prunilla said, drawing out Ella's full name. "Just the Bloomer I've been looking for!"

"Leave me alone, Prunilla. I don't want to be late for class." Ella moved to walk around her stepsister, but Prune quickly stepped back into her path.

"I wouldn't want that, sister dear," Prunilla said with mock sympathy. "It's just that you are so good at cleaning up messes — and I'm afraid there's a rather large one waiting for you in my trunk. I'm sure it won't take you too long to clean out — you already have the rags for the job. Or is that your dress?"

Ella sighed and looked Prunilla in the eye. The "rag" she was talking about used to be Prunilla's. "You might be able to force me to do things in front of your mother, but at school things are different," Ella said.

"Are they really?" Prune asked. The false sweetness was gone, and Prunilla's narrowed eyes looked smaller than ever.

Ella took a small step back. She knew she had just made a big mistake. "Yes," Ella said, her voice cracking.

"*Hungh,*" Prunilla snorted, amused by her own deviousness as she plotted her next cruel act. "We'll just see about that," she growled. "Because if my trunk

219

isn't organized and scrubbed spotless by the time I am out of Fancy Dress class, I am going to tell Mother that it was *you* who ripped her black fur cape."

Ella's mouth dropped open. She wasn't sure what would be worse — getting in trouble at school or at home. And now it was sure to be both.

Prunilla wasn't even finished. "And if you want to be sure Mother's cape is the only thing that gets ripped, you'll scrub out Hagatha's trunk, too!" With one last nasty glare, Prunilla stomped down the corridor.

When the trumpets blew and classes started, Ella was walking away from the Self-defense classroom door. Almost every shred of hope drained out of her poor tired body as she hurried down the hall toward the older girls' trunks.

She knew she had to take Prunilla's threats seriously. She only hoped that if she did what she was told, her stepsister wouldn't carry out her threats anyway, for spite. All Ella could do was scrub out the trunks as quickly as possible and hope that Madame Lightfoot was more merciful than her stepmother. Ella crossed her fingers. If she wasn't, the little bit of hope she was clinging to would be dashed as well. Trouble in school would be the only excuse Kastrid needed to keep Ella from the Coronation Ball.

Ella lifted the curved lid of Prunilla's trunk and

winced. It was crammed with so much stuff she couldn't even see the velvet lining on the bottom.

It's worse than her closet, Ella thought as a waft of stale air drifted past her nose. With a heavy sigh, Ella began to pull things out — books, scrolls, capes, scarves, scraps of food. . . .

"Need some help?" a voice called out behind her.

Startled, Ella turned around to see Rapunzel, Snow, and Rose.

Ella's eyes widened. "What are you doing here? You're late for class. You'll get in trouble!"

"Correction," Rapunzel said. "We've already been to class. We noticed you weren't there and thought maybe something was wrong. So Rose here faked an injury in Self-defense. We're supposed to be on our way to the nurse's chamber."

"It's strange, but my leg is feeling much better," Rose said with a little smile.

"We still have to go to the nurse, but we have a few minutes to help," Rapunzel said. She surveyed the mess on the corridor floor. "What are you doing, anyway? And what's that smell?"

"That smell is odeur de Prunilla," Ella said. "She's making me clean out her trunk. And Hagatha's, too." Ella felt her throat tighten. "If I don't do it, she's going to get me in trouble with my stepmother!"

"I can't believe those awful girls are part of your family," Rapunzel said. "Maybe living alone in a tower isn't so bad after all," she added thoughtfully.

Snow White was carefully studying Prunilla's trunk. "This isn't as bad as the dwarves' cottage the first time I saw it," she said cheerfully. "If we work together, we can get it cleaned up in no time!"

"Which trunk is Hagatha's?" Rose asked. "Snow and I can clean that one while you and Rapunzel take care of this mess. If we hurry we can get it done and still get to the nurse's chamber before the end of class."

"Thank you!" Ella said, her heart lightening. She pointed to Hagatha's trunk, and the girls got to work organizing books and scrolls into neat piles, folding capes, and throwing out aging food.

"What a waste!" Snow exclaimed, holding up a rotten apple she'd unearthed. "Who lets a perfectly good apple go bad?" Her dark eyes were wide.

"A bad apple like Hagatha," Rapunzel replied grimly as she set a *Riddles and Names* textbook on top of the pile she was making.

They were almost done when Rose pulled a burlap sack out of the bottom of Hagatha's trunk. The sack had a small hole in the bottom, and black fur was sticking out.

"Hey, look at this!" Rose said excitedly. She reached

inside and pulled out a black fur cape with pointed fur triangles, like ears, attached near the collar.

"Wait a second," Rapunzel said. "That looks like a wolf costume!"

"The wolf costume one of my stepsisters was wearing when we were in Frog ID," Ella added.

"It's evidence!" Rapunzel said excitedly. "Now we can figure out a way to get even!"

Just then the five-minute horn blasted — class was almost over!

"We'll have to figure out what to do later," Rose said, quickly shoving the cape back into the bag and the bag back into the compartment. "Let's think about it tonight. Tomorrow we'll come up with a plan."

"You should get to the nurse's chamber," Ella said. "I can finish up here."

"Are you sure?" Snow asked.

"Positive," said Ella. "But you have to hurry or you'll be late!"

Chapter Twelve

Castle Skip-trip

The next morning in hearthroom, Rose watched the door like a hawk. She had a great vantage point from her seat, which was on the opposite side of the chamber from the door. She couldn't wait to see her friends and decide what to do about the fur cape they'd found in Hagatha's trunk. She was sure that Hagatha and Prunilla were responsible for a lot of the tormenting — and now the wolf! Seeking revenge on those nasty girls was going to be sweet!

"How are you going to do your hair for the ball, Beauty?" the girl sitting behind her asked.

Rose was so busy staring at the door she didn't answer. "Rose?" the girl tried again.

"I beg your pardon?" Rose tried not to look annoyed as she turned back to the girl. She didn't care about her hair or the ball! At least not at the moment.

Finally Rapunzel came through the door. But instead of coming right over to Rose, she sat down in her chair and began writing furiously on a scroll. *She must be working on something good,* thought Rose.

Snow came in next. She smiled and waved at Rose — and everyone else in the chamber — before she took her seat near the door. Rose was getting to her feet to go talk to her when Ella shuffled into the room like a scolded puppy. She didn't look at anyone as she took her seat in the back of the chamber.

I guess our plan can wait, Rose thought, sitting back in her chair. Suddenly she was much more worried about something else: Ella. Even though Ella's head was bent low, Rose could see the dark circles under her eyes.

Rose felt a pang of guilt. Here she was always complaining about her overprotective parents and the fawning teachers and princesses. She bet that nobody ever fawned over poor Ella. Those nasty stepsisters of hers made her life miserable — and not only at school, but at home, too! She was sure Ella's stepmother didn't adore Ella the way Rose's parents adored her.

I should count my blessings, Rose thought, *and quit feeling sorry for myself.*

Rose wanted to leap out of her chair and go over to Ella right that minute. But before she could move, Madame Garabaldi strode into the room and began to take scroll call. And then the door opened again, and a page scampered nervously up to Madame G. and handed her a roll of paper.

Rose watched Ella sink lower into her chair. A scroll delivered in hearthroom usually meant that someone was in trouble. And since Ella had missed all of Self-defense yesterday . . . well, it didn't look good.

Ella sat as still as a stone while Madame Garabaldi read the notice. When the teacher looked up, her dark eyes were narrowed over her spectacles at Ella. It took her exactly three seconds to cross to the back of the chamber.

"Cinderella Brown," she said, towering over Ella's small, slouched frame. "I have just been informed that you did not see fit to attend Self-defense class yesterday. Would you like to tell me what pressing engagement you chose to grace with your presence instead?"

Ella looked up at Madame Garabaldi, her face full of desperation. But she said nothing.

"Excuse me?" Madame Garabaldi's eyes dared the cowering girl to speak. "I can't hear you."

Across the chamber, Rapunzel opened her mouth to say something. But after a moment she closed it again. Rose couldn't blame her. Aggravating Madame Garabaldi further wouldn't do anyone any good.

"I see," said Madame Garabaldi, rising to her full height. "Perhaps a punishment of double tower detention would demonstrate to you and the rest of the students that attendance in class is *mandatory* at Princess School." She folded her arms across her chest and glared down at Ella, who was by now halfway under her writing desk.

"Sit up straight!" Madame Garabaldi barked. "Cowering is not acceptable for any princess — even one who has been caught blatantly disregarding the rules."

Rose wanted to leap to her feet and tell Madame Garabaldi to stop being cruel. Detention was punishment enough — especially for Ella, who would also get a second punishment at home. It was excessive to ridicule her in front of the class, too.

Madame Garabaldi turned on her heel, strode back to the front of the chamber, and continued taking scroll call. All eyes were on Ella. Rose tried to get her friend's attention but guessed that a sympathetic smile would not be enough to cheer Ella up. Ella appeared to be using all her strength to hold back tears. She sat staring straight ahead for the rest of class.

Finally, when the end-of-class trumpets sounded, Ella broke down sobbing and raced out of the chamber.

Rose was on her feet in an instant, but still wasn't fast enough. By the time she got out the classroom door Ella was a blur streaking down the corridor. Snow was right behind her. Rose lifted her skirts and hurried ahead, hoping she could catch them.

Just then Hagatha appeared out of nowhere, skipping down the hallway after Snow.

"I'm Snow White," Hagatha called. "I spend all day with dwarves and woodland animals, skipping through the forest!"

Rose saw Ella turn, her eyes full of tears and fury. Ella had clearly reached her breaking point.

Don't do anything, Ella! Rose thought desperately. *You'll just get yourself into more trouble!*

Rose rushed forward to stop her friend. But suddenly there was a swarm of princesses between her and Ella.

"I heard you got hurt in Self-defense," one of them said to Rose. "Are you all right?"

"I'm fine," Rose said brusquely, trying to get through. "I'm trying to get to my friends —"

Out of the corner of her eye, Rose saw Rapunzel break through the throng of princesses. With her left arm, she gently took Snow by the elbow, then did a graceful skip-trip with her right foot, sending Hagatha sprawling to the floor.

"Hey!" Hagatha screeched as Rapunzel linked her free arm through Ella's.

"Come on, girls," Rapunzel said loudly. "Let's go find some decent company."

228

Rose pushed her way past a final pair of princesses in time to see Ella, Rapunzel, and Snow disappear through the Princess School doors, their arms linked together.

"Help me up!" Hagatha screeched from the floor.

Rose barely heard her. She was too busy watching her new friends go off without her, leaving her alone in a crowd. Again.

Chapter Thirteen
Needle and Hay

"Do you think she is all right?" Snow asked, turning to look back at the fallen Hagatha. "That stone floor is pretty hard."

"Who cares?" Rapunzel replied with a snort. "She was making fun of you, Snow. She was being mean."

Rapunzel pulled Snow and Ella ahead, steering them out the Princess School doors, down the steps, and through the rose garden.

"Don't you know when someone isn't being nice?" Ella asked more gently.

"Not being nice?" Snow repeated aloud. "Why wouldn't a princess be nice? Everyone should be nice, right?" Since she had escaped living with her stepmother, Snow had not encountered anyone who wasn't nice. Not until she came to Princess School, at least.

"Besides, Hagatha's too mean to get hurt," Ella added, striding over the grass.

Snow nodded but now felt even more confused.

Since when did being mean keep someone from getting hurt? If that was true, her stepmother must never feel *any* pain!

"Really? Does being mean keep you from getting hurt?" Snow asked.

"Well, not exactly," Ella admitted.

Snow pushed all thoughts about meanness from her mind. She wanted to savor this moment. She hadn't even been at Princess School for two weeks, and she was out in the gardens with two new friends!

"Come on," Rapunzel said, steering them toward a cozy-looking building with a grass roof. "I want to show you someplace special before class starts."

Snow gasped again. It looked like Rapunzel was leading them toward the stables! She'd been dying to see inside the stables since she'd started at Princess School, to see where the animals lived. And now she was going to!

Rapunzel pushed open one of the heavy stable doors and pulled the girls inside. Holding a finger to her lips, she stood quietly for a minute to make sure the coast was clear. The only audible sounds were of horses munching hay.

"It's safe," Rapunzel reported. "There's nobody else here."

Snow took a deep breath, taking in the smell of clean hay and horses. "Ooooh," she said, excited. The stables were enormous, with row upon row of wooden stalls painted various pastel hues. A well-organized, cream-colored tack room stood just inside the door, housing gleaming saddles and bridles and halters. A giant hayloft extended over half of the ground floor.

"Look at the beautiful horses!" Snow rushed into a lavender stall that was home to a tall chestnut mare. "Hello, sweetie," she greeted, stroking the bridge of the mare's velvety nose. She gazed into the mare's liquid-brown eyes. No matter how much time she spent with them, Snow was always amazed at the gentleness she saw in animals' eyes.

"If I'd known I was coming today, I would have brought you a carrot," she said softly.

The mare let out a soft whinny, nuzzling Snow's arm.

"Next time." Snow giggled. "I promise." She turned in the direction of her friends. "I could stay here all day!" she called.

"Me too," Rapunzel agreed. "But we don't have all day. Come on!"

"Coming!" Snow called back. She wanted to greet each and every horse but knew she couldn't. So she said a quick hello to a few more, promising she'd bring them treats the next time she came, as she made her way back to her friends.

"I'm so sorry about your detention," Rapunzel was

saying. "And Madame Garabaldi. She was being really severe, even for her."

"Maybe she never gets hurt," Snow suggested, plopping down beside Ella.

Ella's eyes glistened with approaching tears. "I think she has it in for me, just like my rotten steps," she said mournfully.

Snow gave Ella's arm a comforting squeeze. "I know what that's like," she said. "My stepmother was so jealous of me, I had to leave my father's castle!"

Ella sighed. "Sometimes I wish I could leave," she said. "But then of course I'd never see my father."

Suddenly Snow felt a little bit sad inside. She knew *exactly* how Ella felt.

"That Hagatha deserves more than to fall flat on her face," Rapunzel announced, changing the subject. She was lying down on the clean straw, gazing up at the stable rafters.

"Tell me about it," Ella agreed, breaking a piece of straw between her fingers. "And what you just saw was her *good* side. She's even more horrible at home."

Snow felt awful for Ella. After all, Ella was just about the nicest person she'd met at Princess School. She reached out a hand to her friend. "Maybe you could come live with the dwarves and me in the forest cottage," she offered.

Ella's eyes welled up with fresh tears at Snow's kindness.

"We've got to do something about Hag," Rapunzel declared, jumping up and pacing the narrow stall. "And her awful sister, too." There was a moment of silence. "Not you, Ella," she added quickly. "Prunilla."

Ella wiped her tears and smiled. "I know," she said. "And *I know*. We *do* have to do something about them. But what?"

The girls were silent for a minute, thinking. And then, in the distance, they heard the muted trumpets signaling the next class.

"Oh my gosh!" Snow said, leaping to her feet.

Ella was up, too. "I can't be late again!" she exclaimed. "They'll lock me up!"

Falling over the skirts of one another's gowns, the girls burst out of the stall. They raced through the stable doors, across the rose garden, and up the Princess School steps.

Throwing open the front door, the girls burst into the school and ran — *smack!* — into Briar Rose.

Rose stood alone in the main entrance, sucking her finger. Her eyes looked a little droopy.

"Oh, no, are you hurt?" Snow asked, pulling Rose's finger from her mouth to take a look.

"It's nothing," Rose yawned. "Just a tiny pinprick. I'll be fine. Please don't fuss."

"What happened?" Ella asked. "You look kind of strange."

"I don't know, really. I just reached into my Stitchery basket and something jabbed my finger." Rose paused to yawn again and rub one of her eyes. "It was a needle, I think. But the funny thing is, I never leave my needles out. I always put them into my metal box."

Ella, Snow, and Rapunzel all looked at one another.

"Are you thinking what I'm thinking?" Ella asked.

"Prunilla was awfully angry when Rose didn't want to go off with her the other day," Snow said, remembering the scowl on the older girl's face.

"Exactly. And Hag and Prune never miss a chance to get even," Ella confirmed.

"Let's go back to the stables and figure out what to do." Rapunzel already had one foot out the door.

"We can't," Ella said. "If we miss class, we'll all get in trouble — Madame Garabaldi might even expel me. And believe me, there's nothing Hagatha and Prunilla would like better."

Chapter Fourteen
Sleeping Beauty

As her friends hurried her down the corridor to Stitchery, Rose's limbs felt weighted down. Her whole body was exhausted.

This is so weird, she thought. *I feel so sleepy.*

She longed to lie right down on the marble floor and take a nap but forced herself to stay awake. *I have to act perfectly normal,* she told herself firmly. *Or my parents are going to go crazy. And the fairies! They'll swarm the castle if they think there's something wrong with me. They might even pull me out of Princess School . . . just when it's getting interesting!*

"Rose, are you okay?" Ella's voice sounded kind of far away, even though Rose was standing right next to her. Rose felt a hand reach out to steady her.

"I'm fine," she said. "I'm just trying to think of what I'm going to tell Madame Taffeta when we get to class." Rose stifled a yawn. "She'll believe anything I say, so I think I should do the talking."

"Fine with me," Rapunzel said as they reached the door to the Stitchery classroom. She looked intently at Rose. "But are you sure you're okay?"

"Perfect," Rose said, trying to sound convincing. Gathering all her strength, she stood up straight and put her hand on the door. She took a deep breath and pushed the door open, leading her friends inside.

Even in her sleepy state, Rose could tell that Madame Taffeta was furious. Or was that panic? Her usually pleasant, round face was tight and her gray eyes looked as sharp as daggers.

"Where have you been?" the teacher asked in a raised voice. "I was so worried I was about to send a message to Madame Garabaldi."

Rose heard Ella gasp and immediately rushed forward, trying not to stumble. She curtsied. "My sincere apologies, Madame Taffeta," she said in her proper princess voice. "I truly regret that I've made all these girls late. You see, I've pricked my finger." She raised her wounded appendage to show the teacher and hide a yawn.

Madame Taffeta gasped in horror as several girls looked over at Rose in concern. "Why, Rose, whatever happened?"

"I came to class early to begin my work," Rose said, feeling almost lucid for the first time since the pinprick. "But while I was threading my needle I accidentally pricked my finger. I hurried to the little princesses' room to rinse it in clean water, and Rapunzel, Ella, and Snow were kind enough to help me and make sure I got safely back to class."

Madame Taffeta inspected the pinprick carefully, making sure it was not too deep. She looked really worried, and Rose felt a little sorry for her. It couldn't be easy to have Madame Garabaldi looking over your shoulder all the time. She probably waited for the teachers to make mistakes just like she did the students!

"Well, it does appear to be just a pinprick," Madame Taffeta said more calmly. "And you girls did a fine job cleaning the wound." She looked at each of the four of them in turn.

"Under the circumstances, I will dismiss your tardiness. I see no reason to report this little incident to Madame Garabaldi."

Rose saw Ella's shoulders relax in relief. She flashed a drowsy smile at her friends. Being the favorite pupil was finally doing some good! But as relief washed over her, so did another wave of sleepiness. All of a sudden she didn't have the strength to fight it anymore. Every pink stone on the cold hard floor looked as inviting as a feather-stuffed pillow. Her eyelids felt incredibly heavy. She needed a nap.

"I think I'll just lie down for a minute," Rose mumbled. Her limbs felt wobbly, like custard. She was grateful for the supportive arms of Rapunzel, Snow, and Ella as they led her over to a pile of large velvet cushions. She had a sleepy memory of having been worried that these girls weren't really her friends. Now she felt sure that they were.

"Is she all right?" Madame Taffeta's voice sounded as if it came from the other end of a long hallway.

"Of course," Rose heard Rapunzel say smoothly. Rose was grateful for her friend's resolve. Rapunzel always managed to stay calm, no matter what the circumstances. "She's just worn out from all the excitement," Rapunzel explained. Rose smiled sleepily. She wasn't sure about any excitement, but she was definitely worn out.

"Beauty is clearly distraught from her episode," Madame Taffeta said, clapping her hands briskly. It sounded to Rose as if Madame Taffeta were now a hundred miles away, but she didn't care. All she cared about was finally being able to sleep. . . .

A dozen pages responded to Madame Taffeta's clap. Scampering into the chamber, they quickly pulled a tapestry from the wall. Six of them held the sides, creating a curving bed, while the others filled it with cushions and helped Rose lie down upon it.

Rose was drifting off contentedly as Madame Taffeta sent another page scurrying to get some blankets. "Hurry now!" she called. "This princess needs a rest!"

239

Chapter Fifteen
The Perfect Dress

The candelabra beside Ella flickered and she inched closer to it. She could see fairly well in the dim light — she was used to the dark room. But she hoped that the little flames would help warm her cold fingers as she quickly stitched the hem of her ball gown.

Despite the cold and dark, Ella felt unusually happy. There had been no scroll sent home alerting her stepmother of her double tower detention — which hadn't been so terrible after all. She'd used the time to do her homework, and was almost caught up! And since Kastrid had been napping in the afternoons lately, she didn't even realize Ella had gotten home late. Rose had skillfully gotten them off the hook in Stitchery, and — most unbelievable of all — Hagatha and Prunilla hadn't breathed a word of her school trouble for two nights in a row. All her stepsisters talked about was the ball and their beautifully decorated ballot box.

Maybe they don't know about the detention, Ella thought, though it seemed unlikely. It was more probable that they knew that *she* knew about their wolf caper. Knowing Hag and Prune, they were keeping Ella's little secret for now, planning to blackmail her later if she opened her mouth.

It didn't matter. Ella felt too cheerful to let even Hagatha and Prunilla's schemes ruin her mood. With a smile on her face, Ella finished the last stitch on her hem, tied off the thread, and cut it with her teeth. She hung the deep-blue gown before the window and shook out the luxurious fabric of the skirt. With the stars twinkling behind it, the midnight-blue gown looked absolutely magical. It was perfect.

Gazing at the finished dress, Ella felt a little bit like she thought Snow must feel all the time. Without even thinking, she clapped her hands together and began to hum a little tune. It felt good, and before she knew it she was dancing around her tiny room, imagining the fun she was going to have at the ball. She had a dress, she had shoes (so what if they were stuffed with paper and made her a tad clumsy? They were still magic. . . .), and she had new friends. It was too good to be true.

WHAM! Ella's door suddenly burst open, slamming against the stone wall. Hagatha stood in the doorway, panting from the climb up the stairs and holding a torn petticoat — for Ella to mend, no doubt. Her beady eyes grew round when she saw Ella dancing.

Ella quickly tried to appear unhappy. Wiping the smile off her face, she slumped down beside the mending pile with a heavy sigh. Hagatha would take extra delight in tormenting her if she realized she was in a great mood.

"What's going on in here?" Hagatha puffed into the room holding the torn petticoat. "I was just bringing up this mending and I thought I heard singing." Hagatha looked around like she expected to find a chamber choir in the corner.

"Must have been the wind," Ella said, staring down at her lap and trying to look miserable. "My window doesn't shut all the way" — she gestured toward the window — "and sometimes . . ."

Ella trailed off. She followed Hagatha's gaze to the dress that hung from the windowsill and gasped.

She had made a terrible mistake. All she could do was hold her breath and wait to see what Hag would do next.

"It's perfect," Hagatha breathed. She rubbed her hands together as if to warm them before reaching out to touch the beautiful velvet fabric.

Ella cringed. "I, uh, made it myself," she explained. It sounded as if Hagatha's compliment had been almost genuine.

242

"It'll look *gorgeous* at the ball." Hagatha pulled the skirts across her chest. "On me. Doesn't it go well with my eyes? In this dress I will be crowned for sure!"

If she weren't completely horrified, Ella would have laughed out loud. The beautiful blue of the gown *might* match Hagatha's eyes, but they were so small and beady, no one would ever be able to tell. And the thought of anyone voting for Hagatha . . . it was too much.

"You won't be wearing that dress," Ella said, standing and mustering up as much courage as she could. "I will. I made it for myself." Ella swept the dress off the hanger and clutched it to her chest.

"You?" Hagatha scoffed. "You aren't even going to the ball!"

"I am so," Ella argued. "Father said so. Your mother agreed!"

Hagatha smiled slowly. She seemed more and more like Kastrid all the time. "That was before I told her about your trouble in school, Cinder dear."

"You didn't." Ella dropped onto her hard wood-frame bed.

"Of course I did." Hagatha held a hand out for the dress. "I didn't want you there embarrassing us. And don't worry, Mother will think of a suitable punishment so you don't miss class again." Hagatha jiggled her hand impatiently, waiting for Ella to give her the dress.

"Maybe I can't wear this dress, but neither will you," Ella said, standing up and moving to the far side of her small room. "I could tell your mother a few things, you know — like the things we found in your trunk!"

"I'll say you're lying," Hagatha shouted.

"My friends were with me," Ella yelled back.

"I'll tell her you planted it, then!" Hagatha was seething. She stomped her feet. Her face was red and blotchy and she was stepping closer and closer to Ella with each second.

"Girls!"

Without warning, a tall figure appeared in the door and Hagatha and Ella both fell silent. Kastrid appeared so suddenly, Ella was not sure how much she had heard. Or what she was going to say. With one step, Kastrid seemed to fill Ella's small room entirely. Behind her, Prunilla poked her head in, obviously not wanting to miss the fun.

"You *know* I cannot abide bickering," Kastrid said softly with her eyes closed. Then, without warning, she erupted like a volcano. "SO TELL ME WHAT IS GOING ON!"

"Mummy, she won't let me wear that dress," Hagatha whined and pointed at the dress Ella was still holding before wiping her nose on her sleeve.

"Of course she will," Kastrid said, her voice returning to a syrupy smoothness. She held out a long slender hand to Ella, who had no choice but to lay the gown across it. Though Ella had threatened to tell on Hagatha for all of the mean tricks, deep down she knew it was useless. Kastrid would believe whatever she wanted to, and that would be her daughters' lies. Even Ella's father was helpless when it came to dealing with Kastrid. When Kastrid was around, everything always went the way Hagatha and Prunilla wanted.

Kastrid held the dress up, inspecting it. She ran the material between her fingers and a small smile played on her lips.

"It's m-mine," Ella stammered foolishly. "I made it."

Kastrid turned. "With whose material?" she asked slowly, looking Ella right in the eye.

Ella was caught. In a moment her stepmother would be accusing her of stealing. Not that Kastrid would ever have used the remnants — until now they had been mere scraps to her. But the fabric wasn't really Ella's. Ella hung her head and braced herself for the lecture.

She did not expect the one she got.

"It doesn't matter." Kastrid held the gown up to Hagatha, and Prunilla rushed into the room for a closer look. "It doesn't matter because, Cinderella, you will not be going to the ball."

"But you said —" Ella protested, though she knew it was hopeless.

"I said you might go if you were doing well in school. Which your sisters tell me you are not." Kastrid looked at Ella disapprovingly. "I wish I could say I am surprised. I only hope your father can bear the shame should you be expelled."

Ella's face was hot. How dare Kastrid mention her father? He would never be ashamed of her! She would never be expelled from Princess School. Why, with the trouble Hagatha and Prunilla caused, *they* should be the ones to get expelled.

Ella longed to scream back at her stepmother. She wanted to yell at her: *You should be ashamed. Look at your daughters. They are such awful witches, they belong in the Grimm School!*

"The dress won't fit Hagatha," was all Ella could mumble. Her stepsister was much taller and heavier than Ella.

"Well, then, you will have to *make* it fit." Kastrid threw the dress on the bed beside Ella. "In time for the Coronation Ball, of course."

With that, Ella's stepmother turned and swept out of the room and down the long flight of stairs.

Prunilla looked as if she was about to roll on the floor laughing. Hagatha was grinning, too. "And I'll need this petticoat," she said, tossing down the torn garment in her best imitation of her mother. "By tomorrow." Then she turned and followed her sister out of the room.

Ella collapsed across her bed. And though Hagatha had slammed the door behind her, Ella could still hear her stepsisters' wicked cackling over her own quiet sobs.

—

Chapter Sixteen

Wake-up Call

"Maybe I should transfer to *your* school," Val said. He sounded serious. "Nothing that exciting is going on over at Charm — it's all codes and chivalry."

"That's not even half of it," Rapunzel said, picking up a flat rock as they passed the mill pond. "We think maybe Ella's horrid stepsisters are behind the drenchings and the pea incident in addition to the wolf stunt. You would not *believe* these girls. They're like miniature Madame Gothels!"

Rapunzel sent the rock sailing over the still water. It skipped once, twice, three times before sinking to the bottom of the pond. She was enjoying bragging to Val. Princess School really was exciting. "I think they might have been the ones to stash that needle in Rose's bag, too. Luckily she wasn't hurt too badly."

Val flung the rock he was holding and didn't even watch to see how many times it skipped. "Beauty's been hurt?" he asked. His voice was full of concern, and he grabbed Rapunzel's arm. "What happened? Is she okay?"

"She's fine." Rapunzel shook Val off her arm. "Just tired is all." She looked at Val with narrowed eyes. "Is this part of the whole chivalry thing? What's the big deal? She just pricked her finger!"

Rapunzel picked up her books and walked away from Val, down the road toward their schools. She was annoyed. Sometimes Val was a little *too* interested in Rose. Her every move seemed to fascinate him. But maybe there was reason to be concerned. Rose had been awfully hard to wake up after Stitchery. And yesterday she had almost fallen asleep again in every class. For two days her head had been bobbing around on her neck like a sprung jack-in-the-box — hardly a pretty sight.

"Wait up." Val jogged beside her. "Don't be jealous."

"Ha!" Rapunzel laughed. Jealous of what? Rose was even more of a prisoner than she was. It was astounding the way her family doted on her. They were always waiting for her the moment school ended and accompanying her in the morning, trying to get her to wear ridiculous protective clothing. Rose even told her that she thought the fairies spied on her during the day. If you asked Rapunzel, that much attention would be worse than being locked in a tower alone. Everyone was always so worried about Rose.

Rapunzel started walking again, fast. Then she broke into a run.

"Hey," Val called after her. "Hey!"

Rapunzel waved but did not slow her pace. She wanted to get to school early. She had some things to discuss with Ella, Snow, and Rose.

Rapunzel scanned the crowd on the bridge as she rushed across the moat. There was Snow. Snow spotted Rapunzel, too, and skipped over with a wave and a warm smile. Rapunzel raised her head and gave a nod, but she didn't smile. She was too worried. What if Rose had gotten worse after school yesterday?

With a crushing wave of relief, Rapunzel spotted Rose on the other side of the bridge. She was holding a large mug of tea and brushing off her fairies and parents. She still looked tired but very much alive. Rose saw Snow and Rapunzel, too, and started to make her way over.

As Rapunzel watched Rose try to shake her fairies and join them on the steps, she couldn't really blame Val for liking the girl. In addition to being beautiful, she was great. And so were her other new friends, Snow and Ella.

Speaking of which, where *was* Ella? Beyond the bridge on the muddy lane, Rapunzel saw a forlorn figure walking slowly toward the school. The girl's skirts dragged in the mud and her head hung so low it was surprising it wasn't getting wet and muddy, too. Ella.

Without a word, Rapunzel headed for her crestfallen friend. Snow followed. But Rose, who had waved her parents off at last, slumped against the chain of the drawbridge. She yawned as Snow and Rapunzel whisked past. "I just have to rest a moment," she said sleepily. "I'll catch up."

Ella looked worse close up than she did from a distance. Her eyes were red from crying. Her hair was a mess, even by Rapunzel's standards. And her shoulders were so slumped she looked like she was carrying the whole world upon them.

Poor thing, Rapunzel thought as she hurried to Ella's side. *She has to go home to Hag and Prune every night. And her stepmother!*

Ella stumbled in her paper-stuffed shoes and almost fell into the carriage ruts. Rapunzel and Snow got there just in time, and Ella leaned heavily on her friends' shoulders.

"I can't go to the ball," she sobbed. "Hagatha . . . told. . . . She . . ." Ella was crying too hard to even speak. It took several minutes for her to tell the whole story. By the time she finished, Rapunzel was fuming. Even Snow looked angry.

"How could they?" Snow asked, dumbfounded. "Why would they? It's just . . . it's just so *mean*!"

"That's right," Rapunzel said, herding her friends back toward the bridge where Rose was dozing on her feet. "I think somebody needs to teach them to be nicer. Lots nicer."

"That's a great idea!" Snow chirped.

Rapunzel chewed her braid. Ella nodded at her and, in spite of her sad face, Rapunzel could tell by the look in her eyes she was ready to strike back no matter what it cost.

The trumpets blasted a two-minute warning and most of the princesses picked up their skirts and headed inside.

Rapunzel's head was spinning. The ball was only two days away. There was no way she was going to let Ella miss it or her awful stepsisters enjoy it. But they would have to act fast.

"Wake up, Brainy Rose." Rapunzel gently flicked Rose with the end of her braid, startling her awake.

"I'm fine. I'm fine." Rose stood up straight, sloshing the giant mug of tea.

"I'm glad to hear it," Rapunzel said honestly. "Because we need your help." She pulled her friends into a tight circle. "We've got to come up with a plan. And we don't have much time."

Chapter Seventeen

Daring Rescue

Ella peered out of the small open window on the top floor of her father's manor. For once she was glad that Kastrid had moved her room to the distant turret over the kitchen, far from the other bedrooms in the house. There was less of a chance anyone would notice the slim figure climbing her way, stone by stone, up the outside wall. It was so dark, Ella could hardly see Rapunzel herself.

"Are you still there?" Ella whispered into the night.

"Of course," Rapunzel said. Her head appeared just below the window opening and she hitched a leg up over the windowsill. "Could you give me a hand, damsel in distress?"

Ella laughed. "My hero," she said, dragging Rapunzel through the small opening. Rapunzel fell the rest of the way through and onto the knotted rag rug Ella had painstakingly woven from small scraps of cloth.

"Ooph." The heavy sack tied across Rapunzel's

back flattened her to the floor. Ella stared. Even in this inelegant pose, Rapunzel looked regal in a lovely dark green velvet gown with golden ribbons woven through the sleeves.

"No time for swooning, Princess," Rapunzel said as she got to her feet. "We've got work to do if we're going to get you to the ball in time." Rapunzel handed Ella the sack and went back to the window. "Get going. I'll watch for our prince."

Ella could feel her heart pounding in her chest. She had never done anything this risky before. Or this fun.

With the bag slung over her shoulder like laundry, she tiptoed downstairs to her stepsisters' dressing rooms.

In Hagatha's room, Ella's blue ball gown hung at the ready. She had spent hours ripping out stitches and redoing them. And since Hagatha was going to the ball in a newly made gown, Prunilla had announced that Ella would have to refit *her* dress as well, embellishing it with additional ribbons and lace. Ella had taken careful measurements of both her stepsisters. "Mother always said the proper fit is important," she had told them.

"That's right!" Prunilla had snapped back at her. "So don't mess up, dunderhead."

Ella was sure she hadn't messed up. Both dresses would fit like the girls had been sewn into them. They would be . . . breathtaking. Literally. The gowns would be so tight, her stepsisters wouldn't be able to take a deep breath. But Ella knew Hag and Prune would be too vain to admit that their dresses were too small. Instead they would suffer through the evening, puffing and wheezing around the dance floor. Ella almost giggled at her own deviousness. And the gowns were only part of the plan.

Beneath each altered gown, Ella had already laid out each sister's pair of shoes. Now she replaced them with almost identical footwear . . . two sizes smaller.

The shoes had been Rapunzel's idea. But it was Snow who had made it happen. Snow's dwarves were friends with some talented elfin shoemakers who had crafted the replicas in exchange for a few of Snow's delicious pies. Ella ran a finger along the soft leather and giggled. The elves had done a wonderful job.

Ella stooped to retrieve Hag's and Prune's regular shoes but stopped when she felt Rapunzel's sack bump against her leg. There was something else inside. Digging down to the bottom, Ella pulled out a beautiful pair of golden suede shoes with tiny rosettes stitched to the sides. They were just her size. Ella's breath caught. Could they really be for her?

Slipping off one of her oversized glass shoes, Ella slid her small foot into the soft suede. It fit like a glove. She tried on the other and glanced at her reflection in the full-length dressing room mirror. The shoes were truly lovely, and as comfortable as a pair of well-worn slippers.

Ella picked up her stepsisters' properly sized shoes and stuffed them into Rapunzel's bag along with her glass slippers. Then she took one last look in the mirror at the golden beauties on her feet . . . and noticed that the door behind her was opening!

Ella slipped noiselessly out the chambermaid's exit and silently thanked Snow for the shoes. If she'd been wearing her awkward glass slippers she would have been caught for sure.

Upstairs, Rapunzel was walking slowly around Ella's bedroom. "Your room isn't much better than mine," she said when Ella came back in. She smiled down at the sight of the slippers on Ella's feet. "Pretty, aren't they?"

Ella nodded, a smile spreading across her face. "Beautiful," she said.

"Are your sisters getting ready?"

"They were just coming into the dressing room when I left. I almost got caught!" Ella said. She felt nervous and excited at the same time. She and Rapunzel giggled nervously. They could not keep still. Ella was eager to see the results of her handiwork, but she would have to wait.

At last Ella saw a tiny light flare outside. A moment later something shiny caught the light and reflected it into Ella's window. That was the signal.

Hagatha and Prunilla had been sent off in the carriage — the road would be clear.

Rapunzel took a hand mirror out of her pocket and flashed back. Then she unwound her l-o-n-g braid, tying one end around Ella's waist in case she fell. After helping Ella out the window, Rapunzel climbed out slowly behind her.

Ella's stomach flipped when she got all the way outside.

"Just take it easy. Feel the rocks with your toes and fingers and don't move until you've got a good hold." Rapunzel's voice above her was reassuring. "And don't worry — my hair has got you, too!"

"To your left," Val coached from the ground, shining his light up to help the girls.

"Don't listen to him. He can't climb a tree," Rapunzel joked.

"I heard that!" Val protested.

It was easier to climb down the wall than Ella thought. With a final leap she landed on the ground. She felt exhilarated.

"Ella, Val. Val, Ella." Rapunzel gestured between the two while she quickly recoiled her hair.

"Charmed," Val took Ella's hand and bowed deeply. His velvet breeches were caramel colored, and the tunic and cape he wore were deep burgundy.

"Likewise," Ella said with a giggle as Val helped her up onto the horse standing nearby. When Ella was seated sidesaddle, the young prince took his seat behind her and held another hand out to Rapunzel.

Rapunzel refused the hand, swinging up behind Val by holding onto the saddle and boosting herself up on a nearby rock. For the first time Ella noticed that Rapunzel's skirts were split like pants, but the slit was cleverly hidden in pleats. Smart.

"Let's ride," Rapunzel said when the three were all safely on the horse. Val flicked the reins. Ella grabbed the horse's mane and without another word they galloped down the dark road toward Princess School and the Royal Coronation Ball.

The towers of Princess School were bathed in flickering torchlight. Gilded flags flew from the castle turrets. And every guard, page, and trumpeter was dressed in purple and gold and standing in a long line that marked the entry to the school. Tonight was going to be a magical night.

As they raced by on horseback, Ella saw princes and princesses arriving in fine coaches. Even the teams of horses were dressed up with plumes on their heads and silver bells on their halters.

Skirting the edges of the school, Val turned his horse and nudged him with his heels. The horse went from a gallop to a run. Before Ella could cry out in alarm, she and the horse and Val and Rapunzel were sailing over the Princess School moat and trotting toward the stables. When they entered the warm stables Ella slid to the hay-strewn floor with a wide smile on her face. Already this had been one of the best nights of her life.

"You made it!" Snow called. She elbowed Rose awake and pulled her out of the stall they had been hiding in. Snow and Rose both looked lovely. Snow's deep-red gown was the color of her ruby lips and looked so elegant against her alabaster skin that it didn't matter that the hem was too short or that the collar was old-fashioned. And Rose! Her gown was lavender satin with tiny opalescent pearls stitched over the bodice and skirt. Ella noticed that Val seemed to think Rose looked beautiful as well — he was staring at her with his mouth slightly open.

"I guess you'd better see to King," Rapunzel said, kicking Val lightly in the shin. "You know, your *horse*?"

Val quickly pulled his eyes away from Rose and closed his mouth. "Of course," he said. "I'll see you ladies at the ball."

"Did you get the shoes?" Snow asked.

"Oh, yes!" Ella replied. She lifted her tattered gown to show her friends. "They're beautiful. Thank you so much!"

"Ella, look!" Snow exclaimed. "Rose and I brought you something to wear, too!" Next to the horse bridles hung two ball gowns. Ella knew at once which one was Snow's — the hard white collar was a dead giveaway. Maybe Snow could pull off that look with her pale skin, dark eyes, and red lips, but Ella's delicate features would be lost in the stiff whiteness.

The other dress was from Rose's collection. It was pale, pale blue like the summer sky through a thin layer of cloud, but it shone golden on the edges like sun peeking through.

"You have to wear this one," Rose yawned, sitting down on a bale of hay. "It'll look royal on you."

Rapunzel agreed, and Ella slipped the dress on.

"Oh!" Snow cried as soon as the tiny buttons on the back of Ella's dress had been hooked and she spun around to show the girls. Snow couldn't say anything more. The fit was perfect.

"What about the hair?" Rapunzel raised an eyebrow. Ella noticed for the first time that Rapunzel's auburn tresses looked perfect. Her large braid was actually made up of hundreds of tiny braids woven together and then coiled around the back of her head like a bun. The end of the braid (she could never twist *all* of it into a bun) was tied off with a green ribbon that matched her dress. A few wispy curls framed her face. What had happened to the girl who seemed out of place in Looking Glass class? She had obviously been practicing more than communication signals with that hand mirror of hers!

"I think I have an idea," Rapunzel said, sitting Ella down on a hay bale and reaching for the hairbrush Rose had brought. She twisted and wove Ella's yellow tresses while Rose lazily pinched some color into Ella's cheeks, helped her with her gloves and jewels, and wove a satin ribbon through the bodice of her dress. Ella felt like royalty as her friends bustled around her.

"I think that's it." Rose stepped back, trying to hide another enormous yawn.

Rapunzel loosened a few strands of Ella's hair near her face and smiled at her own handiwork.

Standing up, Ella spun around to face her friends. The dress caught the light of the lanterns burning by the horse stalls. Ella's loosely swept-up hair revealed her happy face. She glowed.

Snow, Rapunzel, and Rose drew in their breath. They could not help but stare.

"What is it? What's the matter? Did I get it dirty?" Ella looked down at the shimmering skirts of her gown. "Do I look awful?"

"No. It's just that . . . it's just that you look so beautiful!" Snow exclaimed. Rose and Rapunzel nodded in agreement.

"Here." Rapunzel pulled the hand mirror back out of her pocket. "See for yourself."

Ella gazed at her reflection in the mirror for a long moment. From the curl on her forehead to the tips of her toes she felt beautiful — not just like a princess — like a queen. Like a queen on her way to a ball!

Ella's wet eyes sparkled as she looked gratefully at her three smiling friends. "Thank you," she said, choking up. She rushed toward them with her arms open for a hug. "I could never have made it here without you!"

Chapter Eighteen
The Ball

Smiling and holding hands, the four girls headed out of the stables and across the gardens to the castle.

"We have to go through the front," Rapunzel said, steering everyone around the low wall that separated the rose garden from the main entrance. "So everyone can see the beautiful princess." She winked at Ella, and all four girls giggled. Ella beamed. She really did feel like royalty.

The girls rounded the end of the wall, and the glorious sight of the illuminated castle overwhelmed Ella once again. The flags hanging from the turrets blew gently in the night breeze. The torchlights flickered, casting gentle shadows on the castle walls. The school was truly an enchanting sight.

Making their way across the bridge, the girls pulled Rose along with them. Ella noticed that she was practically sleepwalking.

"Are you all right, Rose?"

Rose yawned, but opened her eyes wide. "I'm completely fine," she replied blearily.

As the girls lifted their skirts to ascend the castle stairs, several of the pages stopped trumpeting to watch them pass. At first Ella thought they were looking at Rose. But some of them seemed to be staring in her direction.

They couldn't be looking at me, Ella thought shyly as they entered the castle. *Could they?* It was all too dreamy. Ella wondered what Kastrid would think if she saw her now. She smiled wider just thinking about it. For once her stepmother would be speechless.

Inside, the girls made their way to the ballroom. When they stepped through the carved double doors, all four of them stopped to take in the breathtaking sight.

The marble floor had been polished to a sparkling shine. Colorful silk streamers hung from the walls and pillars. At one end, a long banquet table was covered with delicious meats and pastries and punch. At the other, an orchestra played a lively waltz on a small raised stage. Just to the right was the ballot box, gaudily decorated with too many ribbons and bows.

That's Hagatha and Prunilla for you, Ella thought wryly.

"Let's dance!" Snow chirped, pulling the others

toward the dance floor, where several princes and princesses were already whirling about.

"I'd love to" — Rose yawned — "but I need to rest a minute first."

"I'll come with you," Ella offered.

"I can stay with Rose," a voice said from behind them. It was Val. Ella had almost forgotten he was with them.

"Of course you will," Rapunzel said, rolling her eyes.

"That would be wonderful!" Snow exclaimed, linking Rose's arm through Val's. "Come on, girls!"

Rapunzel looked a little irritated, but she let Snow lead her and Ella onto the dance floor. Right away the girls began to sway daintily to the music. Or at least, Ella and Rapunzel did. Snow seemed to have her own kind of dance style, which included a lot of leaping and flapping.

I wonder if the deer and the birds taught her those steps, Ella thought, smiling to herself.

"Nice moves," Rapunzel said slyly.

"Oh, do you like them?" Snow cried, hopping up and down like a rabbit. "The animals and I have been practicing!"

"Well, they're original," Rapunzel said, smiling affectionately at her friend. Ella had to laugh. Snow could be silly, all right. But she was also the sweetest person she'd ever met, and full of surprises.

"Excuse me," came a voice from behind them. "May I have this dance?"

Ella whirled around and found herself staring into the blue eyes of a handsome, dapperly dressed prince.

Ella was so surprised, she didn't say anything at first. Was he talking to her?

Next to her, Snow giggled. The prince held out his hand. "I am Allister," he said. "And I would be most pleased if you would dance with me."

Blushing, Ella nodded and took the boy's hand. As he whisked her away, Ella saw the smiling faces of her friends whoosh by. She felt light-headed, as if she might faint. Only she wouldn't, of course. If she did, she might miss something!

Allister was a wonderful dancer. He made Ella feel light and graceful on her feet as he turned her this way and that. Ella's head was spinning faster than her feet on the dance floor. In the Princess School ballroom, surrounded by her friends, she felt completely at home. Cinderella felt . . . right. She sighed as the music ended. She never wanted to lose this feeling. She happily agreed when Allister asked her to dance again.

Ella and Allister danced three times — until another boy cut in.

"May I have a turn?" he asked smoothly.

Allister nodded, bowed to Ella, and stepped away.

"I am Sebastian," the boy said. He was shorter than

Allister, and Ella guessed that he was in his first year at the Charm School. His dance steps were somewhat stilted and he kept counting to himself, but Ella didn't mind. She was having, well, a ball!

Sebastian only got one dance with Ella before another boy stepped in — and another, then another. Ella was grateful that she was wearing comfortable shoes. Her feet never would have survived all this dancing in glass!

Whirling atop the shining pink marble floor, Ella and her dance partner — a handsome, curly-haired boy named Ian — seemed to be in a private pocket of air. Several of the other dancers had stopped to watch them. They were murmuring and nodding approvingly. Ella couldn't recall ever getting so much attention! Peering around the crowd, Ella half hoped that her stepsisters weren't among the people watching. Hagatha and Prunilla were awful enough to ruin even this moment. But with a mischievous smile Ella changed her mind. She hoped Hag and Prune would see her! They would probably be too shocked to do anything.

Ella was just thinking she might need to take a rest when Rapunzel tapped her on the shoulder.

"Come quick," she whispered, sounding a little frantic. "It's your stepsisters!"

"Excuse me," Ella told her dance partner. "I have to attend to something."

His face full of disappointment, the prince nodded and bowed slightly. "Of course," he said.

"Those awful girls are stuffing the ballot box!" Rapunzel reported as she led Ella toward the stage. Sure enough, Hag was standing guard in front of the box. Behind her, Prune was stuffing scroll after scroll into the slot at the top.

"Hurry up!" Hagatha snapped at her sister. "We don't have all night!"

"I've just started. *You* try shoving all these scrolls in here," Prunilla snapped back. "My gown is so tight I can barely lift my arms!"

Ella knew she would get in trouble if her sisters saw her at the ball, but as she stormed forward, she didn't care. She was emboldened by her fancy gown and good friends. No one could tell her she didn't belong at Princess School — certainly not her awful stepsisters. It was time to put a stop to their torment. She would not allow them to rig the vote for Princess of the Ball!

"What do you think you're doing?" she asked, planting herself right in front of Hagatha. She glanced down at the too-tight bodice of her gown and tried not to smile. Her stepsister looked like a sausage!

"You!" Hagatha tried to sneer, but it came out more as a gasp. Her eyes narrowed but quickly widened again as she looked Ella up and down. Even nasty Hagatha could not hide her admiration.

268

"What are you doing here?" Prunilla panted over her sister's shoulder. Her gaze held on the lovely gown Ella wore.

"Attending the ball, of course," Ella said, gazing directly at Prunilla.

"Never mind that," Rapunzel cut in. "What are *you* doing to the ballot box?"

"Ah, yes, the ballot box," Headmistress Bathilde echoed as she approached the girls. The headmistress's stiff silk skirts swished with each step. The people in her path fell silent with awe and drew out of her way. Her willowy frame seemed to float over the ground, making her look taller than she actually was, and her face showed few of her numerous years.

Lady Bathilde cast her silvery eyes on the ballot box. "You must agree it's quite thoroughly decorated," she stated. Beside her, Madame Taffeta watched Hagatha and Prunilla closely.

Ella wasn't sure if the headmistress intended what she said to be a compliment or not, but she thought she saw an unusual sort of smile on Madame Taffeta's face.

"It's time to count the ballots," the headmistress added smoothly.

"Oh, of course," Hagatha said in a sweet but high-pitched voice as she and Prunilla stepped aside.

"We were just guarding it for you," Prunilla peeped.

"To make sure nobody tampered with the voting scrolls." She let out a puff of air and clutched her stomach.

"Yeah, right," Rapunzel said, glaring openly at the older girls.

"Are you all right, Prunilla?" Madame Taffeta asked Prunilla. "You look a bit . . . blue." She seemed to be eyeing the girls' gowns suspiciously, and Ella had a moment of panic.

"We're fine, of course," Prunilla replied. This time her voice almost sounded normal, but she still fidgeted in her golden gown.

"Yes. We were just going to get something to eat," Hagatha rasped.

As Hagatha and Prunilla limped away, Ella tried not to laugh. If either of them ate a single bite, she'd definitely rip a seam!

"Come on," Rapunzel said. "Let's go find Rose and Snow."

Disappointed, Ella nodded and followed her friend away from the ballot box. Part of her wanted to tell the headmistress and Madame Taffeta what Hag and Prune had been up to. But although their actions had looked totally suspicious, they didn't have any actual proof. And besides, why would the headmistress believe a couple of Bloomers? If the teachers didn't trust the older girls, they wouldn't have let them decorate the ballot box to begin with!

As she and Rapunzel crossed the ballroom, Ella struggled with what to do. Then, suddenly, she noticed that people were staring at her.

"What's going on?" she whispered to Rapunzel.

"They're gazing at the belle of the ball," Rapunzel replied with a grin.

Ella thought Rapunzel might be teasing, and whacked her playfully on the arm. But by then they had already reached their friends.

Rose was sitting with Val and Snow on the edge of the dance floor, her drooping head dipping dangerously low to the heaping plate of food she held.

"I'll take that," Rapunzel said, removing the plate before Rose's face fell into the meat pies. "I need to drown my sorrows at our defeat."

"Help yourself," Rose replied sleepily.

"What defeat?" Val asked.

"We think Ella's nasty stepsisters were trying to rig the vote. We caught them stuffing ballots into the box."

"How do you know they weren't real ballots?" Snow asked.

Ella sighed. Sometimes she wished she could be more like Snow — always trusting and expecting the best of people. But living with her stepmother and stepsisters had made that impossible.

"Because we're talking about Hagatha and Prunilla," Rapunzel said.

"Exactly," Ella agreed.

"Excuse me," said a prince as he approached. He stopped directly in front of Ella and stared down at the floor nervously. "Would you like to dance?"

"No thank you," Ella said as kindly as she could. "I'm spending a little time with my friends."

The boy looked crestfallen.

"But I would love to dance later," Ella added.

The boy looked up, grinning from ear to ear. "All right!" he said excitedly as he bounded away.

"I think you've put a spell on everyone here, Ella," Val teased. "Everybody keeps staring at you and whispering."

Ella blushed. "It's Rose's gown, Rapunzel's hairstyling talent, and Snow's shoes," she said modestly.

"Oh, no!" Snow said. "The elves made those shoes for you. They're for you to keep!"

Ella gave Snow a hug. She hardly ever got new items of clothing — and nothing as beautiful as these suede shoes. "Thank you!" she cried.

"And for the record, it's not the gown or the shoes — or your hair," Rapunzel said. "It's *you*, Ella. You're glowing."

"Princes and Princesses," called a loud voice. It was Lady Bathilde. "Please gather around the stage. It is time to crown the Princess of the Ball!"

"Come on!" Snow said excitedly.

272

Helping Rose to her feet, the girls and Val made their way to the stage. Ella saw Hagatha and Prunilla right up front, still fidgeting with their gowns.

Tapping the school scepter on the stage floor and holding a glittering crown aloft, Lady Bathilde stood with her back straight. Her mere presence demanded attention. The crowd quieted, and she slowly began to unroll an ornate scroll that held the winner's name.

"This year's Princess of the Ball is . . ."

"Move over!" a voice rasped out. Ella recognized it at once. Hagatha.

"That crown is mine," Prunilla hissed back.

There was a scuffle as the two girls tried to grab for the crown, nearly knocking over the headmistress. Then Hagatha tripped on the hem of her gown and fell over, dragging Prunilla down with her.

On the stage, Lady Bathilde was ignoring the scuffle quite successfully. Looking over the waiting crowd, she smiled as she announced the winner's name: Cinderella Brown!

Chapter Nineteen
A True Princess

Ella was so shocked when she heard her name that she didn't move. Beside her, her friends squealed with delight.

"It's you! It's you!" Snow cried, clapping her hands together.

Rose gave her a giant hug. "You deserve it," she said with a yawn.

Rapunzel nudged her forward. "You have to go up to the stage," she said. "Your tiara is waiting."

"No!" Prunilla shrieked. On her hands and knees, she was still trying to grab the tiara out of Lady Bathilde's hands.

"It's mine!" Hagatha screamed.

One of the older Charm School princes near the front unceremoniously pulled the girls to their feet. "It's not yours, or yours," he said firmly, eyeing each girl with disgust. "It's Ella's."

"But she, she —"

"She is the Princess of the Ball," the prince said flatly.

Several of the princesses in the crowd began to laugh at Hagatha and Prunilla, who were so dumbfounded by the prince's words that they were actually speechless. As the laughter grew, the girls slinked toward the ballroom door and their waiting carriage, wheezing and limping the entire way.

As Ella watched them go, she realized she would be in big trouble when she got home. But as she stepped onto the stage she didn't care.

Lady Bathilde smiled majestically as she placed the tiara on Ella's head. Then she put her hands on Ella's shoulders and turned her slowly to face the crowd. The ballroom erupted into claps and cheers. Looking down at her schoolmates and her new friends, Ella felt like a true princess.

When the coronation ceremony was over, even more princes were vying for dances with Ella. But after she danced her promised dance with the boy who had asked her earlier, she kindly declined them all. This was a moment she wanted to share with her friends.

"Do you get to keep it?" Snow asked, fingering the tiara on Ella's head.

"I don't think so," Ella said. "They need it again for next year's ball. But just wearing it is wonderful enough."

Suddenly the music was interrupted a second time

and a regal-looking woman in a black gown and flowing black cape took the stage.

"Who's that?" Rapunzel asked, her eyes wide.

"That's Malodora," Val whispered. "She's the headmistress at the Grimm School. Not someone you want to mess with."

Ella shuddered. Just the sight of this woman was enough to scare anyone. She made Kastrid look friendly! She glanced at her friends to gauge their reactions. Rose looked as sleepy as ever. Rapunzel looked wary. And Snow looked three shades whiter.

"Snow?" Ella put a hand on her friend's arm. "What is it? Are you okay?"

Snow's free hand squeezed the one Ella had placed on her arm, but her eyes never left the stage. "That's my stepmother," she said in a frightened whisper.

Waving her hand through the air dramatically, Malodora made an important announcement.

"The Grimm School and Princess School will be holding the annual Maiden Games exactly one month from today," she said in a booming voice. "Everyone will participate, and I myself, along with Lady Bathilde, will oversee the Games. The winners will receive the coveted Golden Ball."

"Wow," Ella breathed.

"Games!" Rapunzel cried excitedly, hopping up and down. "I love competition!"

Rose slumped even more heavily against Val, finally completely asleep.

"Oh, no," Snow said, her dark eyes wide with fear.

"Don't worry, Snow," Ella said comfortingly. "Whatever it is, we'll help you through it."

"That's right," Rapunzel agreed, coming to her other side.

Snow smiled, but Ella sensed that she was still afraid. Ella couldn't blame her. Malodora was clearly a force to be reckoned with. And she knew all about sinister stepmothers.

"Maybe we should move Rose to a corner and lay her down," Rapunzel suggested.

"Oh, I'm fine," Val replied, but he was clearly tiring from holding the sleeping girl up. He'd been doing it practically all night! "I don't mind, really." In a moment of chivalry, he reached down and lifted Rose's hand to his face, kissing it gently.

No sooner had his lips brushed her hand than Rose sat bolt upright, her eyes wide.

"What's going on?" she asked, looking around. "Did I miss anything?"

The girls all laughed — even Snow joined in — and began to fill Rose in on the evening's events.

"Ella is the Princess of the Ball!" Snow exclaimed.

"And Hagatha and Prunilla got laughed off the stage!" Rapunzel laughed.

277

"Wow," Rose said. "And I thought it was all a dream!"

"No, it was real," Ella assured her. "Val has been holding you up all night. When he kissed your hand, you . . . woke up."

Rose looked up at Val. "Thanks," she said.

Val blushed. "You're w-welcome," he stammered.

By the time the ball was finally over, it was very late.

"Anyone want a ride home in my carriage?" Rose asked. "There's plenty of room."

"Yes!" the girls chorused.

As they left the ballroom, Madame Taffeta approached Ella.

"I could not help but notice the interesting stitchery on your stepsisters' gowns," she said pointedly. Ella braced herself. She'd been sure she was going to get punished tonight, but not by a teacher!

Madame Taffeta leaned toward Ella slightly. "I can see you do extensive and, shall we say, creative stitching at home," Madame Taffeta went on, her eyes gleaming. "And your stepsisters seem to require careful watching."

Ella nodded, too surprised to say anything. Could it be that a teacher was on her side?

"In light of the situation, I believe it is only fair that you be excused from Stitchery homework for the foreseeable future."

For the second time that night, Ella could not believe her ears. But one look at Madame Taffeta's smiling face told her that her words were true.

"Thank you!" Ella said, giving the teacher a spontaneous hug. Then she hurried to join her friends and tell them the news.

Laughing together, the group traipsed outside to the waiting carriages. The pages were still lined up along the steps and the bridge, but several had fallen asleep.

Val escorted the girls to Rose's carriage, then bowed to them. I will leave you ladies here," he said. "My horse awaits."

The girls scrambled into the carriage. "Bye, Val," Rapunzel called. "See you tomorrow!"

Val waved while the carriage pulled away. Inside, Ella sat back on the lush maroon seat and looked around at her friends. Two weeks ago, she'd felt completely out of place at Princess School. Now she felt right at home. There was no doubt in her mind that with her friends around her, her future at Princess School was as bright as the sparkling tiara that graced the top of her head.

THE GIRL,
THE DRAGON,
AND THE
WILD MAGIC

Book One of The Rhianna Chronicles

Dave Luckett

To the real Rhian,
who has her own magic

ISBN 0-439-41187-4

Text copyright © 2000 by Dave Luckett.

Originally published in Australia in 2000 by Omnibus Books under the
title *Rhianna and the Wild Magic*.
All rights reserved. Published by Scholastic Inc., 557 Broadway,
New York, NY 10012, by arrangement with Omnibus Books, an imprint
of Scholastic Australia.

SCHOLASTIC and associated logos are trademarks and/or
registered trademarks of Scholastic Inc.

12 11 10 9 8 7 6 5 4 3 2 1   3 4 5 6 7 8/0
                                              40
Printed in the U.S.A.
First American edition, October 2003

CHAPTER 1

"Think, Rhianna." Mrs. Greenapple leaned over the front of Rhianna Wildwood's desk and pointed to the words in the spellbook. "It's just a simple rhyme to say over a sleeping potion. Now repeat after me, *Doremus dorema doremasa sleepy soppy dormousey casa. . . .*"

The class at the Smallhaven village school was quiet except for the turning of pages, but Rhianna knew that everyone was looking at her. She frowned and tried again: *"Doremus dorema doremasa, sleepy soapy . . ."*

"*Soppy,* Rhianna."

Rory Spellwright, two seats to the right, sniggered and whispered something to his friend Fion Oldbuck. Rhianna felt her chest grow tight. She hated giving Rory something to use against her, but it was so hard to get spellcasting right. None of the words made any sense.

"*Soppy* . . . what does that mean, Miss?" she asked.

Rory sniggered again.

"Never mind what it means, Rhianna, just say it." Mrs. Greenapple was a little impatient this morning, and her voice showed it.

"Yes, Rhianna, just *say* it, stupid," mimicked Rory, so low that Mrs. Greenapple didn't quite hear him.

"What was that, Rory?" she asked.

"Nothing, Miss," said Rory, virtuously. "Just going over the chant in my book."

Mrs. Greenapple nodded, and bent over Rhianna's desk again.

Rhianna hated being singled out like this. *"Doremus dorema doremasa, sleepy soppy enormously . . ."*

"Dormousey, Rhianna — oh, no! Stop! I didn't mean that!"

Too late. There was a sudden thump. Rhianna swung around in her seat, and there was Tom Bodger, slumped forward over his desk. The thump had been his head hitting it. He was fast asleep, snoring like a bulldog pup.

Mrs. Greenapple pressed a hand to her mouth. Then she glared at Rhianna. "Now look what you did," she said crossly.

"Me?" asked Rhianna.

"Yes, you." The teacher shook Tom's shoulder. He stayed asleep, snoring a little. "You said 'enormously.' You must have increased the power of the spell." She put her hand on Tom's head and said something in a whisper. It made no difference. Tom was sound asleep.

"But *you* said the next word, the one that —" started Rhianna.

Mrs. Greenapple cut her off. "Never mind what I said. Just help me wake Tom up."

Just like always, Rhianna thought. *First they tell you to listen to everything they say, and then they tell you not to. It isn't fair.*

Rory put on an expression of great concern. "Miss," he called, "has she killed Tom? Should I get my uncle?"

Rory's uncle was the nearest thing the village had to a real wizard. Mr. Spellwright had a spell shop, just down the street.

"No need, thank you, Rory," said Mrs. Greenapple, hauling Tom upright. "He's just asleep."

But Tom wouldn't wake up, not right away. They had to carry him out and put his head under the pump, and all he did at first was blow happy little bubbles. It took twenty minutes and two buckets of water to wake him up enough for him to go home.

The class giggled. Mrs. Greenapple fumed. "The magic shouldn't have gone *that* wrong," she said. The school's spell wards must have run down again. Still, the lesson had been ruined, and it was all Rhianna's fault.

Rhianna sighed. *It was always the same,* she thought.

But there was worse to come before lunch.

"Wands down. Look at me. No talking." Mrs. Greenapple took up a pile of papers. "Here are your results from last week's test of Spell Ingredients. Quite good, and I'm pleased. Mostly." She began to send the papers skimming through the air, using a fly-and-find spell. Each one landed neatly on the right desk, and the fly part of the spell was turned off by each student with a flick of the fingers. "Ariadne . . . Gloriana . . . Ingold . . . Isembard . . . Fion — much better this week, Fion . . . oh, and Rhianna."

Rhianna's paper landed in front of her. She saw the big red marks on it and almost forgot to turn off the spell. When she did remember to flick her fingers, the piece of paper fell off the desk. It crashed to the floor like a sheet of metal, making a noise that echoed around the classroom. Everyone turned and stared.

Rhianna turned scarlet. Mrs. Greenapple took off her glasses and pinched the bridge of her nose, as if she had a headache. "I think you had better see me afterwards, Rhianna," she said.

Rhianna picked up the paper and looked at it. If anything, this test seemed worse than the last one. And she *had* studied for it, she really had. She peeked at the total, just lifting a corner of the paper off the desk, so no one else would see it.

Oh, no! F! Even worse than the D-minus she'd got for Recitation last week. And Spell Ingredients was her best subject, too. That was because it had measures and numbers in it, and they made sense. Not like spells.

Rhianna sat in silent dismay as her teacher called out the names of all the rest of the class, one by one. The dismay was made worse when nobody else was told to wait behind.

The bell rang for lunchtime as Mrs. Greenapple finished handing out the papers. "Look at your marks later. And talk about them outside, *if* you please, Morgana Hedger. Books away. Make sure your wands are properly laid east–west. Who's ready to go?"

Rhianna was ready to go, all right, but there was no chance of being able to get away. Mrs. Greenapple dismissed the class, row by row, line by line, making sure that Rhianna was among the last. There was no way to sneak out past her. She hadn't forgotten.

Rhianna waited, standing by her desk. Her friend Rose Treesong gave her a concerned look as she left the classroom, but Rhianna was too sunk in gloom to notice. The door closed, the sounds of play were hushed, and the bright sunlight outside made the room seem darker still.

"Well, Rhianna." Mrs. Greenapple folded her arms and leaned against her desk. "What's to be done? It seems you didn't take in a thing I said all last week. Or anything in the book, either."

Rhianna stared at the floor and said nothing.

Her teacher sighed. "I must admit, I can't understand it. Your work is neat and clear. You understand all the amounts . . . look, three-and-a-half scruples of butterfly-wing dust plus three quarters of a drachm of thistledown sap makes just about a pinch. . . ."

"It makes exactly a pinch!" Rhianna was stung. The table showing the amounts had been clear in the book. Difficult, mind you. She wished all the measures could go evenly into each other, but all the same. . . . She looked up. Mrs. Greenapple was shaking her head.

"How many times must we go over this, Rhianna?" she asked. "There is no such thing as 'exactly a pinch.' Nothing is exact in magic! Everyone's pinch is different. Far more important than the pinch is what it's a pinch *of.* That's what you were asked about. This is the base for a simple flying ointment. And what did you say it was? 'One pinch of gray goo.' Really!"

"Well, that's what it looked like," muttered Rhianna.

Mrs. Greenapple's face became grim. "Since when," she asked carefully, "has anything ever been what it looks like in magic?"

Rhianna looked down again. There was something about that question that set her teeth on edge. Why shouldn't things be what they looked like? Why should everything be vague and fuzzy and not exact?

But it was no use scowling. Mrs. Greenapple shook her head again. "Well," she said, "I think we need to talk to your parents, Rhianna. I wouldn't mind so much if you just forgot things. Still less if you just got a few of the words wrong or left out a gesture when working a spell. But this is far worse. It's as if you had everything around the wrong way, as if you . . . as if you didn't think magic was *real*. As if you thought there was some other way to make things work." She watched Rhianna's face, what she could see of it. When nothing more happened after a few moments, she sighed. "All right, Rhianna. I don't think there is anything more to be said now. I'll be sending a letter home. Go and have your lunch."

Rhianna trudged out, still scowling.

Rose was waiting for her in their usual place. Rhianna plumped herself down and opened her lunch basket.

"How bad was it?" asked Rose.

"The usual," said Rhianna, trying to look uncon-cerned. "You know, *'Rhianna, you have to remember that noth-ing is what it seems to be. Nothing adds up. Nothing is right.'* Why can't things say what they mean, and mean what they say?"

"Well," said Rose, considering, "I suppose it's because they don't in magic."

"Don't *you* start."

"I'm not starting. You asked me, I told you."

This was so true that Rhianna had nothing to say to it. Her pie was suddenly tasteless, though it was kept fresh by her mother's own spell. She dropped it back in her basket.

Mrs. Greenapple would be writing that letter already, and the sending spell would have it at Rhianna's house by this afternoon. She would have to face her mother and father over dinner.

That was enough to cause any amount of gloom. She'd be sent to her room after school every day for a week, most likely. Told to study. Study! As if it ever made any difference whether she studied or not! The things in the books didn't make any sense at all. Why should a finding charm work if you walked around a circle one way, but not if you walked around it the other? Why? Rhianna always wanted to know *why*. Mrs. Greenapple was always telling her it didn't matter why. *Just do it, Rhianna.*

"Just do it, Rhianna," she said out loud, and there was a rude laugh just behind her. Rory Spellwright's laugh.

It was Rory, all right. "Yeah, just *do* it, Rhianna. Why can't you? What's wrong with you? *I* can do it. All the other kids can do it, even the little ones. Even Rose here can do it, and she's nearly as dumb as —"

Rose whipped her head around, her eyes sparkling dangerously. She whispered a find spell and tossed a squashberry in the air. Up it went, gently, and then it curved in flight as if it had wings, flew faster and faster, and went *splat!* right in the middle of Rory's forehead. Purple juice trickled into his eyes, and he touched his fingers to his face in disbelief.

"Dumb, am I?" asked Rose. "Well, I've got a mean find spell and a basket full of squashberries. Get out of here, Rory, or you'll be so purple you'll think you're a grape."

Rory looked down at his purple fingers. His mouth opened and closed. "You wait," he raged. "You wait. I'll tell. I'll tell Mrs. Greenapple," and he ran towards the school building, his voice working up into a howl as he went.

Rhianna sighed. "You shouldn't have done that," she said. "He'll do it, for sure."

Rose nodded. "It'll be worth it," she said comfortably. "I should have used the whole bunch on him."

"Waste of good squashberries," said Rhianna. She sighed again. "Why does he have to be such a sneak?"

Rose shrugged. "Could be because he doesn't have much power, no matter how right he gets the spell, and he hates that. He couldn't have done that with the squashberry, for instance. Could be because nobody takes any notice of him unless he's acting like he does. But the main reason is just Rory. He just likes himself that way, I suppose." She glanced across the meadow. "Here we go."

Mrs. Greenapple was coming towards them. Rory walked behind her, looking woeful when she glanced at him, and poking his tongue out the rest of the time.

"I'll probably be kept in," said Rose. "You'll have to walk home by yourself."

Rhianna nodded. It was so unfair.

When school was over, Rhianna slouched up the village street towards home. The worst of it was that she had to stop at Mr. Spellwright's shop. Her mother had asked her to pick up some amber for a preserving spell.

Mr. Spellwright was standing at the shop door, his thumbs in his waistcoat pockets. Rhianna's mother had always told her to be very polite to Mr. Spellwright because he was an important man, and well-off, and had the only spell shop in the village. He was tall and portly, with a long face like a hound's, but his eyes were a lizard's eyes, sharp and glittery.

"Good day, Mr. Spellwright," said Rhianna.

Mr. Spellwright looked straight through her and sniffed. His thumbs remained in his waistcoat pockets. Mr. Spellwright didn't like people who were new to the village, like the Wildwoods. And he liked to think of himself as a wizard and a person far superior to Rhianna's father, who was the village blacksmith.

"I need to get ten grains of amber for Mother," Rhianna went on.

Mr. Spellwright grunted and turned his back, retreating into the darkness of the little shop. Rhianna followed him in.

It was darker and cooler inside, with odd shadows in the corners. They formed shapes that melted when you looked straight at them, but came back when you looked away. Magical ingredients of all sorts were stacked in rows on shelves, or filled big glass jars. Many of them looked or smelled odd — sharp or pungent or spicy or musky.

All sorts of strange ingredients were needed for spellcasting. Alum and peat, to make spells of shrinking and drying, for the clothmakers. Mermaids' purses, to make spells to call fish, for the fisherfolk. Lodestone and pelligorny, to make spells to find or hold, soapwort and rue and balsam, to repair or clean. Spells to make things grow, spells to work small changes, and spells to preserve, all with their own ingredients. Most people used some magic every day, and Mr. Spellwright supplied all the things they needed. He had a good business. It seemed that people needed more and more magic.

But that wasn't all there was in the shop. There were oddly shaped dusty glass bottles that never seemed to be used. There were pigeonhole racks at the back of the shop with small colored jars and even smaller vials that were never opened. It was difficult to see what was in them. People said that they contained weirder things yet, ingredients for greater spells than most folk could manage. Spells that needed the bones of strange animals, or leaves of the deadly upas tree, or even troll hide and dragon blood, serpent venom and elf-shot. There was a preserved snake floating in clear liquid in a large jar. Rhianna could never make out its tail. Both ends seemed to have heads — or were there two snakes? The colors of the scales seemed to come and go as she watched, and she thought the little black eyes followed her.

Mr. Spellwright slid behind his counter and took down a jar of amber dust from a shelf. He weighed out ten grains of it, poured it into a small paper bag, twisted the bag shut, and put it on the counter. Without saying anything, he held out a hand.

Rhianna gave him a coin. She picked up the bag and said, "Thank you, Mr. Spellwright," then turned and walked out of the shop, feeling his eyes on her back all the way. To reach the sunshine outside was a relief.

She trailed on up the street towards home. It wasn't a

long enough walk, between the little houses and beyond the village green, but she made it last as long as she could. That note from Mrs. Greenapple would have beaten her home. What on earth was she going to say to her mother?

CHAPTER 2

Going home was every bit as bad as Rhianna had feared it would be.

She slipped in the back door, hoping to tiptoe through to her room and not come out before dinnertime. Her mother's back was turned to her as she peeled potatoes at the bench. Rhianna moved very quietly, but she wasn't quiet enough. Meg Wildwood looked around.

"Ah, there you are, Rhianna," she said. "Late back from school, I see."

Oh dear, thought Rhianna. She smiled. "Yes, Mother. I thought I'd go straight through and get started on my homework."

"Good, good," said her mother, nodding. "That's good, Rhianna. In fact, I think you need to do a lot more of that. You know about the note your teacher sent home, then?" She fixed Rhianna with a considering eye. "Of course you do." She pulled a piece of brownish paper from her pocket. "It says that you failed another test to-day. Mrs. Greenapple thinks you will have to repeat this year's work."

Rhianna stared at the floor.

Her mother looked at the note and frowned. "At least, I think that's what she wrote. I must say, the school really should use better spellpaper. This is falling to pieces already. But" — she put it back in her pocket — "I suppose your father will still be able to read it when he comes home."

Worse and worse.

"Mother . . . I tried. I studied, I really did. But it all gets mixed-up, somehow. It all comes out wrong. I get confused. There are no rules . . . nothing ever makes sense."

Meg shook her head. "Rules? Of course there are no rules. Human beings make rules, not magic. Magic is wild. At its heart, it's not to be tamed. We can only use it because there are ways of handling it that the great wizards work out by trial and error. You have to *remember* those ways. Or you'll never be able to use magic at all."

"Maybe I don't want to use it," mumbled Rhianna. "Father doesn't, much."

Meg's eyebrows went up. "Your father is a smith. There's nothing wrong with being a smith, Rhianna, but it's hard work, and magic isn't much help, with all that cold iron. We wanted something better for you. That's one of the reasons we moved out here from Avalon. Home Island was getting crowded. There's more magic in the country, with fewer folk to use it up. But there's no use in that if you won't learn the spells."

Rhianna shrugged. "Not won't. Can't."

Meg was silent for a moment. Then: "All right, Rhianna. I know you try hard, and it's true that magic isn't easy, not for everyone. Go and do your homework now, and try to remember what you read. I want to hear the chants as you go over them. We'll talk it over at dinner with your father. I'm sure it's not as bad as all that."

Rhianna went to her room, miserably. She sat at her table, opened her spellbook, and tried to learn the spell for that day. It said: *To freshen cut flowers — a pinch of rich earth and the words* Floribunda in abunda floribus *said twice with a pass of the hands, fingers spread, see diagram.*

She looked at the diagram. It was simple enough, and the spell didn't look too hard. There was a bunch of spring wildflowers in a jar of water on her windowsill, and some earth in a window box. She sprinkled the earth over the flowers, made the pass with her hands, and whispered the spell.

Nothing happened. Rhianna waited, disappointment growing. Sometimes, nothing happened. Sometimes . . .

Then the flowers — little spring flowers, pinks and

sunroses and cat's-eyes, bluebells and ladylocks and fairy bonnets — shook themselves. There was a soft tinkle, and the air swirled in strange colors. The flowers raised their heads. They straightened. Then they began to grow. Their stems grew long and strong and leafy, emerald green. And the flowers —

The pinks flushed deep crimson, red as a dragon's heart. Sunroses grew to puffs of bright shining gold the size of Rhianna's hand, their petals stiff as lace and edged with golden sparkles. Cat's-eyes blazed in stripes like candy sticks, shiny like satin. Rhianna watched, fascinated, as the ladylocks became knots of pearl ribbon with silver edges. They brightened until they began to twinkle like stars, tiny points of many-colored fire coming and going at their centers.

It was like . . . like growing your own jewel box. Rhianna stretched out a finger, wondering . . . *Did I do this?*

And as she touched, as her finger stroked the first bloom, suddenly it crumpled, the gorgeous colors faded, and it turned brown and then black. One by one, then all together, the flowers drooped and shriveled, and the dry leaves pattered to the floor, and the stems died back. A minute later, there was nothing but a bunch of dry sticks in a jar of water.

Looking at the ruined flowers, Rhianna began to cry. *I do nothing but make things worse,* she thought. *What use is magic like that?* She sniffled and wiped her nose with her hand. *And it's no use talking to Father about it. He won't understand.*

But when her father came home, late and tired, there was no talk about Rhianna's schoolwork.

Loys Wildwood was a big man, as big and strong as a smith should be, and he was usually easygoing, gentle as large people often are, and smiling. But now he looked thoroughly upset.

Dinner was laid on the table. Meg had given up waiting, and had called Rhianna from her room. The chants and the spell ingredients and the tables of herbs were already blurring in Rhianna's mind, though she had spent *hours* saying them over and over. They lay like cold wet stones in her head, heavy and slippery.

It worried her, but her father's face worried her far more.

"What's the matter, Loys?" Her mother's voice showed the same worry.

He tried to smile. "Oh, nothing. Just a problem at work."

"What sort of problem?" Meg Wildwood was a hard woman to shake off. Everyone said so.

"Just the new fire ward. It . . . won't work."

Rhianna knew what a fire ward was. It was a spell to

stop fires. Her father needed one, because the smithy had a fire going all the time, and there were houses all around. An accident might mean a bad fire.

Meg dished up peas. "I didn't know you needed a new one. Didn't you renew it just last month?" she asked.

Loys nodded. "Yes, I did. And it's failed already. I got Spellwright in to make it again, and he said he couldn't get it to work. He thinks the spot where I built the smithy is cursed. There's no magic there to make the spell, he said. It won't work, anyway."

Meg put down her spoon. "Won't work? That's not right. Spells have to work. If you make them properly, that is. Perhaps you —"

Loys shook his head. "Look, all I can tell you is what Spellwright told me. I'm no magician. He said there's no magic in that spot, and if I want the smithy insured against fire, I'll have to move it. I can't afford to move it, and I can't afford the risk of not having a fire-ward spell. I don't know what to do about it."

No magic there at all? Rhianna stared at her parents. Loys looked at his plate, glum and silent, and Meg watched him in turn, for what seemed like a long time.

Then Meg seemed to shake herself. She dipped into her pocket and pulled out the letter. The paper tore across as she brought it out.

Loys glanced at it. "What's that?" he asked.

"It is . . . well, it used to be . . . a letter from Mrs. Greenapple. Saying that Rhianna is doing very badly at school, and warning . . ."

Loys took the paper from her. He held it in two fingers, and it tore under its own weight. "It came home like this?" he asked. "Brown, tatty, falling apart?"

"Yes. Strange, isn't it? As if the writing spell was . . . was . . ."

"Failing." They sat in silence around the table, and the silence echoed back at them.

Then Loys nodded, as if to himself. "Spellwright says he's asked for a wizard to come out from the Queen's own court. All the way from Avalon. Something has to be done, he says. Too many spells have failed lately. It doesn't bother me much, except for this fire ward, but everyone else is suffering."

That was all he said for the rest of dinner. Afterward, Rhianna excused herself and went back to her room to work on her books again. It was just as it had been before. The spells skittered around in her head like a flock of chickens, hard to tell apart, always just a little out of reach, struggling and wriggling even when she caught one.

At bedtime her mother came in to say good night, as usual. A little line came and went on her forehead, smoothing out when she thought of it, returning after a moment.

"Time for bed, Rhianna," she said. "You've done as much as you can tonight."

Rhianna got up and washed her hands and face in the basin. She put on her nightgown.

"Mother?" she asked.

"Yes?"

"Do you think I'll have to do the year's work all over again?"

Meg sighed. "I don't know, Rhianna. I can't think just now. Go and say good night to your father."

So Rhianna padded out, kissed her father good night, and went to bed. But not to sleep, not at once. She kept saying the spells and the chants and the lists of spell in-gredients over and over to herself, in the hope that they'd stick, but in between them came the worried look on her father's face and what he had said at dinner: *Too many spells have failed lately.*

Including all of Rhianna's spells. Maybe it wasn't all her fault, then. Maybe the magic itself was at fault. Or just the magic hereabouts. Maybe magic itself was the wrong thing to do. Well, it certainly didn't make people better, or any easier to like. Think of Mr. Spellwright. And Rory.

Or maybe it was just the wrong thing for her. After

all, she might not be suited to using magic at all. Like Father. He was a smith, and a good one. Using cold iron all the time meant that he could not weave spells, not even the little ones that most people used, because cold iron and magic were sort of opposites that canceled each other out. Maybe she could become a lady blacksmith.

She fell asleep thinking about that.

CHAPTER 3

The next morning, Rhianna lined up outside her classroom with the others. She hadn't slept well. Her dreams
had been about things running away and getting less and
less. Sand running out of hourglasses; water leaking away
from dams. And it was Wednesday, and that meant Conjuration, first thing. Rhianna hated Conjuration. It was
worse than all her other subjects. The hand movements
had to be done just right, depending on the phase of the
moon and when your birthday was and whether your
hair was light or dark and all sorts of other silly things she
could never remember.

So she didn't notice anything when they went in, and
only looked around when she heard the class murmur.
Then she saw it. Mrs. Greenapple had washed the spellboard. Mrs. Greenapple only washed the board just before the holidays, or if someone important was visiting
the school. And it was still the middle of the term.

But the spellboard was washed and the floor had been swept and polished. More than that, Mrs. Greenapple seemed different. She had to start the opening invocation again, because she said the words the wrong way round the first time. She was wearing her best cape, too, the one she only wore to the opening of term and Parents' Night.

There was no Conjuration period, either, not straight away. Instead, Mrs. Greenapple took a firm grasp on her wand, waited until the class had settled, and then spoke: "Make sure your desks and chairs are neat, please. If there are any class library books, please put them back on the shelves now."

"Miss, I haven't finished reading mine." That was Merry Gladbetook, who read everything and remembered it all, like a sponge soaking up water.

"Nobody has finished, Merry. But I want the books all neatly put away. The school has a very important visitor this morning."

So that was what it was all about. Rhianna tidied her desk. At least it meant they wouldn't have so long for Conjuration.

When they had finished tidying up, Mrs. Greenapple looked at the sundial on the wall outside, across the courtyard. "All right," she called. "We'll start Conjuration, just to show our visitor what we can do, if he arrives. Get out your wands and spellbooks and turn to page fifty-three. The heading is 'Simple fire ward.' Quickly, now."

Despite herself, Rhianna felt a stir of interest. She turned the pages of her spellbook. A fire ward. That was the same sort of spell as the one that Father had had trouble with. Perhaps she could see what was wrong with it. She might even be able to help him.

She found the place and raised her head. Mrs. Greenapple was starting the first series of gestures. "Palms together, like this, fingers pointing upwards. Now, keeping your hands joined at the base, flutter your fingers for four beats."

Rhianna watched much more closely than usual and followed Mrs. Greenapple with care. A flicker of the fingers to show the fire, and then a soothing, broad sweep of the arms to show it being snuffed out. Fanning the face to invoke the heat of the flames, and hands across the eyes to show the sharp, burning glow. Now, water signs: fingers twitching, hands falling to show rain. A rolling of the arms and shoulders to invoke the waves of the sea. Rhianna watched Mrs. Greenapple's hands and did everything she did, making sure the water gestures were stronger than the fire gestures, so that the fire would be put out. Perhaps she should make them a little stronger still, to be perfectly sure. . . .

She was concentrating hard, trying to get it all exactly right, just this once. Concentrating so hard that she didn't hear Rose's yelp of surprise. She didn't even feel the first drops of rain.

It wasn't until she heard the first little clap of thunder that she realized something was amiss. There was a *phut!* sound, like a bag of sand being dropped on a floor. Then a sharp spark of lightning.

The other children were edging away from her and pointing. Mrs. Greenapple had stopped conjuring and was staring at her. Or rather, she was staring at a place above Rhianna's head.

Rhianna looked up.

A cloud was floating between her and the ceiling. It was small but inky, like a mass of black cotton wool. As Rhianna watched, it grew even darker and expanded like a balloon being blown up. It spat a sudden fork of lightning, thin as a thread, but blue-white and dazzling. Another crackle of miniature thunder sounded. It began to rain harder.

And there was something on the floor, something clear and wobbly like a jelly, and it was coming towards her, leaving a trail of water that soaked into the floorboards. It rolled like a great big drop of water, but it was getting bigger and bigger, gathering itself from some place that Rhianna couldn't see. The rain from the cloud fell on it, and on her. She realized that she was soaked to the skin.

Mrs. Greenapple found her voice. "Out! Everyone out!" she cried. "Open the door!"

The door slammed open. The nearest children tumbled out, and the others followed, while Mrs. Greenapple waved her arms in drying gestures. She started a drying spell: *"Desicca inati evapo summa . . ."*

But the words took no hold. The bubble of water, clear as glass, slid up to Rhianna and rubbed itself against her like a cat, growing larger all the time. Rhianna couldn't move. She knew she ought to do something about this, and she knew, in some dark place in her mind, that this was all her fault, but she stood numb with surprise and dumb with amazement.

Then a shadow fell across her, and she heard a new voice.

"Dear me. What to-do."

Drenched, the water globe washing against her knees and seeping into her shoes, Rhianna turned and looked.

A little man stood there, framed by the door and the light from outside. He wore a tall pointed hat, black but blazing with the signs of the moon and the sun and the stars. To balance the hat, he had a long pointed beard, like corn silk near his mouth, but white as snow elsewhere. It was long enough to tuck into his belt. The belt was jeweled, and there were more jewels sewn into his dark robe and cape. He held a staff of silver-gray wood in one hand.

"Water elemental, eh?" He smiled. "My, this must be an *advanced* class. In my day we didn't summon elementals until we passed third degree at Wizardly College."

Mrs. Greenapple dashed water out of her eyes. "We didn't summon . . . I mean, we didn't *mean* to . . ." Her voice was high and panicky.

"Didn't mean to?" The little man's eyebrows climbed. "Then this is an accident? Dear me, your spell wards must have failed completely. You really should be more careful, you know. Dangerous beasties, elementals."

The water globe heaved and rippled. It was as high as Rhianna's thigh now, and still growing.

The little man gazed at Rhianna, at the thundercloud, at the driving rain inside the classroom, and then at Mrs. Greenapple. It seemed as though he were looking at something interesting and cheerful, like a ride at a carnival. He took a closer grip on his staff. "I say," he asked, "would you like me to . . . ?" He glanced at the globe of water and made shooing-away gestures with the staff.

Mrs. Greenapple nodded rapidly. "Please, oh, please, Magister. I can't seem to . . ."

"Oh, of course not. No. Not with a stronger witch summoning it. Now let me think. Hmm. Yes, I see. Young

Lady" — to Rhianna — "just you think of . . . ah . . . dry toast, for a moment. *Dry* toast, mind. And no tea."

Rhianna thought of toast. Dry, hard toast, without butter.

The globe of water drew off a little way. The rain might have eased a little.

"Ah," said the wizard, approving. *Magister,* Mrs. Greenapple had called him. That meant *"master."* "That's right. Now." He flung his cape wide and his staff leaped into the air, drawing a fiery circle there. His voice came, powerful, driving, different from the vague and absent-minded way he had spoken before. *"Dehydra diminisha dranus desicca . . ."*

The globe of water stopped growing. It began to shrink. Rhianna thought of dry toast as hard as she could. The cloud also shrank and lost its intense blackness. After a moment it became gray, and then it began to break up into smaller wisps and tendrils, which faded away as she watched.

The globe became smaller and smaller, draining away into what was apparently thin air. The Magister continued to chant. The globe continued to shrink. At last there was a faint *pop!* and the water elemental, which had become a bead on the floor, disappeared.

The Magister stopped his chant. The three of them stood and stared at each other, Rhianna in dumb horror,

Mrs. Greenapple as though unable to believe her own eyes, and the little magician with a certain self-satisfaction.

"Well, that's that," he said. "Although I must say it wasn't easy. No wonder you're having trouble with magic drain hereabouts."

Mrs. Greenapple looked around her, openmouthed. Everything in the classroom was wet. Her good cape was dripping about her shoulders. Her hair hung in rats' tails. And the important visitor to the school, the one she had wanted so badly to impress, was watching her. Her eyes drifted over the utter ruin of her classroom — the soaked books, the stuffed pelican that would never be the same again, the chalk marks on the floor that had run into a milky puddle, the spellboard that had been given another, quite unneeded, washing.

Her gaze came to Rhianna, standing alone and dripping in the middle of the room. Her mouth closed. She didn't know *how,* she didn't understand *why,* but she did know *who.*

"Rhianna!" Mrs. Greenapple's voice didn't often crack like that. "Mrs. Wesbarrow's room. March!"

Rhianna's shoulders slumped. She had no idea what she'd done, but she could only agree with Mrs. Greenapple. It was clearly the most dreadful thing that had ever happened in the history of the school, and it was all her doing. Tears prickled at the corners of her eyes.

The little magician saw them. "No, no. Dear girl. Cheerful. Smile, please. No tears. You'll bring it back again, and we mustn't have that. Like calls to like, you know. Be angry, if you must be anything. At least anger is a fire caller. We really can't do with any more water just now. Laugh, please, if you can."

Laugh? Rhianna had never felt less like laughing. She had turned in obedience to Mrs. Greenapple's order, and was halfway to the door where the master magician was standing. For all his obvious power, his face had uncertainty in it.

She stopped. "Excuse me, please," she said. "I need to go to Mrs. Wesbarrow's room." The thought made her chin wobble again.

The little magician flapped his hands like someone trying to chase hens out of the house. "Oh, yes, I suppose so. We'd better go together. And" — he glanced at Mrs. Greenapple — "we'd best ask the young lady's parents to come to the school as well, don't you think?" He smiled as he said it. *Almost twinkled,* Rhianna thought.

Mrs. Greenapple's mouth thinned out and became a flat line. "Certainly, Magister. I was about to suggest that. I'll call them on the spellcaster myself."

The Magister beamed at her. "Excellent!" he said. "Now, miss, if you'll just come along with me. . . ."

They marched across the open green together,

Rhianna on the Magister's right, close by his staff. Children stood in groups, talking excitedly. Rhianna couldn't watch them.

They passed Rory Spellwright, who sniggered and said something under his breath to Merry Gladbetook. Both boys laughed, and Rory called out: "Rhianna's goin' to get expelled, hah!"

The Magister stopped and faced him. "Ah?" he asked, mildly. "You seem to know all about it, my young friend. Why would that happen?"

Merry had enough brains not to say anything, but Rory's mouth had always ruled his head. "'Cause she's so-o-o stupid. Really, really thick. She'll have to go back to the city, an' good riddance." He laughed again.

Rhianna felt her insides curl up. She wanted to go somewhere, anywhere, and die.

"You think so?" asked the Magister. "But then, you would think that. It's wrong, of course, but *foolishness comes from the mouths of fools*." He seemed to grow suddenly taller, looming over them, dark and awesome. A cold wind sprang up out of nowhere. His voice deepened and took on the sound of distant thunder. "Your words are worth so little that I think it might be better if you spoke no more today, boy."

The staff in his hand started to glow. He raised it,

spoke a single word, and walked on. Rhianna went with him, looking over her shoulder at Rory and Merry.

Rory opened his mouth to speak, but nothing came out. Merry watched him with wide eyes. Still Rory tried to say something. He was *still* trying when Rhianna turned away from him.

"I do apologize for that," said the Magister. They had come to the door of Mrs. Wesbarrow's room. No one else was near, and Rhianna realized with a shock that the little magician was talking to her. He continued: "I really should keep my temper better." He tried to look severe with himself. "One must never use the power in anger, that's the first rule. You probably know that already."

Rhianna looked blank. She had never thought about such a thing.

"It was fun, though, you must admit," he went on, as though confessing to something. "And it will do that particular young fellow no harm at all to keep silence until the sun sets. By the way, my name is Northstar, Antheus Northstar. What's yours?"

Rhianna's mouth moved, just as Rory's had done. But she managed to find her voice. "Rhianna Wildwood, um, so please you, Magister."

He nodded vaguely. "Wildwood . . . Wildwood. That's your mother's name, of course. What was your father's?"

"Um . . . Periman, Magister."

"Ah. I should have known. Descendent of old Michaela Periman, I should think. High Witch of the White, and a great spellmaker. And Wildwood. Branch of the Hightree Wildwoods, I'll be bound. Strong High Elven strain on both sides, then. Your power's not to be wondered at."

My power? thought Rhianna bitterly. *My lack of power, you mean.* The knot in her stomach, which had slacked off a little, seemed to tighten again.

The Magister knocked twice on Mrs. Wesbarrow's door, and then threw it open and strode in. "Congratulations, colleague!" he boomed. "You must be very proud."

Mrs. Wesbarrow was a small, mousy woman with permanently pursed lips. She swung around from the spellcaster and blinked. "Proud?" she asked. *"Proud?"* Her eyebrows went up. "I've just been reading Ivy Greenapple's spellcast to Rhianna's parents. I can't imagine why you'd think I should be proud. Classroom soaked? *Water elemental?* Whatever next!" She glared at Rhianna. "You just wait until your parents get here, young lady. Why, I've a good mind to —"

Nobody would ever know what Mrs. Wesbarrow had a good mind to do. Magister Northstar's own eyebrows went up like snowflakes in a draft. "Dear lady," he said in the Wizard's Voice, the voice that stilled others, "I wonder if you understand what you have here. A Wild Talent is not seen frequently, but I had thought that teachers were trained to see the noses in front of their faces."

There was a moment of silence. "A Wild Talent?" Mrs. Wesbarrow asked, her voice high, almost squeaking. "I went to the lecture, but . . . a Wild Talent? I don't think I've ever seen one. Are you sure, Magister?"

Even Rhianna knew that one thing you must not do is ask a wizard what he knows or how he knows it. Magister Northstar frowned. "I am sure, madam," he said coldly, and that was the end of it.

CHAPTER 4

Loys and Meg Wildwood arrived to find the school deserted, the children taken on a sudden outing, and Rhianna's classroom being mopped out by the school caretaker, old Mr. Moss. He directed them to Mrs. Wesbarrow's room. "She'll be there, for sure," he remarked, chuckling.

Meg looked at her husband, stricken.

Loys set his jaw. "I don't believe it. She wouldn't have done this — in fact, I don't think she *could* do it. But she wouldn't, and that's the important thing. They've got it wrong, you'll see. I'll sort it out."

Meg caught his arm. "Be polite to them, Loys," she said. "They can —"

"I know, I know." He knocked on the head teacher's door.

They were expecting to see Rhianna in the corner,

Mrs. Wesbarrow with a face of thunder, and a distinguished wizard looking outraged. But when the door opened, there was their daughter, sitting and eating elfbread, and Mrs. Wesbarrow chuckling as if at a joke. As for the distinguished wizard, he was drinking tea and telling a story:

". . . never got over it, you know. Frogs everywhere. Frogs in the drainpipes, frogs in the sink. Frogs all over the spellroom floor. What was worse, they just kept popping out of nowhere. Hundreds of them. I have never seen a plague spell, you know, but I have an idea that it would be something like that. And that was the last, and only, time I saw a Wild Talent before today. At Wizardly College, when I was just a lad myself. Do you know, it took half the faculty to dispel the summoning, because the Talent couldn't stop thinking about frogs! Runes, books of spells, half a day of incantation, a pentacle of suppression, the lot. Never saw so much fuss. And the Talent, as I said, was a young fellow not quite right in the head . . ."

The Magister was seated in the only armchair, with his back to the door. Mrs. Wesbarrow glanced past him as the door opened. He noticed it, set his teacup down, and stood politely to meet the newcomers.

Rhianna stood, too, putting down her half-eaten

piece of elfbread. She had been enjoying herself, but the sight of her parents brought her troubles back with a rush.

"Rhianna?" her mother asked. "What *have* you been up to?"

The magician smiled. "Nothing at all, dear lady, except that she listened too carefully and copied her teacher too exactly."

There was a moment of silence, and then Mrs. Wesbarrow made introductions. Two more chairs had to be brought in. The little room was crowded. Magister Northstar resumed his place in the armchair. Although it was Mrs. Wesbarrow's room, there was no doubt who was in charge.

The Magister steepled his fingers and spoke. "Now, Mrs. and Mr. Wildwood. No doubt we shall have to confirm it, but there is no doubt in my mind, from the events of this morning, that your daughter is a Wild Talent. You've heard the term, I suppose?"

Loys and Meg glanced at each other. Both nodded.

Magister Northstar nodded in return. "But," he went on, "most people have never seen such a thing. A Wild Talent. Wild, meaning that it's difficult to control; Talent, meaning great power. I have a fair amount of power myself, but it has to be carefully shaped, like most people's. The right spells, the words and the pentacles and the conjurations and so forth. By using them, power can be called and then controlled. But Rhianna's Talent is more like the Old Magic, the magic that existed before the Magic Guild began to organize and channel it. It accepts no rules. It makes of itself what it wishes. Giving it spells and words and the rest only unleashes it, and the results can be frightening. That's what a Wild Talent is."

Loys and Meg exchanged another astonished glance. Meg leaned forward. "But, Magister, Rhianna . . . well, she's always had trouble with spells, and this year was worse than before. We were going to get her special tutoring."

The Magister waved one hand, palm towards her, as if to stop her from going on. "No, no, no! That would be the worst thing you could do. A Wild Talent? Special tutoring? Dear me! I'm very glad they called me in. In another year . . . well, who knows?" He took a sip of tea, and they watched him, frowning, puzzled.

He patted his lips with a napkin and continued. "Wild Talent is rare. There have been only two in the last thousand years with all their wits in the right place. One was the Archmagistra Selina of Sary."

"And the other?" Rhianna found herself asking him.

He turned and looked at her. "A man from Caradhas. You've never heard his name." His voice was flat certain.

Rhianna's puzzlement must have registered on her

face. The Magister's lips tightened. "He was never able to learn control. Or perhaps he never wanted to learn it. At any rate, he went to the bad, a thousand years ago. It took the College, the Queen's army, the Ring of the Sea, and the life of the hero Tam Longstrider to sink his black castle beneath the waves. And he may be there yet, brooding under the sea, waiting for the day when the Land is swallowed up by the waters and the Wild Magic is loosed on the world again."

The bright room darkened a little. There was silence, and the Magister brooded.

"And you're saying that Rhianna is like them?" Loys Wildwood hardly seemed to believe his own words.

The Magister shook himself. "Well. That much, I don't know and cannot say." He looked at Mrs. Wesbarrow. "What I *am* saying is that I'm sure she has a Wild Talent. It would explain much. As for having all her wits, I think you're the best judges of that."

There was another silence. Rhianna was thinking: *So maybe I'm not so dumb after all?*

"At any rate, it will be necessary to remove her from school for a few days while I do what I can. And then she must be taught in a special class. One of her own." Those calm words made everyone stare. Magister Northstar stared back, as if he had said nothing unusual. "Obviously," he added, and sipped his tea again.

"Ah . . ." Loys Wildwood looked doubtfully at his wife. "We did want her to have an education, Magister. Perhaps a special class would not be . . ."

"We have no such facilities . . ." began Mrs. Wesbarrow.

The wizard held up a hand. "Please. It will be a special class because she must learn different things from other children. Other children, with small power, as most of us have, must learn how to make the most of it. With Rhianna, the problem is different. She doesn't need spells and ingredients and pentacles and spellchanting. *She must learn control* — never to use any more magic than she absolutely must, never to take more than the least amount possible, and to bind with bands of iron what she does use." He smiled at Rhianna. "But she can learn the first steps here, among her friends. In years to come, perhaps, she will come to Wizardly College to study further."

Rhianna watched him, a little nervous of him despite the smile. "It sounds hard," she said.

He nodded. "It is. It is a difficult art, a hard road. But do you know, there is a law of magic: *Magic is never more than will.* If you will it so, you can control it. Your will is strong enough."

Meg leaned forward. "But what about a properly qualified teacher? No offense, Mrs. Wesbarrow."

The Magister pursed his lips. "Well, in one sense, I imagine that I am properly qualified to teach. At least, I should think so. If not, perhaps as Chancellor of Wizardly College, I could award myself some more diplomas. And so are her teachers here. In a different sense, though, nobody is qualified to teach Rhianna. A lot of what she must learn, she must come to herself." He frowned. "It is a lonely path, but she need not walk it entirely alone. I will go the first steps with her myself. Indeed, I think it would be best if I were to take her as an apprentice. It would give her a sort of bond with me, and another outlet for her power."

Silence. Loys cleared his throat. "Well, Magister, we'll think about what you say . . ."

The Magister was shaking his head. "I'm afraid there is no choice. Her power must be controlled, and it must be done now." He said it quietly, with sorrow.

Loys swelled, turning red. "What do you mean, no choice?" he demanded. "Look here, I don't know who you are, and I don't know who you *think* you are, but you can't just come in here . . ."

Magister Northstar gazed at him, his eyes huge and commanding, and the little room and the sunlight and the walls and the furniture faded away and were lost. Loys stuttered to a stop.

Magister Northstar spoke, his voice slow as ages and

heavy as doom. "I'm afraid I can, and I must." He sighed. "Although I do ask your pardon. I seem to have expressed myself poorly. When I said that there was no choice, I meant it not only for her." He turned to Rhianna, who sat gazing at him with her mouth open. "It's required, you see, for the Land itself."

Mrs. Wesbarrow took a hand. "Do you mean, Magister, that Rhianna's Talent must be tamed, or it will be a danger to her — and to others?"

"Mm? Oh, yes. That, too. But the real reason is quite different. You see, the country around here can't supply her."

"Can't supply her?"

"Yes. With enough power for her Talent. Talent seeks power, you see. Calls it up out of the ground, the air, the water. Rhianna's Talent is calling up that power and storing it. What might happen if it should all come out at once, I hate to think. But as she is taking up the power from the country around her, there's less for everyone else." He smiled a little. "They called me all this way to ask me why spells are failing hereabouts, and I walked in on the reason, not even knowing."

Loys and Meg stared at their daughter. Rhianna stared back. Her mind ran on like a rat in a cage.

Loys moistened his lips. "You mean . . . ?" he asked.

The Magister nodded. "Yes. The reason why your

spells are failing is sitting in that chair. It's Rhianna. And that's why I must do all in my power to control her magic. I will help her in any way I can, but by my oath as Wizard and as Mage on the Queen's Council, my first duty is to the Land and the Realm. That's what I meant about there being no choice. Control her power I must, or the Realm will suffer. And it must be done as soon as may be."

CHAPTER 5

"Oh, dear. Oh, *dear!* Oh, good heavens!"

Magister Northstar hopped from one foot to the other. A canary clung to the end of his staff. Two more settled on his pointed hat. Another dozen popped out of thin air in a whirl of lemon-yellow feathers. They joined the throng in front of Rhianna, whistling impatiently, pattering on the tiled floor. Small groups took off to fly around the room.

Rhianna stared at them in dismay. Already the kitchen of her house looked like the center of a lemon-drop snowstorm.

"Avaunt!" cried the Magister. "Rhianna, think of . . . um . . . something heavy. But don't think too hard." He made passes with his staff, the canaries fluttering around him. "Blast! The pentacle isn't holding them at all."

"The canaries aren't magical themselves, Magister," Rhianna reminded him.

"Oh, dear! Of course not. Get off! Shoo!" The canaries on his staff flew off to join the others, a whirling yellow cloud. More kept appearing, though not as fast. "Now. *Unflutter by butterfly unwingless belessing . . .*"

Rhianna thought of heavy things. Big, clumsy, gray, heavy things. Then, because she did not want to start summoning elephants, she thought of stars and planets, and then of other things as far removed from canaries as possible. The Magister chanted, and the flow of canaries slowed, became a trickle, and finally stopped. He chanted another line to make sure before falling silent, pushing back his tall hat and wiping his forehead on a large cotton handkerchief he had pulled from the pocket of his robe. Finally he used his staff to trace the rune Liss, the rune of guarding, on the place in the air where the canaries had been appearing. Glowing slightly, it hovered for a few moments before fading.

The Magister found a chair and collapsed onto it, fanning himself with his hat. Canaries flew in clouds around the room, piping and calling. The air was full of the sound of whirring wings.

"Open a window or two, there's a girl," he said. "That unsummoning spell has quite drained me. You're getting stronger all the time, you know."

Rhianna jumped up and did as he asked. The butter-colored cloud began to thin as canaries in singles, pairs, and small groups took their leave, flying out of the windows. Magister Northstar looked up at them fluttering into the bright sky. "Thank heavens it isn't nighttime," he said after a minute or so. "We'd never get rid of them." He pulled his hat on again. "Right, now. How did that happen? We were supposed to be getting lemons, you know. Not much harm in lemons, and you can sell them." He looked at Rhianna severely.

Rhianna started to hunch her shoulders, just as she used to, but she remembered that Magister Northstar disliked that habit very much. She tried not to scowl, as well. Still, it was difficult to stare straight at him. "I — I think it was the birds singing in the trees outside while I said the spell, Magister. I thought, just for a moment, how pretty they sounded, and it got mixed-up with the lemons in my mind, and so . . ."

"We got a flock of lemon-colored birds. A great big flock of them." Magister Northstar nodded. "Well, it makes sense. I suppose I should be thankful that we're not close enough to the river for you to hear the sound of the water. We'd have drowned before I could have done anything sensible. And in lemonade, too. Well, you'd best come away. So strong a summoning must have lowered your own reserves, for the time being."

He pushed open the door and ushered Rhianna out into the back garden. Once there, he muttered a simple call spell, and the remaining canaries flew out of the windows in clouds. They settled on the grass in front of him or perched in nearby hedges, whistling and calling. "Is that all of them?" he asked wearily.

Rhianna looked, and nodded.

The Magister let the spell lapse and the birds began to fly off in all directions. Then he stood, leaning on his staff for a moment. "Come along, Rhianna," he said.

They passed through the back gate and into the meadow beyond, the Magister silent, walking, his staff making his pace. Rhianna was silent, too. She twisted her fingers together and wondered what she could do to make things better.

"Control, Rhianna," the Magister said after a while. "How is it to be controlled?" He walked on a few more paces. "That was a case of using too much magic," he said. "You put too much power into the summoning spell. And the summon wasn't exact enough. You didn't have the right thing in your mind."

He frowned, then stopped short. "The right thing in your mind?" he murmured. "Or the thing right in your mind? Hmm. I wonder." He pulled off his hat, looked at it, and put it back on again. "I asked you to summon lemons. How often do you see lemons?"

Rhianna shrugged. "Not very often, Magister. There

are no lemon trees here — I think it's too cold for them. But I know what lemons look like. There's a picture in one of my books."

The Magister nodded. "Ah. I think I see. And I understand what my error was. How could I ask you to summon something you knew only from pictures? You have to . . . ah! That's it!" He clapped his hands together, a sharp sound, letting go of his staff to do it. The staff stayed in place, upright.

Rhianna watched him. He was squinting off into the distance, where the sun shone above the far hills.

They were on the top of the slope that led down to the village. Smallhaven lay in a little valley that ran down to the sea. Rhianna's home was up on the slope above the village, and from the meadow you could look down onto the cottage roofs. You could see the pier where fishing boats unloaded their catch, a row of houses along the harbor wall, and then the single cobbled street that led away from the shore like the downstroke on the letter T. The school, the inn, and the few shops — and Loys Wildwood's smithy — lined that street, before it broadened out to become the village green and marketplace. Around the green stood more houses, and then the street became a road that turned left and wandered up the valley toward the farms and the hills. Beyond the hills, tall mountains ranged, blue with distance, snowcapped. Wild country lay out there, with strange people and stranger things than they. Trolls, some said. Faerie folk. Dragons.

Magister Northstar stared as if he wasn't watching any of that. He was stroking his beard. Then he nodded once, sharply. "We'll try again tomorrow, Rhianna, when I have finished the binding spell to apprentice you. I need some ivy tendrils and a swan's feather for that. I suppose the spell shop in the village will have them. Come to think of it, I'll need Mr. Spellwright's signature on the apprenticeship paper. It has to be witnessed by a wizard. When I've done that, I'll have some control over your magic, and I'll set you a task that should be a little easier."

Rhianna said nothing. She wasn't sure she understood, exactly.

The next morning, the Magister came early to the Wildwoods' cottage, and he and Rhianna walked down to the village with Meg, who would sign the papers, too. They waved to Loys, who was hard at work in the smithy, and then crossed the street and entered the spell shop.

It was as if Mr. Spellwright hadn't moved since Rhianna had seen him last. He was leaning on his counter, gazing towards the door. The shop, as usual, was dim and cool, although the morning sun was bright at the windows.

Magister Northstar nodded politely, and an odd sort of expression came to Mr. Spellwright's face. A frown, almost, but then it cleared, and his mouth stretched sideways. A gold tooth winked in the gloom. Rhianna realized that Mr. Spellwright was smiling. He removed his hands from the counter and clasped them in front of his chest, bending slightly from the waist.

"Good morning, colleague!" Magister Northstar greeted him. "I wonder if you could oblige me with two handspans of ivy tendrils — fresh, if you have them, but dried will do — and a swan's pinion feather. A mute swan, mind. For a binding spell for an apprentice, you understand."

Mr. Spellwright stopped smiling. He looked from Magister Northstar to Rhianna and then back again. He blinked, and it couldn't have been because of the light. "An apprentice binding? For her?" he asked.

"Yes, indeed. For Rhianna. I'll be apprenticing her — and I'm certain that the village will have cause to be proud of her. And I'll ask you to witness the paper, if you would."

Mr. Spellwright moistened his lips, made to speak, hesitated, and then leaned forward, as if to speak privately into Magister Northstar's ear. But the Magister drew back, and Mr. Spellwright had no choice but to say it out loud: "Well, actually, Magister, I was meaning to ask you about apprenticing my nephew Rory. A smart lad, that, well ahead in his studies. I'm sure he'd make a fine —"

The Magister shook his head. "I'm sorry, colleague, but I do not normally accept apprentices. Miss Wildwood here is a special case. No doubt your nephew is a fine student; I'll send you the names of any of the magicians in Avalon who are looking for an apprentice. But for now, all I need is the ingredients I mentioned, if you would oblige me, please."

Mr. Spellwright straightened. He tugged at his apron. His eyes rested for a moment on Rhianna and her mother, and then returned to Magister Northstar. The Magister raised one tufted eyebrow, just a little, and Mr. Spellwright nodded jerkily.

"Just a moment," he mumbled. "Not much call for swan feathers. They're at the back."

He had to use a pair of steps to bring a jar down from a top shelf, but he produced a long white feather and a moment later some pieces of dried tendril that Rhianna supposed must be ivy. She knew what these were for: ivy to bind, a mute swan's feather to keep secrets.

Magister Northstar nodded his thanks and put down a silver coin. He drew a rolled-up paper from his pocket and placed it flat on the counter, where Mr. Spellwright had a quill pen and ink. The Magister dipped the quill in the ink and signed his name at the bottom of the paper.

"You sign here, Rhianna . . . that's right. Now you, Mrs. Wildwood. Thank you. And now, if you would witness it, Mr. Spellwright . . . ?"

Mr. Spellwright took the quill and looked down at the paper. He coughed. "Are you quite sure about this, Magister . . . colleague? It seems a little —"

Magister Northstar raised both eyebrows this time. He studied Mr. Spellwright's face as if he wanted to remember it. "I thank you for your opinion, Mr. Spellwright, even though I did not ask for it. But I am quite sure. I only require you to witness the deed, not to approve of it. Please do as I ask."

Rhianna heard the chill in his voice. She hoped she would never hear it meant for her.

Mr. Spellwright hesitated a bare moment longer, then bent and signed the paper in a hurried scrawl.

Magister Northstar blew on the ink to dry it, and then carefully tore it down the center. He gave one half to Rhianna, and put the other in his pocket. He nodded to Mr. Spellwright. "I thank you," he said coolly. "Come, Rhianna. There's a good charcoal fire in your father's forge. Good day, Mr. Spellwright."

CHAPTER 6

Unlike Mr. Spellwright's shop, the smithy was always warm. It was sunlit, too, with an open front so that you could watch people passing in the street. Folk walked by, and most waved or called a greeting. A long, narrow charcoal fire burned in a brick tub, and Loys Wildwood pumped the bellows with his foot to heat iron until it glowed like the setting sun before he beat it into shape with his hammers.

He was finishing a set of firedogs when his wife and daughter came in with the Magister, and they watched as he shaped the bar iron. Firedogs were racks to hold a burning log in a fireplace. They were just iron bars, really, but they stood on either side of the fire, and they were made to look like long, thin dogs, with noses and tails that pointed upward to hold the log in place. Rhianna smiled as she saw them emerge, paws and eyes and ears and noses, under her father's skilled hands. Or rather, under his hammer, nippers, chisel, and punch, for these dogs were made of red-hot iron. Blacksmithing was a great skill, and it suddenly came to her that it was as great and as useful as magic itself.

Loys held the glowing iron in his tongs, looked at it from various angles, and nodded, satisfied. He plunged the finished dog into the water barrel to quench it, and a cloud of steam went up.

"I've always wondered how they did that," said Magister Northstar, admiration in his voice.

Loys Wildwood laughed. "No great trick for a wizard, sir," he said. He wiped his brow with a handful of tow, his broad face good-humored.

"I wouldn't say that," answered the Magister. "I couldn't make so much as an iron nail, and I have the feeling that cold iron may be more than my art, in time to come. But we have come to do some magic here. I didn't feel like doing it in Spellwright's shop."

"Just imagine, Loys," said Meg, "Mr. Spellwright wanted Magister Northstar to apprentice Rory, his nephew, instead of Rhianna. He was quite insistent."

"Rory Spellwright? The one with the shifty eyes?" Loys looked annoyed. "You, er, didn't . . ."

"No, I did not," answered Magister Northstar stoutly.

"And I am about to work the apprentice binding here and now. I wonder if I might borrow the fire, just for a moment. So long as I touch no iron, it should be perfect."

The apprenticing spell took only a few minutes. Magister Northstar said the words, the ivy and the feather were burned, and master and new apprentice breathed in a little of the smoke. Rhianna's parents watched with pride as their daughter was made into the official pupil of the highest wizard in the Realm. They knew, and she knew, that her life would never be the same again.

Still, Magister Northstar's eyes widened as some of Rhianna's power flowed into him, and his staff flared a little. "Whoo!" he puffed. Color came and went in his cheeks. "Just as well I was fairly drained. You're like a roaring great fire, Rhianna. We'll have to try to cool you off before you cook yourself."

Rhianna nodded. She didn't want to be cooked. And she was eager to get on. They took leave of the smithy, Loys Wildwood tousling his daughter's hair with a big, gentle hand.

They returned to the cottage and sat at the kitchen table. They would not be summoning lemons this time, Magister Northstar explained.

"Control, Rhianna. You need to control. There's only one way to control, and that's to shape the magic you use just exactly right for whatever you want to use it for.

Never too much of it, never the wrong shape or size or style or type. To know those things, to know just how much to use, you must know exactly the thing you are trying to spell. Other people can afford to be sloppy. For them, it hardly matters. Not you. Your knowledge must be exact."

"Exact?" Rhianna's ears pricked up. "I can be exact? I can say exactly what I mean?"

He nodded. "Yes. That's what you have to do. Any magic that doesn't exactly fit the spell is uncontrolled. And it would be very bad if your magic went out of control."

He frowned, but Rhianna almost laughed. *How funny,* she thought. *All I ever wanted was to have rules that made sense and didn't change. And now I've got one.*

"So," he continued, "we need to start you off with something you know very well indeed. Something you see every day, something that's part of you. But nothing too heavy or sharp or dangerous. What's that yeasty smell, Mrs. Wildwood, by the way?"

Meg smiled. "It's the bread sitting in the pan by the window, Magister. I've just punched it down so it's ready for its second rising. Now, I'll leave you to it. I have to pick some beans for dinner." She stepped outside.

Magister Northstar removed the cloth that covered the bread dough and brought the pan over to the table.

339

"The very thing. What could be simpler, what could be more familiar, or safer, than rising bread? Eh, Rhianna?"

Rhianna nodded doubtfully. It was true, she had helped her mother knead dough and bake bread before. It was something she was familiar with, and a rising spell wasn't difficult. A good cook could produce a sponge cake so light it nearly floated away.

They went over what she needed to do. No words or spells. She would use the Wild Magic on its own, just a very little of it, to make the bread rise. Magister Northstar readied a counterspell and nodded.

Rhianna concentrated on the bread dough. It stirred slightly. She reached out for it in her mind and felt how it was, warm and squishy and heavy. It should be lighter, more airy.

As she thought that, she felt a trickle of magic. Just the tiniest bit. The dough began to rise slowly, getting larger and bulkier. Rhianna grinned. It was working!

The dough shook itself, trembled, seemed to quiver — and then it slowly unstuck itself from the bread pan and began to float gently up toward the ceiling. Rhianna shook her head at it. That wasn't supposed to happen! *Not like that. I said light, but not so light you float.* The dough darkened alarmingly, becoming shiny and solid. Rhianna frowned. *No, no, you're supposed to rise. Not like that.* She made a movement and her concentration broke. The magic tumbled out of her like water over the top of a dam.

The dough shot up, obeying Rhianna's last thought. It took off like a rocket, faster and faster, streaking towards the ceiling. Rhianna jerked her head up to follow it, but it was only a brown blur when it hit. There was a loud crack, a rending crash, and, just after that, another crashing sound. Plaster and bits of wood rained down. Then a slate, from the roof above their heads. It fell through the hole in the ceiling and shattered on the floor.

Magister Northstar jumped and peered upwards. Plaster dust was still sifting down, but he squinted through the hole in the roof into the patch of bright blue sky overhead. When nothing more happened, he slumped in relief.

He turned to see Meg Wildwood standing in the doorway, openmouthed, staring at the hole in her kitchen ceiling.

Magister Northstar winced. Again he looked after the rocketing ball of dough. "I can't see it anymore. I doubt if it'll stop before it reaches the moon," he remarked, and then, to Meg, "I do apologize, dear lady. My fault entirely. I'll just step down to the village and ask the local tiler to call around and repair the hole. I'm sure he will drop everything else for me. I'll call in at the baker's, too, for another loaf of bread. Come along, Rhianna."

And he hustled her out the door before her mother could say anything.

On the road, he removed his hat, scratched his head, and looked at Rhianna. "Well, that does it. I was watching every moment, and I didn't have a chance to do anything sensible at all. It happened too fast for either of us. You have too much power. It's like trying to paper over a volcano."

Rhianna couldn't hide her disappointment. Her lip trembled. A fat tear escaped and rolled down her cheek. "It was going so well, at first," she faltered. Magister Northstar offered her his handkerchief, and she wiped her eyes.

"There, there." He patted her shoulder. "It's not your fault. It's the magic itself. It won't be confined or controlled. It insists on coming out in larger and larger amounts, just as it wants to." But he was speaking in a distracted sort of way, and it was clear that he was worried.

"What can I do?" wailed Rhianna. "It's too strong for me. It feels as if I'm trying to ride a horse that I can't control — and it keeps running away with me." She wiped her eyes again.

The wizard stroked his beard. He nodded. "You're right. I was a fool to think you could manage this in a week or two. Nobody could do that. It's my own fault. I had no idea how hard it would be."

Rhianna sniffled into the handkerchief. Magister Northstar watched her sympathetically. They stopped walking and stood under a shady tree, so that nobody would see her.

"There's nothing else for it," the Magister continued, after a moment. "You're too strong. If this goes on . . . well, anything might happen. Like that water elemental you called. There are other things that might answer when you call, and many of them are worse than elementals. Much worse." He shuddered, and a shadow fell over the sunny sky. The mountains loomed blue in the distance. He seemed to shake himself. "If it will not allow control, then it must be shackled, just as you tie up a horse that kicks."

"Shackled?"

"Yes. I don't like it, because so great a Talent as yours, Rhianna, should be used. But so be it. We can delay no longer."

Rhianna felt her face grow tight around the eyes. He noticed it. "Oh, don't worry," he soothed her. "I won't take your gift away. Indeed, I can't. But we have to stop what it's doing — collecting power from everything around you. You're taking up much of the supply for the whole district, you know. The more power you collect, the more it's going to overflow — and there's no knowing where it will go, or what it will do."

"So," Rhianna asked carefully, "what will *you* do?"

He sighed and looked away. "It will mean a special sort of spell. Power comes from the Land, from the earth, the water, and the air. Well, what we will do is make a device, a thing you wear all the time, like a ring or a locket. It will be pretty — I'm sure I can choose something that you will like — but it will have a spell on it. We can't stop your Talent from taking up power, but we can store the power in the jewel, and then empty it out from time to time, like bailing water out of a boat. Better to fix the boat so that it doesn't leak, but at least bailing it out stops it from sinking. As long as you bail the water out as fast as it comes in."

Rhianna thought about it. "But if you did that, I'd have no magic at all."

Magister Northstar looked down and shuffled his feet. "Um. Yes. That's true. But if we do it any other way, the power will simply build up again. Until it overflows again. And sinks your boat."

"Oh." Rhianna frowned.

Magister Northstar misunderstood the frown. "Um . . . yes, I can see how that would worry you." He smiled, a little uncertainly.

Rhianna's head was aching, and a tight little dry feeling scratched at the back of her eyes. It had been a long week, and a hard one. "You're worried about what will happen if I don't wear this thing all the time," she said. "Worried that I'll be difficult about it. Because if I am, you won't know what to do next."

Magister Northstar raised his eyebrows. His staff was leaning against the tree, as always within his reach. His hand moved toward it, and then withdrew. For a moment he had seemed to grow taller, just as he had when he had struck Rory Spellwright dumb. Then he sighed, and the moment passed.

"I'll try no wizardly tricks on you, Rhianna," he said. "No fooling, either. You're too sharp, and anyway, you're my apprentice."

Watching him, Rhianna suddenly saw that he was indeed only a little man, and that his spangled robe and his staff and his tall hat didn't really matter. What mattered was that he was a wizard on the inside as well.

It was with his eyes on the staff that the Magister spoke: "I am the Chancellor of Wizardly College and the Mage on the Queen's Council. I speak for the magic of the Realm. You are my apprentice, and I am responsible for you. I will not allow you to come to harm; and yet my first duty is to the Realm itself." He looked at Rhianna. "And you are a danger to it."

Rhianna's lip quivered. "I don't —" she started.

He waved a hand. "Oh, you don't mean to be. Not at all. I know you now, Rhianna Wildwood, and I'd trust your heart to the end of the world. But magic needs more than heart. It needs a firm, sure hand. It needs skill. You will learn the skill — but until you do, you are in danger, and you are dangerous." He sighed. "So far, the things that have gone wrong have been little things, and funny, really. But sooner or later something serious will happen. It might be anything, but whatever it is, it will be wild and strong. Fearful, too. At least, *I* fear it."

Rhianna nodded. "I fear it, too, Magister," she said.

"That's wise. So will you wear this trinket?"

She thought, and then decided. "Yes," she said.

CHAPTER 7

"It's the Law of Magical Means," said Magister Northstar. "The greater the magic, the more costly the piece. Rhianna's power is very great, though at present uncontrolled. The magic of any jewel that stores it will take the whole College the better part of a day to make, and therefore the piece must be of the very highest quality. I must go at once to have it made — in Avalon. I'll be sailing on the evening tide. There is no time to waste."

It was later that day. Magister Northstar was explaining matters to Rhianna's parents. He sipped rushwash tea and sat back. They looked at him, and then at each other.

"Will Rhianna be going with you?" asked Loys, in the sort of voice that meant he was going to argue if Magister Northstar said yes.

The little wizard shook his head. "I would not take a child from her family and home without the clearest need. I'll go myself, have the jewel made and bespelled, and send it back with some other things. Lessons for Rhianna, and a spellcaster that will reach me at any hour of the day or night."

He sighed. "I've been away longer than I planned. There'll be a mountain of work on my desk, and in three days there is the monthly meeting of the Queen's Council. I cannot miss that." He smiled at Rhianna. "I'll look in again as soon as I can — within a month, hopefully. Meanwhile, wear the jewel that I shall send. Do the lessons — you can work on them at school. I'll send them to your teacher. You must go to Mr. Spellwright every week to have the jewel drained of magic. He can do that. I've just spent some time instructing him. An odd fellow."

Later they saw Magister Northstar down to the harbor. It was evening, and the first stars were twinkling. The ship that would take him across the water to Home Island and Avalon was waiting.

At the head of the pier Magister Northstar put a hand briefly on Rhianna's brow. "A blessing," he murmured. "And no taking the jewel off, Rhianna. Not until you've mastered your magic. Mr. Spellwright will have a lot to drain and return, I can see that. Good night to you all. Expect my packet in four days."

He turned and stepped down into the ship. The sailors cast off, and the sail rose to the evening breeze.

The steersman leaned on the tiller. A few moments later Rhianna could see nothing of the wizard but the pale glow of his staff. It lifted in farewell.

Rhianna spent the four days fretting and waiting, thinking about magic as little as possible. But on the fourth day the packet arrived, as well as another one addressed to Mrs. Wesbarrow at the school.

There were two small boxes and a letter in the Wildwoods' parcel. The letter read:

Greetings.

Please forgive this short scribble. Here is the magic-storing jewel I promised. Rhianna is to wear it at all times except when it is being drained out. Here, also, is the spellcaster, which has its own instructions. If there is any problem, any problem at all, you are to call me at once, at any hour.

I have sent lessons to Rhianna's teacher. We will be starting with simple, familiar things — the meadows around your own house. I will check with her, and with you, every week, by spellcast.

Remember, Rhianna, exactness. If you are to achieve control, you must know exactly what you are trying to do.

In haste,
A. Northstar.

One of the boxes was small, square, and wooden. In it was a globe of glass and a slip of paper. Meg read the paper and nodded.

"Not too difficult," she said. "What's in the other?"

It was a flat boxwood case with a clasp. Rhianna opened it, and it was as if the sun had just peeped above the sea. She heard her mother's sudden inward breath.

Lying on a silk lining was a pendant on a chain. The chain was fine gold. In every third link a deep red stone glowed like a drop of blood, and in the middle of the chain . . .

It was a rune, the rune Liss, the sign of warding and guarding, a shape like a straighter letter S turned on its side, with two dots, one inside each curve. But this shape was made of gold, and the two dots were jewels, larger than the others. They had fire like a dragon's heart at their centers.

It was the most beautiful work of hands that Rhianna had ever seen. She reached out a finger to it, almost fearing to touch it, and then looked up at her mother.

Meg Wildwood's face showed her amazement. "He asked what your birthday was. June the twenty-third, a fire month and a fire day. Your birthstone is the greatest of the fire stones: ruby. You were born on a Sunday, the day of gold. I'd say that jewel is made of real rubies and solid gold. It must be almost beyond price, something fit for the Queen to wear." She was whispering, as though she feared to make noise.

Rhianna looked down at the beautiful thing in the box. A little voice sounded in her mind: *Don't forget, this is to stop you from having any magic at all. This is to take it all away.* She reached out and picked it up. It lay warm in her hand.

The moment she touched it, it seemed to her that a background noise she had always heard had stopped. It was as if there were some change in the light of the day. She looked around at the familiar kitchen and it was just the same. The sun was not less bright, but something was different.

Well, what else would you expect? she asked herself. The jewel was magical, after all. She put the chain around her neck so that the rune sparkled at her throat.

"Do up the clasp for me, please, Mother," she said.

Two weeks later Rhianna lay on her stomach, her workbook open in front of her, in the grassy meadow by the schoolhouse. Her class was learning Spellcasting this morning, but she had her own work to do.

She was drawing a long grass leaf that she had plucked. She drew it with great care, the tip of her tongue showing between her teeth, trying to get the shape and the size and the parts of the leaf all exactly right. It took a long time.

There were so many things to learn. There were hundreds of different kinds of grass in every field, all of them with different leaves and heads and growth and seeds. It would soon be summer, and they were all in different stages of sprouting and setting. But she had to know them all, in all their parts. If she ever wished to use magic on grasses, she must know every leaf and every shoot of them. And grasses were just the beginning.

The drawing went slowly, but it felt sure, and it looked right. The more closely she looked at the leaf, the more she saw, and the more she understood.

Everything was like that, she thought. The clouds over her head and the pebbles under her feet. The trees that covered the hills and the hawk on the wind. All of it was rich and full of details that she had to find out and understand perfectly before she could begin to work magic. Yet that was all right, in its way. It was a thing she could understand, not like the nonsense words in the spells she had to learn at school.

Only the flies bothered her, and saying the little spell that kept them off made no difference now, not with the pendant taking away all her magic. Rhianna shook her head, partly to get rid of a fly, partly from annoyance. She wished she could just be like everyone else. It had been fun telling her class about the jewel and what it was for, and everyone had admired it, but still . . .

The drawing was finished. Rhianna wrote a name for every part, and then she compared the drawing with the real leaf. They looked exactly alike. She glanced around. Perhaps she could give herself a test on it.

She closed her book and held the leaf up, checking every part, every shade of color, every vein and bend. She was sure she had it right.

She looked around once more, and then she slipped the pendant chain over her head and laid it on the grass beside her. She felt the magic filling her up, like a rising tide from all around, from the earth and the air and the trees. It was — normal. She *should* feel like this. The jewel was beautiful, but when it was around her neck, it was as if she were deaf and blind. Now she could feel the magic. She had never done that before. *Just like fish,* she thought. *I'll bet they don't feel the water.*

She looked at the leaf again, and when she was absolutely sure, she shaped a little of the magic around her. Just a little. No spell was needed, no passes with the hands. The magic was in her and worked through her, and she thought of exactly how the leaf was, and then of exactly how she wanted it to be.

The leaf trembled, and then it curled gently into a

circle. At the same time a different color washed up from the stalk. Spring-fresh green became gold. The gold brightened until it was the metal of the pendant, rich and sparkling, with the tiny veins a darker, goldlike toffee. The tip of the leaf touched the stalk. It had become what Rhianna wanted it to be — a thin golden bangle in the form of a leaf curled into a circle. The droplets of dew had turned into tiny shimmering crystals. A beautiful jewel, and she had made it.

A feeling of wonder rushed over her, like diving into a pool. *She* had done this thing. She had changed the leaf. By changing it, she had changed the world.

She held in her mind just how the leaf had been, checking against the drawing in the book. Then she used just a tiny bit more of the magic that flowed in from all sides. The golden bangle relaxed and straightened and flushed a spring-green and was a leaf again. And no more.

Rhianna laughed, and slid the pendant over her head again. In an instant the magic disappeared, like a light blown out. But now she knew. She knew what she could do, and she knew how to do it. Magister Northstar was right. It was hard, and it took great exactness, but it could be done.

Now, what about burdock? How were its leaves different? She started another drawing.

When the bell rang for lunch, she put her book away and sat with Rose in their usual place.

"I think you ought to know," said Rose, opening her lunch basket, "that Rory Spellwright got into trouble this morning."

"You're breaking my heart," said Rhianna with a grin.

But Rose was frowning. "No, really. Mrs. Greenapple told him off for daydreaming. He was staring out of the window."

"Rory? He never daydreams. He's not the daydreaming type."

"You're right. He's always too busy looking out for himself. But I had a look out of the window, too, and I saw you drawing in your book."

Rhianna paused, an apple halfway to her mouth. "He was looking out of the window at *me*?"

"Yes. Odd, isn't it?"

Did Rory see me take the pendant off? Rhianna wondered. And then she thought: *No, he couldn't have, because if he had, he'd have told Mrs. Greenapple as fast as he could put his hand up.*

Just as she thought that, a shadow fell across her. She looked up. There, looming over her, was Rory himself.

"Rhianna. We need to talk," he said. He smiled brightly.

Rhianna shrugged. She didn't trust that smile. "So talk."

"In private." He flicked a glance at Rose.

Rose glared at him. "Say it, Rory, and go away," she told him. "Or, better still, just go away."

Rory shook his head. "Rhianna wouldn't want me to say this in public, would you, Rhianna? You wouldn't want me to tell people what I saw, eh?"

Rhianna's heart sank. Rory had always had that effect on her. But when she looked at his face, she knew suddenly that she couldn't let him do it anymore. Rose was gazing at her, and her eyes were questioning.

Rhianna swallowed. "Rose, what Rory means is that he saw me take the pendant off, just for a minute. I shouldn't have done it."

Rory blinked. He hadn't expected that. But he came back quickly. "You didn't just take it off. You made something right there. Something real nice." He smirked as Rhianna went rigid. "Relax. I don't have to tell anyone you did it. See? I can be nice to you. And what I reckon is, if I'm nice to you, you should be nice back to me. Thing is, it seems you can make all sorts of stuff. Now me, I could really use a new penknife, and maybe one of those little crossbows, and a few —"

"Forget it, Rory." Rhianna's voice surprised even her. It was hard and unbending; perhaps it had a bit of the

Magister's own power in it. "I made a mistake. I'm not making another. Go peddle your goods somewhere else."

Rory's face went still, but his eyes flickered. "What are you going to say to Mrs. Greenapple, then, when I tell her?"

Rhianna sighed. "I'll tell her the truth, Rory. The jewel stores all my magic and your uncle empties it out every week. I took it off once, and never again. The end. Now go away. You annoy me."

"Yes," said Rose. "Go ahead and tell, Rory. It'll get you nothing."

"You watch. I will, I'll tell . . ." Rory started to back off, his eyes hard as stones. And then he stopped. He was still for a moment, and his face cleared. He nodded, smiled, turned, and walked away.

"I'll back you up," said Rose. "I'll tell Mrs. Greenapple you never took it off at all. He's just a liar. Everyone knows it."

Rhianna's voice was stubborn. "No. It won't do. If I'm asked, I'll tell the truth."

The day passed. Mrs. Greenapple said nothing to Rhianna other than "Good work" when she saw the workbook. Nothing happened at all, and there was Rory at his desk, still smiling. Rhianna wished she knew what he was smiling about.

*   *   *

At the end of the week, Rhianna had three pages of drawings in her workbook, and Mrs. Greenapple had given her a gold star for them. Magister Northstar would be pleased with her. And then it was time to take the jewel to Mr. Spellwright to have the magic emptied from it and returned to the ground.

Rhianna's mother walked with her down to the spell shop. "I'll just pop down to the market while you have your pendant emptied out," she said. "Mr. Spellwright said it wouldn't take long. Meet me at the market when you've finished." She nodded at another shopper who was passing. "Good morning, Mrs. Brewer."

Mrs. Brewer sniffed, and walked on briskly without a word. Meg looked after her, openmouthed.

"Yes, Mother," said Rhianna. She pushed open the door with its bell that tinkled, and went into the shop.

Inside it was cool and dark as always. Rhianna looked around her. Minor charms in bundles, herbs, magic spell ingredients. Witchlights, alarums, refilling bottles, healing bandages, horse quieteners, ripening salve, wart removers, tonics, chillers, firetouch sticks. And those odd jars with still stranger things in them. And Mr. Spellwright, leaning on his counter.

"Good morning, Mr. Spellwright," said Rhianna. Mr. Spellwright didn't move, but Rhianna saw his eyes swivel towards her. "I've come to have my magic emptied," she continued.

Mr. Spellwright's hand slid across the counter, pale in the gloom, and opened, palm up. He said nothing.

Rhianna took off the pendant and laid it in the open palm. The chain flowed over it, a spill of bright gold, the rubies glowing. Mr. Spellwright's fingers closed. He pulled himself upright, running the gold between his fingers.

"Wait here," he said. "And don't touch anything."

He shuffled into the back of the shop, passed through an open door there, and pulled it shut behind him. Rhianna could hear a scraping noise, and then a light showed under the door. As she watched, the light slowly changed color, from the normal bright yellow of a candle flame to a sharp mint-green.

She sighed, found a stool by the counter, and sat down on it.

Minutes passed. The green light slowly dimmed, then flared suddenly, once, twice. There was a tinkle, a jingling. The light grew softer, lighter. It went back to being a warm yellow. Then, suddenly, it went out altogether.

After a short pause, footsteps sounded. The door opened. Mr. Spellwright stepped out, and Rhianna saw a smile on his face. When he saw her, the smile went out as sharply as a snuffed candle.

Without words, he held out the pendant, the jewels dangling from his hand like sparks. She took it and put it on.

"Same time, same day next week. Without fail," said Mr. Spellwright. He was looking straight over Rhianna's head.

She nodded. "Yes. Thank you, Mr. Spellwright," she said. He didn't respond, but just stood watching her. She pulled open the front door and, turning, saw him hurry into the back of the shop again as she went out into the street.

Meg Wildwood was buying apples in the market. Cooking apples, for a pie. Rhianna smiled at that as she walked up to her.

As she came into earshot, she realized that her mother was unhappy. "You're asking twice as much for apples as you did last week," she said to the stallholder.

"Prices go up, Mrs. Wildwood," said the stallholder. He looked at Rhianna and his face was cold. "There's been a lot of brown spot on the fruit. Ripening spell failed, I hear."

Meg shook her head. "I'll take only three," she said. "It'll be a small pie."

The stallholder shrugged, and thrust three apples into a bag. He held out a hand for the money before he handed them over.

Meg took the bag and walked away, looking puzzled. "What's got into people?" she asked.

Rhianna didn't answer. She didn't know either. But she saw that her mother was hurt and bewildered. She took her hand and gave it a squeeze. Meg smiled, and they climbed the hill towards home.

CHAPTER 8

Weeks passed. Rhianna's workbook filled up, and she started a new one. She drew and learned about all the plants of the meadows: the grasses, the small flowers, the clovers, the weeds. She knew them by leaf and stem, bud and flower and seed, their colors, their patterns, the way they grew. Next month, maybe, she would start on shrubs and bushes. Then, as autumn came on, she would learn about the leaves of the trees as they changed. In winter, about water — rain and snow and ice, rivers and streams. And more, and more. Her head spun at the thought of all there was to know.

Each week, on Tuesday, she went to Mr. Spell-wright's shop, and it was always the same. He sniffed, took her pendant into his back room, did whatever he did, came back, and returned it to her without a word, looking straight past her the whole time. Rhianna had never liked going into that odd shop with its dried-herb smell and its strange things in jars. Now she liked it less than ever.

Then the storm broke, and she had no idea that it had been building up.

One afternoon her father came home early. He was calm, too calm, and the expression on his face was flat and controlled, not open and friendly as it usually was. Rhianna was writing in her workbook, describing and drawing the seeds of smallflax, when he came into the kitchen.

"Hello, Father," she said, a little distracted. The shape of the seed case was tricky, and she was thinking mostly about that. Then she looked up and saw his face. "What's the matter?" she asked.

"Rhianna, we have to talk," he answered. She put down her pencil. He sat down at the table, opposite her. "Meg, come in here, will you?" he called. When Meg came in, wiping her hands, he went on, "Rhianna, this is important. We told you that you mustn't take the pendant off, except when you're getting it emptied out. Magister Northstar told you that, too. That's right, isn't it?"

Rhianna nodded.

"So," Loys went on, "why have you been taking it off?"

Rhianna stared at him, unwilling to believe he had just asked her that. "What . . . ?" she started, and stopped again. She got hold of herself with an effort. "I haven't," she said firmly. "Only in Mr. Spellwright's shop."

Loys frowned. "You're telling me that you've never taken the pendant off, all the time you've had it, except when Mr. Spellwright was emptying the magic out of it? Are you sure of that, Rhianna? Word of honor?"

Rhianna licked her lips. "Well . . . once. Once only." Her father nodded. "I took it off, for just one minute, to find out if I could use magic on the grass leaf I had drawn. And I could! I changed it into a golden bangle. But then I changed it back, put the pendant back on, and never tried again. It hasn't been off since then except in Mr. Spellwright's shop. Not at all."

Her hand had gone to hold the pendant. It felt heavy, warm with her own warmth. Her father's eyes were still narrow, not sure. He looked down, then up. "Then why are people still complaining that the magic is going missing?" he asked quietly. "They're saying that it's even worse than before. Spells are failing all over. Spells for cloth, spells for growth, spells for fishing, spells for this, that, the other thing, and everything else. The whole village has lost its magic. Why would they be saying that to me?"

Rhianna sat, stunned. "I don't know, Father," was all she managed, at last.

Loys sat back and looked at the ceiling. Rhianna suddenly thought that this was what Mr. Spellwright did: he looked over the top of her head, too. "Very well," said Loys, and his voice sounded as if it came from a distance. "I think we had better call Magister Northstar. He'll know what to do about this. I hope."

"About what, Loys? What's been going on?" Meg's voice was worried. "People have been acting oddly with me, too."

Loys ran his fingers through his hair. "What's been happening is what I said. Three times in the last two days, people have asked me what I'm going to do about that daughter of mine who's taking all the village's magic. I think Mrs. Greenapple must have been talking. Anyway, this very afternoon, Sam Farmer came in and told me that he wasn't going to pay me for that plowshare I'd made him. He said he'd take it off the bill I owed him for his ruined crop. He also told me to come to the Village Meeting. They're having one to discuss what to do about the losses caused by *my* daughter. How's that for a pleasant afternoon's work, eh?"

"It wasn't . . . they can't say . . ." Meg began.

Loys folded his arms. "They *can* say it, and they *are* saying it. We had better get Magister Northstar as soon as possible. The meeting is tomorrow afternoon. Where's that spellcaster?"

Meg got the spellcaster from the cupboard, put it on the table, and said the spell rapidly. Inside the ball of clear glass, if you looked at it the right way, there was a swirl of mist. Meg spoke the last words of the spell, *"Antheus Dexter Northstar!"* — Magister Northstar's full name.

For a second or two nothing happened, and then the mist parted and Magister Northstar's face appeared in the globe.

"Hmm?" he said, and Rhianna heard a dull clap, the sound of a book being closed. The wizard was in his study in Avalon, a hundred miles away. He peered at them and smiled. "Ah. Mrs. Wildwood. Mr. Wildwood. Rhianna. How pleasant to see you. What can I do . . ." He peered more closely. "What's the matter?" he asked sharply.

Loys told him what was happening in the village, and Magister Northstar's eyebrows drew down.

". . . and they're having a Village Meeting about it. Tomorrow afternoon," Loys finished.

In the glass, Magister Northstar's hand came into view, stroking his beard.

Meg leaned forward. "Could there be something wrong with the jewel, Magister?" she asked.

Magister Northstar pursed his lips. "It is always possible," he said, but not as though he believed it. "The magic is still going missing, you say? You're sure of that?"

Loys shrugged. "Sam Farmer told me that his crop had come in all patchy. It'll hardly be worth harvesting, he said. And the earth witch he hired to put a growing spell on it told him that there was no power in the Land to cast it. He was very annoyed."

"I see. Hmm. And Rhianna. You have not taken the pendant off, except at Mr. Spellwright's shop and that one time in the meadow at school?"

"No, Magister, I haven't."

"Could she have used so much magic doing that one change, Magister?" asked Meg.

"No, I think not. Making gold from leaves would be a fairly heavy use of magic, but Rhianna didn't make much. Just as well, and also just as well she turned it straight back."

"Why is that, Magister?" Rhianna wanted to know.

"Mmm? Oh, it's just that spell-wrought gold causes . . . difficulties. Never mind that now. Put your hand on the glass, Rhianna."

"Over your face, Magister?" asked Rhianna, startled.

"It isn't my face, Rhianna, it's just a piece of glass. Please."

Rhianna leaned forward and put her palm on the cool, round surface of the spellcaster. She could still see the edges of Magister Northstar's face around and through her fingers.

"That's right," he said. "Now. Tell me again that you did not take that pendant off, except as you have already said." Rhianna said it. He nodded. "Fine. That will do. Thank you. You can take your hand away now."

Rhianna sat back, and the globe showed Magister Northstar's face looking worried.

"I'm sure Rhianna is speaking the truth, and . . ."

At that moment his voice cut off and the globe went blank. The swirl of gray mist at its center rolled and then faded. A moment later it was just a ball of clear glass again.

"What happened?" Loys looked at his wife. "It's stopped."

Meg picked up the spellcaster, held it in her hand, frowned. "I think the spell has worn off," she said. She darted an anxious glance at her daughter. "It should have lasted longer than this."

A minute passed. Finally, Loys looked at Rhianna. Directly at her. "But it lasted long enough for Magister Northstar to say that Rhianna spoke the truth. So it's something else that's wrong. That's enough for me. I'll tell them at the meeting."

Rhianna did some figuring in her head. She hoped that Magister Northstar would think that the Village Meeting was important enough to come himself, but he was a long way away. Even the fastest ships took a day and a half to cross from Home Island. So probably the meeting would just have to take place without him. *And even if he did come,* she thought, *what could he do?*

CHAPTER 9

The following afternoon people came to attend the meeting, which was held on the village green. They walked in, talking low among themselves, and sat down on benches and stools. Many people — forty or fifty, all from nearby. Most of them seemed worried or angry, and few were prepared to greet Rhianna or her family. Rhianna stared around her, as worried as they.

Someone sniggered behind her — Rory Spellwright. All the children were at the meeting, and so was he, thumbing his nose at her. He said something to the other children, and they laughed.

Rhianna turned away. No use getting upset about Rory. He didn't matter now.

Mrs. Fisher was the Elder this season, and at last she moved away from the knot of people she had arrived with and walked out to the front. The sun shone brightly on her face.

"All right," she said. "Quiet, please. The meeting will come to order." They stopped talking, more or less, and sat. "This is a Village Meeting. We are here to discuss the matters set out in the Bill of Calling. I'll read it to you." She unrolled a paper and squinted at it, then shaded it with her hand to see the letters. As she did so, the paper tore across with a weak, soggy noise. There was a mutter from the villagers.

"That's just the sort of thing we are complaining about," stated Sam Farmer loudly, getting to his feet. Mr. Farmer was a bulky man, red in the face — even redder now. He had a large farm up the valley, and was said to have money, too. "We don't need to read a paper to know that the magic is running out. It's become weak and un-reliable. Spells are failing. But we know what the cause is, and we want to know what that family" — he turned his head and looked squarely at Rhianna and her parents — "is going to do about it."

Loys Wildwood stood up. Many pairs of eyes were fixed on him, none of them friendly. He cleared his throat. "None of us knew about Rhianna's Wild Talent," he said. "Not us, not you, not even the school." He glanced at Mrs. Greenapple. "It's very rare, I'm told. And nobody had the smallest notion that she was taking up so much of the magic of the Land, least of all her. But she isn't doing it anymore."

"No," said Mrs. Brewer, who made and sold ale. "She's left little enough to be taken."

"That isn't true. She is wearing the magic pendant that returns it all to the Land. Look!" Loys pointed.

The crowd was silent. Then a voice sounded. "She hasn't always been wearing it, though."

It was Mr. Spellwright who had spoken, and now he stood up. "Rory, my nephew, told me that. He's a truthful lad."

"He's a sneak and a coward," called Rose Treesong. People shushed her, and Mrs. Greenapple frowned at her.

Mr. Spellwright ignored the interruption. "Rory, tell the people what you told me," he said, folding his arms.

Rory could always look noble and pure-hearted when he wanted to. "I cannot tell a lie," he said. "I saw her take the pendant off to work magic. It was when she didn't think anyone could see. I bet she does it all the time."

"But *you* saw, you sneak. You're always sneaking about, looking for someone to tell on." That was Rose again, and Rhianna was grateful to her. But Rose wasn't making matters any better.

"Look, we know about that," said Loys, but he sounded weak. "She shouldn't have done it, but it was only that once. Magister Northstar said —"

Mr. Farmer cut him off. "I've heard quite enough

about that wizard. He isn't here now. We want to know what you're going to do about our losses."

"You owe me for the cost of three barrels of ale, soured and ruined," called Mrs. Brewer.

"And half my crop," added Mr. Farmer.

"And my cloth, of course. Three bolts, all useless. Fulling spell failed. You must pay for it." Mr. Natter, who made cloth, seemed to think that was obvious.

Loys shook his head. "I can't . . . we can't. We don't have that sort of money."

There was a silence. The folk looked at each other. Then Mr. Farmer clasped his hands behind his back. "If you won't pay —"

"Not won't. *Can't*," protested Meg.

"Whatever. It's your daughter's fault. You must make it good."

"It wasn't Rhianna's fault," cried Meg. "She can't help having the Talent. The school didn't —"

"Well, it isn't *our* fault," said Mrs. Greenapple loudly. "You can't blame us for it."

"I didn't say it was *anyone's* fault —" But Meg wasn't allowed to go on.

"You can't just come here and take our magic," called someone else.

"We didn't . . . we came because —"

"I lost a churn of milk just last week. All soured, gone to waste. The preserving spell failed. It's all your fault."

"Hear! Hear!" said someone else.

Voices were rising. Faces were taut and angry.

"It's cost us money!" called someone.

"Crops . . ." That was another voice.

"What about my hides? Curing spell failed . . ."

"Nets got torn across like cobwebs . . ."

"My well went dry . . ."

"Cow did just the same . . ."

"Chickens won't lay . . ." There were too many to answer, all talking at once.

"Order! Order, please." That was Mrs. Fisher. "No doubt we can all work out what we've lost and present our accounts. And then . . ."

But Mr. Farmer stepped forward. There were calls of "Move!" "Let's hear it, Sam!" and "You tell them!"

Mr. Farmer nodded. "Move, you say. So I will, then. I move, Madam Elder, that the Wildwoods pay in full for the damage their daughter has done, or . . . or" — he cast about for the worst thing he could think of — ". . . be banished. Let them forfeit their property and go back to where they came from. Yes, let them be banished. Forever. They must take their child and go and not . . . and not . . ."

And then he fell silent.

For behind him, behind them all, the sun suddenly seemed to dim, and a great blazing light sprang up. Their shadows were sharp-edged shapes before them, twisting and writhing in the flame of that hard white fire, and they swung around, everyone at the Village Meeting, all at once, as if it were a dance step. Magister Northstar had emerged onto the green from the street that ran between the houses, and they had not seen him arrive. Or perhaps he had not wanted them to see.

His staff, leaping into his hand, lit and burned with a cold light that was blinding. He rose up as tall as a mountain, his beard and eyes white flame in the light, and his robes swirled like storm clouds. They all shrank from him, Rhianna as well, for a wizard in his power is a frightening thing. And then he spoke. It was as if the Land itself spoke, slow, deep in the silence, cold and heavy in its anger. The noisy words that had gone before seemed like the squeaking of bats.

"I have heard enough," he said, and the very air shimmered and rang. "This is greed and waste. You use magic as if it were a thing to be traded and sold like a pot or a sheep, and you use it up. Farmer, how many years standing have you cropped that field, using growing spells? More than two, I'll be bound, and now you whine that your crop is poor. And you blame a child for it." He swung around so that they all were under his eye, and that eye was stony hard in judgment. "Beer and nets and hides and wells and fowls! Is there nothing you will not load on her? And all with not a voice raised to defend her, save Rose and her own parents! I tell you that this day's work is ill done, like all your work. You have much to do to make it up."

Silence. Mr. Farmer stood still, his mouth opening and closing. Magister Northstar turned to him. "You may sit," he rumbled.

Mr. Farmer wet his lips. "But . . . look here, you can't —"

"What is this you say I cannot do?" Magister Northstar gestured sharply. Mr. Farmer sat down, folding over as if broken in the middle. The wizard eyed him grimly. "I am the Mage on the Queen's Council. It is not for a Village Meeting to say what I can and cannot do. Still, for the sake of your instruction, I will answer my own question. I cannot bring the Land to harm. I cannot allow treason against the Queen. I cannot allow injustice to her subjects or wrong to a child. All the more because the child is my apprentice and under my protection. If you wrong her, you wrong me. And I say you have wronged her."

He stared at them, and this time nobody would meet his gaze. He nodded, and it was as if a mountain had moved its snowy head. "I am glad that I thought it was worth raising the wizard's wind in my sails, to come as fast as could be. For indeed, so it was. What you were about to do would have been shameful. Shameful."

Silence. Then a voice in the stillness:

"But Magister, however shall we manage if all the magic has gone away?" And Rhianna was shocked to find that the voice had been her own.

Slow time passed, a long time, it seemed, and then the Magister nodded. "Gone away, you say. Well, so it has. Let us find out where it has gone. Give me that pendant." He held out his hand.

Rhianna almost ran toward him, lifting the pendant off her neck as she came. He smiled a little, murmured a word of thanks, and took it. For a moment he let the jewel rest in his palm, and then he spoke again, while the villagers sat hushed to hear him.

"Magic is here, but not so much as to drain a district. The magic has gone somewhere else. Let us see . . ."

He handed the jewel back to her and swung his head from side to side, as if he were trying to hear where a faint sound was coming from. Then he turned and looked down the village street. "That way," he said.

Down the street he paced, following its crooked length towards the harbor. The villagers followed, carefully staying ten or twenty steps behind him as he walked, his staff clicking on the cobbles.

The houses were deserted. Everyone had gone to the meeting. The shops were closed, including the spell shop. Looking around for him, Rhianna suddenly realized that she hadn't seen Mr. Spellwright since Magister Northstar's arrival. Or Rory, either. Well, Magister Northstar had outshone everything, rather.

They passed the buildings, one by one, and Magister Northstar never paused.

At the end of the street there was a strip of green grass along the harbor wall, and then the pier jutted out as if to continue the street into the sea. Beside it rocked a single ship, tied up. Four figures stood together on the pier, their voices loud in the quiet. Magister Northstar quickened his step.

One of the figures turned. It was a man wearing a traveling cloak and hood. In his hand he carried a bag, a loaded valise that swung heavily.

Under the hood, the face was Mr. Spellwright's. He dropped the bag and it fell with a clank. His smaller companion was Rory. The other two were sailors, the crew of the vessel at the pier.

Magister Northstar's expression hardened. He swept up to the group, halted, and leaned upon his staff, three paces from them. "Well, colleague?" he asked quietly. "Going somewhere? A family outing, perhaps?"

One of the other men answered, one who wore a sailor's stocking cap. "He wanted us to take them out, right now, going anywhere, Magister. I told him you'd hired us, but . . ."

"I understand." Magister Northstar stared at the village wizard. "A sudden decision to take a sea voyage, Mr. Spellwright? I see you took some magic. Your bag is full of it, and very strong it is, too."

"I had a sudden call," blustered Mr. Spellwright. "The spells are needed."

"There's a lot of magic there for a few spells. Enough to drain a district. Perhaps I should look to make sure there isn't too much for you."

Mr. Spellwright glared. "Too much for me, you say? Why always too much for me, but not for you? It's all very well for you, with your power and your fancy robe and your wizard's staff and your college. I never went to college. Not enough power, they said. Good enough to run a stupid little shop in a stupid little village, but no better. I never had —"

Magister Northstar held up a hand. "Let me say it for you. You never had the power that you needed and wanted. But one day, it just walked into your shop. All the power you could never have. And so you took it."

Mr. Spellwright looked away, his eyes hot and resentful. Magister Northstar shook his head. "What did you use the magic for? If it was not used, it would just drain back into the earth and the stones. You could never contain so much. What did you do with it all?"

A shrug. Mr. Spellwright's face didn't change.

The staff in Magister Northstar's hand twitched. The bag shook itself, and its lock clicked. It fell open and tipped on its side.

A torrent of bright gold nuggets, smooth and rough, large and small, fell out onto the boards of the pier. Pebbles, small stones, cobbles — all had been turned into gold.

A murmur went up from the crowd.

Magister Northstar stared at the gold, and the blood drained from his face. Slowly his gaze lifted. His lips were white with anger. The sailors backed away and then broke past him into the safety of the crowd behind, leaving Mr. Spellwright and Rory to face the Magister alone. Rhianna stood behind him, watching in amazement.

"Spell-wrought gold," Magister Northstar whispered, and the whisper was as cold as the wind in winter. "You fool."

Rory began to blubber. "I told him not to!" His voice rose in a howl. "I didn't want to come! He made me!"

His uncle made a grab at him, but Rory ducked and

ran for the crowd, bawling in fear. "Made you?" shouted Mr. Spellwright. "It was you who put me up to it! 'Make some gold, like she did,' you said, 'and we can blame her.'"

But he was answered only by Rory's running feet.

People drew apart to let Rory through, holding themselves away from him as if he were dirty. He ran on, up the street, still blubbering and howling, and disappeared between the houses.

Magister Northstar had not moved. "Did you never stop to think about what you were doing, Spellwright?" he asked harshly.

"What's wrong with making a little money?" asked Mr. Spellwright. He laughed, a short bark. "Making money . . . that's what I did, all right." He laughed again.

Magister Northstar shook his head. His eyes had never left the other's face. "Do you think it's as easy as that to get rich? Did you never stop to ask why no wizard does this? Why we do not live like kings by making spell-wrought gold?"

Mr. Spellwright sneered. "Don't you live like kings, anyway? Ah, but I suppose if there was too much gold, it wouldn't be worth so much. So I only made enough for me."

But Magister Northstar had turned his back on him. He was looking up to the hills behind the village, and past them to where the mountain range reared its snowy summits into the clear sky.

"No," he said, and his voice was low and sad. "No, that's not the reason." He looked down at Rhianna. "Remember how I told you once that some things will answer if you call?" She nodded, staring up at him. "Well, making spell-wrought gold is a manner of calling, too. But it calls in a special way, and it's rather a special thing that answers."

He nodded towards the mountains. Far, far off, high in the sky beyond the peaks, there was a speck that sparkled in colors like a faceted glass in the sunlight, a speck that flew. It slowly grew to a dot, still an immense distance away, yet Rhianna knew somehow that it flew on great sweeping wings, and the light sparkled off scales that were polished like metal mirrors. As she watched, spellbound, her hand opened by itself, and her jewel, beautiful and sparkling, fell to the rough timbers of the pier. Nobody noticed.

"A dragon," said Magister Northstar. "And I am already weary."

CHAPTER 10

"All of you, quickly." Magister Northstar was using the Wizard's Voice, the voice that stills others. "Get out of the village, out into the fields. Go as far from here as you can. The dragon isn't interested in you. Not yet, anyway. Spellwright, if you're any kind of wizard, add your magic to mine. Rhianna, go with your parents."

"Magister, my place is —"

"As my apprentice, your place is to obey me. We have no time. Go."

"Come on, Rhianna." Her father pulled her away and picked her up like a baby, his blacksmith's arms strong under her. He ran, and Meg and the others ran, too — the sailors, the villagers, all of them. Rhianna looked back over her father's shoulder at the Magister and the village wizard on the end of the pier, above the lapping sea. Magister Northstar stood, leaning on his staff; Mr. Spellwright sagged like a badly filled sack.

The villagers ran up and out of the little valley until they reached the nearest fields. There they stopped, gasping, looking down at the village and the pier and what was happening there.

"Turn the gold back to stones," Mr. Spellwright shouted. His voice broke. "The gold's what brought it, you say."

The Magister shook his head. "It would take as much magic to unmake it as it took to make it. Magic is already short because of your folly. Soon we will need all we have. And if we thwart the dragon, it will only waste the district and slaughter the people in its wrath."

His eyes never left the dragon as it slowly grew larger in the sky. It flew on vast airy wings, pulsing like a beating heart, wings of crimson shot with gold. It was not perhaps the greatest of its kind, no more than the length of the ship that rode at the pier, but it had scales like the painted shields of a hundred warriors, gold and scarlet and emerald and purple, armor that no weapon could pierce, and teeth as long as a man's arm. From its jaws rolled smoke from its living fires.

Closer it came, and closer, until it was overhead, its shadow covering pier and mages and ship, and then it began to descend. It settled, settled, and the wind from its mighty wings blew dust and wood shavings in blasts. Magister Northstar held his tall hat to his head, and

Mr. Spellwright crouched at his feet, face gray, lips moving.

The dragon landed beside the harbor wall, on the short grass before the place where the pier extended out over the sea. Dragons are creatures of air and fire, and they do not care for the great waters. Perhaps that was why the Magister had chosen to meet it there. But that was no great advantage.

It set its front hawk feet like a giant cat, and its tail, barbed and spined, trailed up the village street behind it. Its great eyes stared at the two figures at the head of the pier.

"A wizard," it said, its voice like the roaring of a huge fire. "And a hoard of spell-wrought gold. Is it your gold, wizard?"

Magister Northstar answered, his voice calm. "No. Nor anyone's."

"Then it is mine." The huge eyes flared, and a dart of flame jetted out of the open mouth.

The Magister shook his head. He looked small and slight, standing there leaning on his staff, before the jeweled length of the dragon. "Well do I know that giving gold to a dragon — spell-wrought gold above all — only strengthens it. I would not make you any stronger than you are, dragon."

The dragon hissed. It might have been dragon laughter. "What do you know of my strength, little man, little mage? It is enough that you know this: that it is far greater than yours. Stand aside, or the jewels of your robe and the ivory of your bones will be part of my hoard, too." Its head snaked forward on its long neck, and flames crackled in its nostrils.

Magister Northstar set his staff in his hand, raising it. "If your strength were as mighty as that, you would offer no bargains, dragon, and you would take as you pleased. Therefore, you have doubts. Heed them. You shall not pass. If you try to take, you shall die."

For answer the dragon breathed in, and then fire gushed from its jaws, a flood of flame. The Magister and Mr. Spellwright were caught up in it.

Mr. Spellwright yelped and scuttled in circles, crouching, his arms over his head. At the same instant the staff in Magister Northstar's hand leaped up, and the fire divided itself around them like the tongue of a snake. For a long moment the two figures were in a bubble within a sea of flame.

Yet even a dragon cannot flame forever. It pulled its head back, and the flame died.

"Quick, Spellwright," Magister Northstar called. "Join your magic to mine. You have some, at least. Boost the power of my spell."

He reached out a hand to the other man, but Mr.

Spellwright was past all reason. He knew only that he had to escape. Gibbering with fear, he ran in the only direction possible — straight at the dragon.

It reared back and hissed, and that was indeed dragon laughter. It let him pass, watching him out of its great cat eyes, and like a cat it let him think he was out of its reach. Mr. Spellwright passed the first house and dived into the space between that and the next. Then the dragon grinned and turned its head. It breathed again. Flame gushed, washing around the walls like a torrent. There was a great roaring of fire, a crackling of roof beams as they took light. Perhaps there was a terrified cry that was suddenly cut off.

Magister Northstar closed his eyes briefly. He set his feet and his staff. Still he stood between the dragon and its hoard, and the great beast turned its eyes back on him.

In that moment, Rhianna, watching from the rise above the village, wriggled out of her father's grasp and set off down the slope toward the sea, running as fast as she could. She could see what the others could not: that Magister Northstar was exhausted, and his magic was low, and there was little nearby to help him.

She heard shouts behind her, and then running feet, but they didn't matter. All around her the Land fed her its power, for the pendant still sparkled on the pier, dropped and forgotten.

Magister Northstar had taken a step back, and his shoulders were hunched, as if he were walking into driving rain. His wizard's staff still stood upright in his hand, and his other hand was tracing the rune Sophas, the rune of power, in the air.

"You shall not pass, dragon," he said again. His staff shaped the air also, and the sea grew an arm that reached out of the water. Long and thin, it whirled up, a waterspout where there was no wind, and shaped itself into a spear. The spear shimmered and whitened in the air, becoming a crystal weapon, a spear of ice. Magister Northstar gestured, and it launched itself at the dragon's heart, flashing like lightning.

The dragon had just breathed, and it had used its fire for the moment. But it was as agile as a great cat, and it leaped aside with a beat of its mighty wings. The spear flashed past, scraping a wound on its flank.

Drops of black blood rolled slowly down, but the hurt was not mortal, and the dragon reared up in its rage and its pain. It struck out blindly, and its claws were not to be batted aside like its fire. Magister Northstar was suddenly in midair, clinging to his staff as it rose like a lark into the sky. The claws passed under him, all but the tip of the uppermost; yet that was enough. The talon caught the edge of his robe, tore through and out, and the shock hurled the wizard backwards, tumbling him to the timbers of the pier. His staff fell from his grasp.

"Ha!" roared the dragon. It pulled its hindquarters under it, more like a cat than ever, to leap on him as he scrambled on hands and knees, his hat knocked off, his staff out of reach. One leap, a quick rending strike with its mighty jaws, and the fight would be over. It would take its hoard, drive out the villagers, live in the largest house, sleeping on its gold, mightier than ever before . . .

Rhianna reached the corner of the last house. She gasped, then called out —

And as the dragon's huge limbs prepared to spring, suddenly the grass it crouched on was growing over them. Hundreds, thousands of small plants, angel-eye and cow-parsley, oat grass and graywort, clover and dock and sinthel and mockweed, more than it could count, all grew in a moment, tangling and knotting themselves over its clawed feet and its barbed knees, lashing its tail to the ground, anchoring it down with millions and millions of rootlets. The dragon tore up one foot, then put it down and tore up the other, and while it did that the foot on the ground was overgrown and anchored down again.

The dragon roared, and the sound was like a mountain in the grip of an earthquake. Still Rhianna ran, gathering power as she went, power from the Land, from the sea, from the wind, from the fire. Out onto the pier she flew.

The dragon was confused, but still it had its mighty strength and its flame. It drew its head back and pulled breath in.

Rhianna had nearly reached Magister Northstar. He was on his knees and had seized his staff.

The dragon breathed out, and again the river of flame rushed down. Again the wizard's staff sprang between, and again the flame twisted and divided and roared past, hot as a furnace. But it was the Magister's last gasp. The embers of his magic flickered and died. He sank to the ground, overspent, his limbs suddenly unable to bear him up.

The spilled gold lay in a bright tumble at Rhianna's feet, and suddenly she knew what she had to do. She saw it as it was and as it must be, and she gathered the magic all around her, thin as it was, and demanded that it do her will.

The dragon tore up its huge limbs and freed itself at last. It seemed to have used up its flame, just as the Magister had used his magic, but it still had its might and its teeth and claws. It took a step towards them, and then it stopped. A hiss came from it, but this was not laughter.

For the gold it was striving for had lost its sparkle. It

dimmed and dulled, there in its careless heap on the rough timber of the pier. It took on the colors of the earth and soil again. It lost its buttery richness, its luster of metal, and became rough and common and ordinary.

Rhianna looked up. At her feet was a heap of stones.

The dragon stared. Its eyes narrowed and its head drew back. "You have taken my gold," it hissed. "Give it back."

Rhianna felt as though someone else spoke with her voice. "No, dragon," she said. Her words were calm, and seemed to come from a long way off. "I will not." She gathered up the Wild Magic, the last scraps and tatters of it, and held it as if she were drawing a bow. "It was and is a heap of stones, and a heap of stones it shall remain. Will you fight me over it, or will you go in peace?"

The dragon cocked its huge head as it considered. Then it spoke again, its voice lower than before. "There is the jewel there. It is of great price, and magical besides. Give me that and I will go. Wild as your magic is, will you measure it against mine?"

Rhianna glanced down, and there was the jewel that took away her magic, lying on the pier a pace away. Slowly, she shook her head. "No, dragon. The jewel is mine. You shall not have it. Will you fight me for it?"

It hesitated, and might have turned then. But at that moment, from around the corner between the burning houses, the villagers came running, bearing pitchforks and hatchets and scythes. At their head was Loys Wildwood, wild-eyed, his heaviest hammer whirling in a bright circle.

Rhianna could not prevent her shout: "Father! No, don't!" She stopped short.

Too late. The dragon flickered a glance at her, faster than thought. There was terrible knowledge in those eyes. Then, as fast as it had glanced, it made a grab with an armored claw, and Loys Wildwood was struggling in a grasp of steel. He struck with all his blacksmith's strength, and the heavy hammer rang off the scales and fell away, leaving a mark, a bruise. The dragon hissed in pain, but settled back on its haunches, holding its catch writhing under its clawed foot. The villagers shrank back.

"Well, now, little mage," said the roaring-fire voice. "We can bargain, you and I. *Father,* you called him, and it is said that humans value such things. Certainly he is worthier than these." The dragon's eyes dismissed the cowering villagers. "I have something you want, it seems." It nodded at the gleaming jewel on the pier. "You have something I want. Shall we trade?"

Rhianna was silent. It was her father who shouted: "No! No, Rhianna. Give it nothing. It fears you . . . ah!"

The dragon stirred. "Quiet, warrior, or I lean a little

harder and listen as you crackle." It cocked its head again. "Well, little mage? What say you?"

Rhianna looked from the jewel to her father's straining face to the dragon's slit-pupiled eyes. She nodded slowly. "Your word on your name, dragon, that he goes free unharmed and that you will depart in peace and not return, if I give you the jewel."

A groan came from her father. The dragon grinned, and lifted its huge, spike-taloned foot. "I swear it on my name," it hissed as Loys Wildwood rolled free and staggered away. "Now give me my prize."

Rhianna bent and picked up the jewel. Instantly her magic blew out like a snuffed candle. She walked toward the mighty beast, holding out the pendant in both hands.

Delicate as a duchess taking tea, it threaded the tip of a claw through the chain. It grinned again and held it up dangling from the needle point of its talon, exulting as it inspected the gleaming gold, the gems splintering the light.

But even as it did so, its eyes narrowed and became vague. The metal colors of its scales flickered and died. They became dull, first rusty, then gray-green like stagnant water. It shrank, and it became squat and uncouth in form; the long neck shortened to become a hulk of furrowed flesh. The wide wings drooped and took on the appearance of mere flaps of excess skin. It opened its mouth as if to protest, but only a lizard's hiss came out. There was no flirt of magical fire in its throat, and its eyes had become those of a beast, without understanding, dull and stupid. Its terrible grace, catlike, elegant, was gone. Stumpy legs splayed out under it. Its magic had departed. It was a great slow lizard, nothing more. The jewel had taken its magic; and dragons must have magic to be dragons.

The upraised foot it placed back on the pier, puzzled, shaking its head. What were gold and jewels to a lizard?

It was a wrong thing. Rhianna watched, knowing it would happen, and yet pitying. A dragon is a dragon, and not to be judged as if it were a thief or a bandit. She watched and knew that she could not allow this.

"Dragon," she said softly, "I will slay you if I must, but I shall not take your magic and leave you to die as a beast. It is not right."

She tugged the jewel free from under the splayed foot. Dull eyes blinked at her in bewilderment.

Holding the jewel, Rhianna walked away. As she did, color came swirling back into the dragon's scales. A dragon does not merely work magic, it *is* magic, Wild Magic in its very nature. As soon as the draining jewel was taken away, its nature returned. It grew again, long and sinuous. Its scales and claws regained their gemmed brightness and metal hardness. Its head reared up and its flashing wings filled out in enameled colors. Its limbs and body became spare and elegant and beautiful again. In its eyes grew understanding — and the understanding of its loss.

It turned its great eyes on Rhianna and hissed. Again this was dragon laughter.

But it was Rhianna who spoke. "Do you still want the jewel, dragon?" she asked.

The huge head weaved from side to side. "No, little mage. I want nothing of it."

"Then there is no more to be said. Yet I gave you the jewel, and so I hold you to the oath you swore by your name, dragon."

The dragon angled its head down to her. "You did well to spare me, and better to restore me. That is the act of a great mage." It might have meant its dip of the head as a nod of respect. "Two wizards I have defeated, but my third opponent is the mightiest of the three. I will tell my brothers and sisters this: that another Wizard of the Wild Magic has come into the world. Little mage, little mage, I think that we will meet again."

Spreading its wings with a snap that raised dust in clouds, it sprang into the air. It turned, and the great wings bore it higher, higher, faster, faster. The sun glinted off its scales as it diminished, becoming a metal eagle in the sky, then a dragonfly, a glittering wasp, a rainbow dot. To the mountains it flew, climbing above even the peaks, until it was lost, a mote in the darkening sky.

Magister Northstar pulled himself to his feet. He leaned on his staff, one hand pressed to his side. Rhianna ran to support him. Slowly and carefully they limped back towards the harbor wall together, and the villagers watched them as they came, too stunned even to cheer.

It was Loys Wildwood who scooped up the small wizard in his strong arms and carried him to where he could rest.

CHAPTER 11

The burning houses were put out, the whole village working with buckets, hauling water from the sea. The roofless shells still smoked, their blackened window frames staring out at the harbor and at the strip of green where the dragon had sat and talked. Spots of dead grass pocked it where the dragon's blood had fallen.

Farther up the street, Magister Northstar stumbled to a bed in the inn. He lay with open, restless eyes, his hands twitching as though in a waking dream. They put his staff beside him, and Rhianna sat with him and fed him power little by little as the Land fed it to her, until his eyes closed, his breathing eased, and he slipped into natural, deep sleep. He slept the sun down and the moon down and the sun up again.

As soon as the Magister was really asleep, Loys Wildwood carried Rhianna home to her own bed. Caps were removed as he passed among the people, for the dragon had called him *warrior* and his daughter *wizard,* and those are titles of respect.

Rhianna, too, slept long. Even when she woke, late in the bright morning, the memory of weariness still seemed to soak to her very bones. Her father had gone to the smithy, making light of his scrapes and bruises, for nails and ties and strap iron would be needed to rebuild the burned houses, and he would have to make them.

Meg sang in the kitchen as her daughter emerged, tousled and still sleepy, from her room. Rhianna was eating a very late breakfast when she heard Magister Northstar's step at the door. She jumped up to give him a seat, and Meg set a bowl of porridge before him.

He thanked them and sat with a sigh, as if his knees pained him, but he ate with a good will. When he had finished, he pushed the bowl away and sat looking out of the window. Tall summer grasses were waving in the warm breeze.

"You learned your lessons well, Rhianna," he remarked. "Who'd have thought you could bind a dragon with chains made of grass?"

Rhianna shrugged. "It was all I had, Magister, and all I knew. That, and stones, and the cobbles of the street."

"It was enough to turn a dragon, and that is a very

great deal. And did you hear what he said as he departed? 'Mightiest of the three,' he called you, and it is true. Trust a dragon to know magic."

"Can you trust a dragon to speak the truth?" asked Rhianna, and the Magister smiled at the question.

"Sometimes. I think this was one of the times." He leaned back. Perhaps his beard was even whiter than it had been, the last gold gone from it now. There were more wrinkles at the corners of his eyes. When a wizard spends his power, he spends more than just his power. But his voice was firm: "You are my apprentice, and will remain so for a time, Rhianna. But the day will come when you will grow beyond me. I always knew that; now I am certain. And the dragon said one thing more. Do you remember what it was?"

Rhianna remembered. "He said that he and I would meet again."

"Yes, he said that. And perhaps that was another truth from a dragon. I don't know." He rose. "I've just come to say farewell, Rhianna, Mrs. Wildwood. I must return to Avalon. There have to be some changes made. It's well and good to use magic to heal or to calm the storm or to hold the flood or the fire, to find a lost child or to send an urgent message. But no more of this magic for everything. It will exhaust the Land. I can see that we of the

Queen's Council have done amiss to give it to every farmer and weaver and fisherman. We must confront the matter. I will go and see to it."

Rhianna nodded. Her hand came up, as if by itself, to touch the jewel at her throat. The pendant was in place again, and perhaps the village could start to get its magic back.

The Magister saw the gesture. "The College will send out a young wizard to take over Spellwright's shop. It will be, perhaps, less easy to buy magic than it has been, but a village like Smallhaven needs a wizard. He will discharge your power back into the earth again, until you have learned what you need to learn. And when you have progressed a little further in your studies, you must come to Wizardly College yourself." He looked across at Meg. "With your permission, Mrs. Wildwood, and your husband's. But I would most earnestly recommend it. In another four or five years, perhaps."

Meg nodded. Rhianna looked disappointed, though she smiled. Four or five years. A lifetime!

The Magister smiled, too. Perhaps he knew what she was thinking. "I'll look in every couple of months," he said. "I'll be watching how you grow."

The three of them walked down to the harbor together, and the folk they passed nodded and lifted their caps. At the smithy, Loys racked his tools and walked with them past the dragon-burned houses to the end of the pier, where a ship was waiting.

The wizard stepped down into the ship, the lines were cast off, and the craft heeled to the wind. He raised his staff in farewell. "Until we meet again," he called, across the widening blue water.

They waved until the ship was a white fleck of sail on the ocean. And that was the end and, in a sort of way, also the beginning.

ABOUT THE AUTHOR

DAVE LUCKETT writes in many genres, but his first loves are fantasy and science fiction. He has won many accolades for his work, including three Aurealis Awards.

Although he was born in New South Wales, Dave has lived most of his life in Perth, Western Australia. A full-time writer, he is married with one son.